CITY OF SAND

A WAR OF BANES AND DEMONS
BOOK THREE

KEVIN HARKNESS

SHOUTING ROOM BOOKS

CITY OF SAND

Cover design by Design for Writers

Editing and typesetting by Liminal Pages

Chapter opening illustrations by Galen Dara

https://kevinharkness.ca/

To those who write, those who edit, those who publish, and those who read. 'Tis a long chain of curiosity, hard work, and delight.

Also by Kevin Harkness

A War of Banes and Demons Series:

City of Demons (Book 1)

City of Masks (Book 2)

City of Shadows (Book 4)

City of Blood and Fire (Book 5)

CONTENTS

CHAPTER I
RED SAND

S he stopped when she saw a patch of red sand, then another, darker than the rose colour of the dunes. She bent down, her features hidden behind the hood of a long, red cloak. Wet grains of sand stuck to her fingertips when she touched the patch. The next stain was farther up. She studied the face of the dune, a slow wave moved only by weight and wind. The grains carved from its crest filled the air, and she pulled up her mask until it met the bottom of her eye shields. It was late to travel. She judged time and survival against the rising sun. The blown sand dropped as the wind shifted. What had been an erratic gale now came steady, deliberate, and from a single direction.

A north wind! Whose death do you bring?

It had blown from either the west or south-west since dawn, troubling Yala's day-sleep and whistling in her dreams, but now it came straight from the north, speaking death. She touched her right shoulder. An answering movement eased her fears. She reached inside her shirt to find where Chit-chit's tube was tied to her upper arm. The fear lizard pushed out its head and touched an inquisitive tongue to her fingertip. Yala breathed out. If Chit-chit was calm she did not need to fear that particular death, not today.

She pushed her sled's runners into the slope. Leaving it secured, she climbed the face of the dune with practised steps, switching back and forth to find purchase for her boots. Just below the crest, she set an arrow to her bow. The death wind was stronger here, and she hesitated. Taking her fingers from the bowstring, she peeled back the collar of her shirt. Again, Chit-chit stuck out his small, brown snout to taste the air.

She smiled at his curiosity and gently pushed him back into his nest, flipping a leather stopper over the opening. She didn't want to lose him if she had to run. The little lizard hissed a bit, but she paid it no mind.

Raising her head over the crest, she saw something in the shadows between this dune and the next. A figure lay there, a man with limbs outstretched, left there to be covered by the moving sand. There was nothing else. None of the desert's scavengers had begun to feast. She looked up and saw a hawk circling in the half-lit sky, waiting for her to leave so it could feed.

The wind spoke of this man's death, not mine.

She stood and half turned to fetch her sled and continue to Old Carving Well. This outsider was no concern of hers. She had seen town-dwellers at the trading post, had watched them sidelong as they moved and talked like human beings. On this, her first trading journey, she had not spoken to any of them, carrying out trade through sandwalker intermediaries who were more used to the one-souled.

2

Yala stood there, on the crest of the dune, balanced between the two slopes.

He could be alive . . . and I could die finding out.

She slid down into that pocket, using the angle of her body to break her speed and keeping both hands on her bow and the nocked arrow. Even beside him, she hesitated. To become entangled in a stranger's sorrow risked making it her own, and her people's. Another would have walked away, not even bothering to see if there was still breath in that thin, crooked form.

She turned the body over, moving the arms and legs into some semblance of dignity. The face, hawk-nosed and bearded, was a Southerner's. He was dressed in rags, his neck was bound in iron, and a chain ran from that collar to pool snake-like at his bare and bloody feet.

He did not speak when she turned him, nor move. She knelt, considering. Then the man groaned. The sound came from deep within and spoke of great pain. She could see why. He was cut across the back from shoulders to hips, long oozing wounds that had already turned sour. She scanned the crests of the surrounding dunes, fingers back on her bowstring.

Whipped! But who were the whippers, and where are they now?

After the groan came speech, halting yet understandable to those who knew the town-dwellers' tongue, as any sandwalker would.

"Slavers," the man said. "Help me."

His eyes remained closed. The young woman stood and looked down at him. She shivered once, a movement of the head and shoulders that ended as quickly as it had begun, and knelt again. She lifted the man, holding him upright, and began the arduous task of helping him back up the dune and down the other side to her sled. Beside the Southerner, she seemed smaller than when she stood alone atop the dune, though the only watcher to note this was the bird floating high above.

The hawk screeched and followed his stolen meal until the sight of a distant death sent it racing away.

The girl tied the man to her sled and rocked the runners free. The wounded man would need more water and food than she carried, but she had been on her way to a shelter of the Slow Sand Well when she had seen the blood. There would be supplies there, and she had trade goods to leave as thanks.

She gave him what water she had, then set the harness around her shoulders. The runners were newly polished, but she knew the additional weight and the loose sand would slow her, leaving them to roast in the morning sun before they reached the refuge. Since standing and thinking covered no distance, she leaned into the harness and began to pull.

It took as long as she thought. In the last stretch, she took off her cloak and covered the man, leaving herself unprotected. Every sandwalker was taught to travel by night and rest by day. Those who didn't never returned to their wells.

Yala tried to swallow and could not, for her mouth was as dry as the sand and her water flask was empty. Had it been farther, she might have died, but the Slow Sand Well shelter was there, in sight though trembling in the heat waves. It was not much, but the three stone walls and mat roof were enough to keep off the sun. Around it, a few broken lines of stone, none higher than her knees, stretched into the sand. Such ruins were common enough in the desert, appearing and disappearing as the sand wished.

She set the man against a shade-side wall and drew water from the stores to wash his wounds. She saw no hope of saving him now. The whip cuts were corrupted, and the red lines of blood poisoning were everywhere.

He woke again in the evening and took some water, though he could not keep any food down. "Who are you?" he asked. His dark eyes were on her, though he closed them again when a coughing fit shook him.

"Yala," she said.

"Inla-phor," he said. He raised a hand towards her. "You're a sandwalker?"

After a moment, she nodded. To share too much with the one-souled was dangerous, for they could use the details in their spells, and then the water would sink back into the sand and the dunes would cover the fields. Wells had been lost this way, the old women said.

Yet I brought him here.

She should leave him to get on with his dying. He was an animal, and she was a human being, or so her people believed, but Yala was not so sure about this or many other things. A chaos of winds had pushed her all day, feeding this confusion in her souls. Then the death wind had steadied and told her what she would find. Wind had more wisdom than anyone's words.

And the wind was still from the north.

"Inla-phor, do you have any message for your kin?" she asked.

"Is it so, Yala?" he asked, and the hand dropped back down. He did not wait for her answer. "Yes. If you have paper and ink. My family is in the Far South. I beg you give it to traders going that way."

She nodded and reached into her pouch to pull out a roll of reed strips meant for the trading and counting strokes and a small pot of ink. She searched further and found the bone-tipped pen. She handed all to Inla-phor and held him up to write his farewells.

When he was done he lay back down, but laid a hand on Yala's arm.

"You are a good woman, Yala of the Sandwalkers. I will help you from the other side, if the gods allow it."

He closed his eyes again, and Yala laid his hands over his chest. She would have removed the chain, but she had only her sand shovel and dared not risk its edge against the brute iron of the collar. While the man fitfully slept, she let Chit-chit loose to hunt for dew beetles among the broken stones.

He died in the night, waking her with his death rattle. She moved him to the farthest line of stones and left him, huddled against an eroded block, waiting for the sand. She said no words over him, for she did not know his rites; she only knew that the one-souled did not properly honour their dead. Tales told at her well said the river cities in the North burned their kin, and the town-dwellers in the South sealed them in dark stone caves.

Yala shuddered. How could one's true soul find freedom reduced to ashes or in the dark below the ground? She had already started carving an open niche in the pillars of the dead near her well. When she was very old and gave up the last syllable of her name, it would be ready for her, keeping her body-soul safe while her wind-soul ranged over the earth.

She turned from the thought.

I have time. I am young and will have many years to finish it.

When the sun fell into west, she readied her sled, but hesitated before leaving the shelter. The wind still blew from the north. She gathered herself and pulled into it. Any watcher would have seen her only for a moment before her red cloak merged with the sand and hid her from sight, but there were no living eyes to see, for even the hawk had gone. Behind her, the body of Inla-phor bore the assault silently. By daybreak, it would be buried, and the only part of him left on this earth would be the message Yala carried away.

CHAPTER 2
THE CITY OF FOUNTAINS

It was near evening, but the sun still pressed on the City of Fountains, easing its citizens from their usual rush to a more deliberate pace. Though they slowed, they kept moving, enduring the heat to go here and there on business, for the people of this town were single-minded when it came to their tasks. At least, that was true for most of the town, but for anyone passing a certain inn on the edge of the festival grounds, that focus was rudely broken. Those unfortunates stopped, tools and goods forgotten in their hands, as a loud string of curses flew out of an open window on the second floor.

"Claws, Vinir! I thought you were joking about chaining me up," a high-pitched voice cried out.

"Marick, come down here!" a young woman shouted back.

The townspeople shook their heads and walked on. It must be the foreigners. Two things were free in this city: water from its hundred fountains and gossip from its ten thousand tongues. Everyone knew about the three travellers who had sailed from the river cities that lay north beyond the desert and planned to stay for a season in the town. Who else could be yelling so? No citizen of the City of Fountains would hurt their name or the name of their tower with such an embarrassing display. After a bit of listening, each townsperson went on about their business. There was no telling what foreigners would do or say. As everyone knew, the south brought war, the desert offered death, and the north was as mad as a whirlwind.

Up in that room, Master Vinir of Shirath Banehall had little thought for her name, or the reputation of her home-land, and was far beyond worrying about any personal embarrassment. Her normally calm features were flushed and one of her long braids had come undone, giving her the crazed look expected by those listening outside. She held a length of rope in one hand and was grabbing at a boy's dangling foot with the other.

Marick peeked out from behind a roof beam. His friend Dorict was standing by the door, holding a cudgel and guarding against any sudden dash for freedom.

"It's not a chain, it's a rope," Vinir said, jumping up and just missing an ankle. "I only want to tie a line from your leg to my bed post, so I'll know if you try to sneak out!"

"And what if I untie it?" Marick demanded, drawing up his leg out of reach. "Will you tie my hands too?"

"A good idea," said Dorict. He darted in and pushed his friend off the beam with the tip of his staff. Marick held on by one arm, but Vinir wrapped her arms around his waist before he could climb back up. She pulled him down and thrust him into a chair, keeping him there with one hand on his shoulder.

"Claws! I wish Salick or Tarix were here to tame you," she said. With her free hand she brushed back strands of loose hair.

Marick looked mulish, but Dorict laid his staff across the boy's legs when he tried to wriggle free.

"Fool! You know what's at stake," the larger boy said.

Marick kept wriggling. "Let me go! Of course I know!"

While Dorict kept Marick in the chair, Vinir closed the window and came back to stand in front of him, arms crossed and blue eyes narrowed. "Truly? So, you haven't forgotten the thousands killed by demons?" she said. "Nor our duty to protect the men and women of Shirath?"

Seeing no hope of escape, Marick stopped moving and said, "No, of course not. I'm a demonbane, aren't I?"

Dorict shook his head. "Are you? A bane obeys their master."

Vinir nodded. "And that would be me, scamp!"

"I know, Vinir," Marick said, smiling up at the frowning young woman. "And a master well-made! But you can't expect me to sit around doing nothing. I'll go mad!"

"And so would we," Dorict muttered.

"Be patient," the young woman said. "If only for the sake of the people who died when the demons came in force against us last year."

"I know. I was almost one of them!" Marick said and continued in a less aggrieved tone. "I'll try to be patient," he said. "I swear on Heaven's dome! Now, let me up."

Dorict lifted his staff.

Before he could stand, Vinir laid a gentle hand on Marick's shoulder and squatted down to look him in the eye. "Think hard about this when you measure your scheming against our mission. Demon fear and misery for the last six hundred years! We can change that now," she said, "but I need your help, Marick. We all do. You're on this mission to find where the demons spawn because you can sneak into places and pry out information like no one else I know! You proved that when you found out where the Masks were hiding and showed us who led them. We need you again, but you have to be wise as well as brave. Can you do that for me?"

Such a personal appeal from Vinir was impossible to ignore. He might risk his life for something as simple as a prank, but he would not chance losing Vinir's friendship.

Marick stayed in the chair and nodded, his head bobbing up and down.

"Yes, yes, of course, Vinir. Master Vinir, I mean. You know I would do anything for . . . the banehall."

She stood and smiled down at him.

"Thank you, Marick! I knew I could count on you. Don't worry about calling me 'Master.' I'm too young to be one anyway, and Hallmaster Branet wouldn't have given me the Red Sash if he'd had anyone else to send."

She reached across to take a sheaf of paper off the room's single table.

"I know how sitting around frets you," she said, "so, now that I have your promise to behave, I'm giving you a job. I want both of you to explore this city and make a map. We can't search if we keep getting lost! You can start now with the streets around this inn."

She dropped the paper in the boy's lap and reached back to gather her loose hair. While Marick rolled up the paper, she braided the golden strands with deft movements of her long, scarred fingers. Marick and Dorict had the same blond hair, as most of Shirath's citizens did, and similar scars, as all demonbanes bore. Hunting demons, and training to defeat them, left its own map upon the body.

"Do a good job!" Vinir said. "If we have to sneak about for information, we'll need to know the tricks and turns of these streets. This is an odd place! A city without wards, and it climbs uphill like a long set of stairs." She finished fixing her hair and smiled. "Now, while you're doing that, I'm going to talk to our innkeeper about which art masters are taking students. Be back by dark. Agreed?"

Marick fairly snapped to attention, propelling the chair several feet behind him. Dorict sighed and set his staff beside the door.

"I'll leave this here, since I saw no one armed in the streets. It seems a very peaceful place."

Marick grinned at him, his expression leaving no doubt that, if he had his way, this peace was about to end.

CHAPTER 3
OLD CARVING WELL

The opening in the high south wall of the well was narrow, and Yala pulled the sled carefully through it. A scraped frame would be noticed, especially after her first solo trading journey. The old women would smile behind their hands, and her mother would waste no time lecturing her in private. She slowed her pace. The wheels now fixed below the runners made the load top-heavy, and she had to pause more than once to balance the cloth-wrapped packages.

A last twist, and she left the stone corridor and looked out onto the well proper. It was always a surprise to come in from the desert and see so much green spread across the men's fields. Old Carving Well had many such fields, and many men to tend them. That was good, for they kept the women busy trading spice, oils, and the things they made with their clever hands.

Yala bit her lower lip and gave her trade goods a nervous glance. She hoped they would meet with the approval of the old women. A trading journey gone awry would be met with frowns. Two or three such journeys might see her sled taken away and given to another. If that happened, she might have to go back to her before-name, Yalasa, and live as a child until she regained the well's trust.

She paused where the road divided. Should she turn towards the tent of her mother or take her goods to the trade-house right away? After a long breath, she turned towards the trade-house. Whatever cutting words the old women might have would pale before the judgment of her mother, especially when she learned of Inla-phor's message.

Yala's grandmother, Ke, was in the trade-house. The building was long, low, and made of wood, a fantastic expense of trade and haulage that was the envy of other wells. The old woman came and sniffed over the packages Yala stacked against the wall.

"Hmmm, soda lime and tincal for glass and enamel. The men will be braying for that at the wall! Sea salt, fever bark, and what's this, tincture of wound-heal? Well, well, at least you weren't cheated too badly. There should be more though, even for a new sandwalker."

She lifted her watery, brown eyes to look at her grand-daughter's face. With veined hands, she pulled off the young woman's hood.

"You look away. There's a story in your eyes, and not a good one, I think. Well, tell me before you tell your mother. Practice in lying is always useful," she added, and made her bird-chirp laugh.

Yala poured tea and brought it to her. They sat beside the wall, and she told Ke of Inla-phor, the chain around his neck, the whip-marks on his back, and the message to his kin.

When she was done, Ke looked down at the clay vessel, now empty, cupped in her hands.

"I would have preferred a lie!" she said. "And I know your mother will be as mad as a pit-killer at your . . .foolishness. Why did you talk to him? The chain was enough to tell us the slavers had returned. Aiii, little one, why take on the sorrows of the one-souled?"

Yala was silent, though her thoughts kept speaking.

Because they are sorrows! Because I wondered if a chain hurts the one-souled just as much as it does us. Because, because, because . . . the wind blows me on and back again, and I can't keep a straight line in the sand.

She hung her head until Ke's thin fingers lifted her chin.

"The day you were born, the winds blew from seven different directions, and I told your mother that you would live a troubled life. Ahh, it is sad to be always right!"

Yala smiled. She had heard this story before, but it had always been three winds or four, never seven.

"Ke, do you think my mother will remember that and listen to me?" she asked.

The old woman leaned back against the dry planks. She shook her head.

"The day your mother was born, the wind blew only one way, and it hasn't shifted since."

CHAPTER 4
THE ART MASTERS OF THE TOWN

There was no strong wind in the bowl of rock that held the City of Fountains, only the sea breeze of morning that came ghosting up the tiers of the town. It kept the streets cold, for the highland at the town's back left them in darkness for that first part of the day. As the sun rose, shadows vanished from the top down. First, the highest tier of tombs and crypts glowed. Their plain stone façades – so rare in this town – took the warmth and radiated it back into the morning air. Next, the sun lit up tip after colourful tip of the seventeen towers that thrust upwards from the retreating shadows.

Soon, the bright hues of the houses blazed and the light moved down the town until it reached the lowest levels. The people, up and about their business before full light, shivered a bit as the sun chased the last of the night-chill from their bodies, but they kept at their tasks.

In the harbour, the ships at dock were the last to be lit, mast-tips first, then spars, and finally the decks of a dozen merchant vessels secured to wooden wharfs or rocking gently on the protected waters. The City of Fountains was famed for its busy docks, though the sailors slept longer than the townspeople. Those on the bobbing ships still stretched and dreamed while the people of the town moved about like ants.

"Keep up!" Vinir called over her shoulder. She turned and wound her way through the ever-present crowd.

Dorict grabbed Marick's arm and dragged him along.

The smaller boy turned his map this way and that. The rough sketch was his own work and bore no street names nor legends to help him find their way. Dorict tried to hand him the other map, a handsome thing in different coloured inks and with neat titles below each landmark, but he waved it away.

"Don't trust it," he said, shaking his head. Marick had a low opinion of the map-making skills in this town. Besides the city map, Dorict had brought back several others, including one that showed a great stretch of land from the territories south of the City of Fountains to the river cities along the Ar, Shirath among them. To Marick's confusion, the whole river valley, from Solantor to Old Torrick had been labelled "North," when everybody knew that the Five Cities of the South were, well, south! The North was where Salick and Garet had gone, a snow-blasted land peopled by those who left the Ar Valley six hundred years ago when the demons came. Dorict had lectured him about "relative viewpoints" and other nonsense, but it was clear the people here didn't even know where they lived!

So, Marick had spent two days roaming the city, making his own plan of the town, though it lacked the beauty – and the accuracy – of Dorict's purchased map. "We should go left here," he said, comparing a crossroad to the sketch in his hands.

Vinir shook her head. "Claws, Marick! That would take us through a building. Dorict, what does your map say?"

Marick bristled but kept quiet. Vinir was too easily upset these days. Her usual cheerfulness had gone, replaced by a growing fear that she would not find a teacher.

"Up one more block and then turn left," Dorict said. "It should be the . . . ah, purple, yellow, and green tower." He stopped to cover a gigantic yawn. When it was done, he glared at Marick. "Heaven's shield, I'm tired! You woke me up twice with your thrashing and moaning," he said. "I thought you didn't dream."

"I didn't used to," Marick replied, stifling a yawn himself. "Not until I came to this clawed place. This town wants to trouble both my days and my nights!"

Vinir called out for them to hurry and shifted the flat leather case she carried over one shoulder. Playing the role of her servant, Marick should have carried it and had offered, but Vinir only shook her head. She strode up the street, as determined as the people around her.

Unsurprisingly, Dorict's map was right. A garish tower rose before them, one of many in the city. It was a jarring sight for any traveller from Shirath. The houses in Shirath were plain and for good reason; no one wanted their house or tenement room to stand out lest it attract a hungry demon's notice. But Shirath's people felt safer walking in a crowd during the day, so they let their personalities come out in brightly coloured clothing. A market crowd in Shirath looked like a dancing rainbow.

Not here. The City of Fountains was a bizarre reversal of normal life. The people wore dull clothes, mostly greys and browns, while the buildings were painted every colour imaginable, and some that should have never been imagined.

Marick shuddered. "I still say it looks like someone reached a hand down this town's throat and pulled it inside out," he said.

Dorict shuddered. "So you've told me. Many times, and I still haven't gotten that picture out of my head, thank you. But I'm getting used to it – the colours, I mean. I don't think it's confusing to the people who live here."

"How do they even find their way home?" Marick asked and went on in a nasal voice. "Do I live in the red house between the pink and blue houses, or the pink house between the orange and green houses?"

Dorict laughed and shook his head. "They'd probably wonder how we find our own houses with no colours at all to make them stand out," he said.

"I doubt they'd wonder about that or anything else," Marick said. "All they do is work."

Dorict couldn't disagree, because it was true. Wherever they went, people passed them by with little more than a nod, intent upon their own business. Aside from quiet knots of students gathered around street teachers, writing and questioning, everyone else seemed to be on their way to some very important destination.

"Like blood rushing through the veins," Dorict had said on their first day, admiring them, but such diligence held little interest for Marick. For one thing, no one had time to talk, and that was hard on the curious and sociable bane.

After many attempts at casual conversation, he ignored the industrious and instead looked for disreputable characters, like the many he knew in Shirath, but to no avail. Thieves, drunkards, and rogues seemed absent from this town, or at least invisible. It was abnormal, and frustrating. How was he to learn anything without a shadow to explore?

The only glimmer of hope so far had been when they left the inn two days ago, on the third day of looking for an art master to take Vinir as a student. Marick had spotted a bald man peering at them from one eye. The other socket was hollow. He wore the same drab clothes as everyone else, but at least they were filthy and frayed at the sleeves. When Marick saw everyone else give the man a wide berth and suspicious glances, he felt an instant kinship, but Vinir called him on, and the man disappeared into the constant flow of work.

That had been a bad day all around. An old woman who taught drawing and painting to beginners had turned up her nose at Vinir's excellent sketches and waved away her request to study before turning her back on them all.

"The nerve of that old hag!" Marick had said, when they were out on the street. He was dismayed to see tears in Vinir's eyes. Dorict patted her arm, but Marick fumed and stamped his foot.

"Don't cry, Vinir," he said, and turned to glare at the art master's door. "A knife across those paintings, or a pot of ink, and she'll regret—"

His threats ended with a strong grip on the back of his neck. That hand lifted and twisted him around to reveal a very angry bane master.

"You will do no such thing!" she hissed and wiped at her face with a sleeve. "Did you see those painted shadows? The candle flames that looked so real? I would give so much to do as well. It was like looking into a real room, and you want to destroy it?"

She dropped him and continued in a more controlled manner. "You will never, I repeat, *never* harm any art in this city. If I'm not fit to study it, you are definitely not fit to destroy it!"

She had not spoken to him for the rest of the day, and it was only careful behaviour on his part that restored some peace between them. Dorict had been no help at all. The bigger boy agreed with Vinir about the town's art, and his approval for every other aspect of the City of Fountains was obvious. That had been the first night Marick dreamed, a confused retelling of the sea journey from Solantor to this town. All storms and angry sailors, he had been glad enough to wake, sweating and shaking in the dark of the room.

Today, their goal was the purple, yellow, and green tower. With Dorict's map, it was easy enough to find but, as always, there was some negotiation needed before they were allowed inside to speak to the art master. Several people who either worked at the tower or were just passing by consulted each other in hushed tones. Runners were sent inside and came back with messages. A young man brought out tea, and everyone drank from the small cups and continued talking.

Marick fumed, and even Dorict fretted a bit at this delay. In Shirath, banes were not kept waiting on a doorstep but greeted with honour for their sacrifice and service.

"Courtesy is upside down in this place!" he said to Dorict. "Even if we're strangers, we're still guests, and guests are treated better in Shirath."

Dorict looked at him – down at him, actually, for he had grown much since the Battle of the Bridge last year, as if that horrifying day had thrust him into an early adulthood.

"Not always," he said. "Remember how badly the bane-hall treated Garet when he first came to Shirath?"

Marick frowned at that. The hallmaster of the time, an odious man named Adrix, had made their friend's life miserable until Master Mandarack replaced Adrix as leader of the banes.

"Relax," Dorict said and sipped his tea. "Things could be worse. This is a pleasant enough city, though very hot."

He waved his folded map, trying to manufacture a breeze. The heat didn't bother Marick. Nor cold, for Marick could ignore everything unpleasant except boredom.

I'm starved for fun here, and I'll never make my own if Vinir doesn't let me loose.

Vinir took the delay with an air of grim patience. This was the ninth place they had enquired for a master. Some had been in other towers; others had been at private homes or shops. All had rejected the foreign woman from the North who came looking for a teacher.

Marick was sure that stung, for the ruse of a Trader's daughter coming south to study art was a crucial part of their mission. In Shirath, the masters of the banehall, the king, and the king's councillors had all agreed: the three must hide their true identities.

Their reasoning had been this: little was known of the Far South. Of course, Shirath's merchants travelled there and might have told them much, but some of those Traders, as the city had recently found out to its horror, were untrustworthy and had very dangerous ambitions. Both the hallmaster and the king had doubted their claim that demons were unknown in the Far South, and so a plan was made to search there in secret. By hiding their identities, Vinir, Dorict, and Marick could be sure that any local allies of those traitors would be ignorant of the banes in their midst.

Needing new identities, the three banes could have gone as merchants, for the City of Fountains shipped many trade goods, but being banes and knowing nothing of business, King Trax decided another cloak was needed to hide their true purpose and all agreed that Vinir was the best one to wear it. First, she was a bane dependable enough to be newly promoted to the highest rank of Red Sash. Second and more importantly, Vinir had a peculiar way of spending her spare time between patrols and practice. She drew pictures, and she was one of the few in the city – and the only bane – who did.

Shirath's citizens, living in a city besieged by demons for six hundred years, had little time for painting and drawing. They only showed their creative side in the colourful clothing they made to wear, but Vinir was close to being a true artist. She had started by using sticks of charcoal to make portraits of her friends and teachers. She soon moved on to create detailed sketches of the banehall, the temple, the palace, and even ordinary tenements.

In the last year, she had begun drawing demons. In fact, her rendering of those horrors was so good that the masters had taken her off patrol for several days to make the illustrations for a new edition of *The Demonary of Moret*. The text of that ancient book had already been revised by Garet, a former bane who now served as advisor to the king. Such a reworking had been long overdue. The original *Demonary* lacked information about the new types of demons that now appeared, and the behaviour of the beasts it did list was increasingly at odds with the latest observations.

Vinir had finished her work before leaving for the city of Solantor to take a trading ship to the south. The new *Demonary* was now with Shirath's stewards for copying. It would be kept not only in the banehall, but also in the palace, the ward lords' houses, and lent to any who wished to read it. That would have been unthinkable even a few seasons ago, for the banehall had kept its secrets for six hundred years, and Moret's book had only instructed new banes. Now, King Trax and Hallmaster Branet decreed that every citizen in Shirath had the right to read it and know their ancient enemies as well as any bane.

This openness had not been welcomed by everyone. The traditions of the city were old and set in stone; this new knowledge turned them all on their heads. Banes no longer had private knowledge, and the citizens were learning things they might have wanted to avoid. A year ago, even the word "demon" would have brought a quick finger to their ears to flick the unlucky sound away. Now they had to hear it. Of course, some still flicked it away, for luck's sake.

"It's frightening," Vinir had said to Marick before they left on this journey. "Everyone in Shirath who wants to read Moret's book will be looking at my drawings!"

Some would be more than just looking. A select few would be studying their ancient enemies so they could add their arms to the fight for Shirath's future. Lord Andarack, a man of great intellect and curiosity, had discovered a way for non-banes to fight their demon foes using silkstone. Made into armour, or at least a mask, the substance allowed an ordinary, though well-trained, man or woman to withstand the force of fear cast by a demon, the choking, paralyzing terror that was their most terrible weapon.

And that was the second part of Vinir's mission. Even if there were no demons in the Far South, they were to look for any signs of silkstone. Banes were those who had already learned to live with a great fear, to move and act despite its clutching fingers. When ordinary men and women stood shaking and weeping, waiting for the claws to fall, banes fought back. So it had stood for six centuries, but now citizens in silkstone armour could join the bane-hall's ranks, driving back the demons, perhaps to their undiscovered source. Cheering as this was, an army of citizen-soldiers was unlikely any time soon, for silkstone was rare along the River Ar, where Shirath stood. With what little they had, the masters of the banehall were already training ex-Duellists, palace guards, and even others in its use, but a new source would add greatly to their defences.

Marick thought on this and looked up at the tower's top, a garish eruption of swirls and arches. Their whole mission depended on quietly finding these two things: demons and silkstone. And that seemed to depend on him doing nothing, or at least not drawing attention to their presence here. He knew Vinir feared that if certain traitorous Shirath merchants did have allies in the City of Fountains, a mistake might find them on a ship bound for home. Or dead.

He sighed. The idea of running for their lives was wonderful.

While the tower wardens argued among themselves, Marick reached down and patted the top of his dusty boots to make sure his lockpicks hadn't slipped free. It was a shame he couldn't use them to pry open the mouths of these busy, boring people. That would be Vinir's task, for she was the friendliest person Marick could imagine. Once accepted as a student, she would have a place – and a reason – to ask questions of her teacher and fellow students. Whatever information she uncovered could then be investigated by Marick and Dorict.

That Vinir's part would take time – and leave little for Marick to do – was depressing. He was used to asking his own questions, usually in the shadows, or spying out the truth from the rooftops. He had all the skills of a thief, not surprisingly, since he had been one as a child in the city of Old Torrick, surviving by climbing walls and jumping from roof to roof when chased by his victims. In Shirath, he had used these talents to good effect, first during the rebellion of the Duellists, and later, when some of those same fighters put on silkstone masks and tried to replace the banes as Shirath's protectors.

Marick still had scars from that last fight, though he bore the Masks little ill-will. They had made life interesting for a while.

Now all was dried up and dust. He must sit on his hands outside this tower and wait, like any ordinary fool. Worse, he might have to wait alone, for Dorict had come up with his own plan. The bookstore where he had bought the map was run by an old man of great curiosity. Despite the man's near blindness, Dorict was teaching him Northern writing. In exchange, the man was teaching Dorict the slightly different Southern script, and the old man let him try to read what he wanted after their lessons. When not accompanying Vinir, he planned to stay at the shop.

The night before, at dinner, Dorict had spoken enthusiastically of his research. "That place has books on everything, from boat building to creatures only found in the red-sand desert," he said around a mouthful of beef stew. "Nothing on demons yet, but there's a lot to look through. Even Shirath's stewards don't have as many books in their school! And Bortor doesn't mind me reading them as long as I'm careful."

Vinir seemed pleased, but Marick had only grunted. He knew Dorict was never happier than with his face in a book, though his face in a plate of food might run a close second. Marick, who viewed books as useless, was left with nothing to do but follow after the others holding their coats.

One thing he was not allowed to do was to investigate in his own particular way.

"Breaking into houses and following one-eyed people from the rooftops?" Vinir had said. "No, no, no! Or, not yet at any rate. Let Dorict and me try first. If all else fails, then I'll turn you lose upon this city. Then Heaven shield both them and us!"

And so I trail along like a dog waiting for a bone.

He looked up just in time to see Vinir follow a dully dressed man into the tower. Marick and Dorict jogged into the darkness after her.

The tower was several buildings in one, the central spire connected to arched wings and wandering extensions. As in the street, men and women, and even children, bustled about carrying trays of paper, building supplies, or pushing small carts full of mysteries.

Waiting where they had been instructed, Marick picked up one such puzzle from a cart left by the side of the hall. It was a glass jar, beautifully made with smooth, regular sides. Inside was more glass, a jumble of red shards. He shook it to see if there was anything valuable inside, but the jar was snatched out of his hand and he turned to see a girl, not yet his own age, he judged, glaring at him from under a fringe of jet-black hair.

"I've just sized these, so don't go making them smaller by smashing them around in the jar!" she said, and pushed him away from the cart, shooing him like he might chase away a small, irritating dog.

She put the jar back and looked the three visitors up and down.

"You're the ones from the North. No wonder you don't know anything! People say you're" – and here she pointed at Vinir – "looking for a teacher. Well, I don't know if you'd want old Sarth here to take you on. My employer is always complaining about how hard he is to study under, but Chal-lat's a big baby."

Vinir blinked and then smiled. "I apologize for Marick's rudeness. It was unintentional. My name is Vinir, and this is Dorict. Your name is . . . ?"

"Son-neen," the girl said. She reached out and stroked the cloth of Vinir's sleeve. "I can take you to a better shop for clothes. These colours make you look so odd! Five percent commission, and that's a deal because you're all so ignorant."

"That's enough of that," Marick growled. He shoved forward, but Son-neen only glared back at him.

Dorict pushed between the two. "Thank you, Son-neen. We'll let you know about the clothes. Can you tell us anything that would help my employer get a teacher?"

Son-neen considered this. She pulled on a lock of her black hair and frowned.

"Fair trade for fair trade," she said. "Tell me something first."

"What?" Marick demanded. He tried to push past Dorict, but Vinir held him by the collar.

"Some people say that Northerners are really monsters who eat babies in their cribs," Son-neen said. "Is that true?"

"Claws take you!" Marick shouted but gasped as Dorict swung an elbow into his chest.

The bigger boy spoke as if nothing had happened. "No, we don't, though we do have monsters there. We call them demons, and they eat more than just babies. Have you heard of them?" he asked.

Before she could answer, a querulous voice called from the inner room.

"Chal-lat, you sent that girl for the tesserae a lifetime ago. Where is she?"

Son-neen pushed past them and wheeled the cart away from the wall.

"Coming, Sarth!" she yelled. "Don't have a fit and die before you finish your latest masterpiece."

"Imp!" the old voice shouted back.

Son-neen paused for a moment and tugged on Vinir's sleeve.

"Look, I don't know if he will take you on. He's angry as a struck beehive most days, but I'll tell you this: speak straight to him, no false compliments or he'll toss you out on your ear. Whatever he asks, answer as truthfully as you can, even if it makes him mad. Fair trade?"

Vinir nodded, and the girl pushed her cart through a side door.

"Well, don't just stand out there, foreigners," the old voice called. "Come in before I do have a fit!"

The three entered the side room and stopped, held by the scene before them.

It was a very high room, and scaffolds lined three of the walls. Scrambling up, down, and sideways along the slender poles were dozens of workers. They perched up there like a flock of birds in paint-splattered clothing as colourful as feathers, but there the similarities stopped. Some of the workers were dark-skinned, some light, and most in-between. A few scrambling about were as blond and pale as Marick and his companions, and others, like Son-neen, were paler, some even had red hair, a thing unknown in Shirath. This was just one more jarring effect for Marick, who wondered if they arranged themselves like this on purpose: dark, light, blond, red – just like they painted their houses.

"Over here," the voice called, and they found its owner, a thin old man, bent at the shoulders and with a twist to his head that made him appear a bird looking for worms.

He wiped his hands on a stained apron and held them out. After a moment's confusion, Vinir gave him the flat leather case that held her drawings. The old man spread them out on a trestle table, finding room amid the pigment pots and stacks of brushes.

"Fair," he said, holding up a study of a young woman with a scar on one cheek and a fierce look in her eyes. Marick smiled in recognition.

That's Salick. I wonder where she is now? She and Garet were supposed to go north on the same mission we're on, finding demons and silkstone.

The art master dropped that one on the table and flicked through the rest. At length, he stopped at one and held it up to the light.

"What is this, a fever dream?" he demanded. "I want students who can take what is real and make it immortal! I don't need fantasies such as this!"

He dropped the drawing on the floor, and Marick scooped it up. It was a sketch of a Basher demon – a large, fierce beast that could break down any barricade set against it. Vinir had given it a sense of movement with her charcoal strokes, and the creature looked ready to charge off the page. "What do you mean 'fantasies?'" he demanded.

The old man peered at him, eyes at a level due to his crooked back.

"There are no such things in the world," he said, clearly pronouncing each word.

"Yes, there are," Son-neen said, before Marick could speak up. She took the paper from him and waved it.

"Everyone knows there are baby-eating monsters in the North, Sarth," she said. "They're called demons."

A young man came up behind the girl and tapped her on top of the head with a finger. "And I know you still have work to do, or am I paying you to talk instead?"

He was tall, taller even than Vinir, and had a thin, dark face with high cheekbones. He took the drawing from Sonneen, who grinned and went back to where she had been arranging her jars of glass pieces on another table.

"Master, this is very good!" the young man said. "Look at the musculature of this . . . thing. And the dynamic composition is—"

"Yes, yes, Chal-lat!" Sarth said. "Be quiet. Come here, foreigner. Look at this mosaic and tell me what's wrong with it."

From what Marick could see, standing behind Vinir, there was nothing wrong or even very interesting about it.

It's just a picture made of those glass pieces. The sea, some stupid fish, an old boat, some rocks. That's all.

"I think," Vinir began, and then stopped.

Though she had killed many demons, Marick had never seen her so nervous.

"Think! Think what?" Sarth demanded. The old man was peering at her in his canted, bird-like way, waiting for the worm to show itself and be devoured.

Vinir blushed but raised a trembling finger to point.

"The colour is not right in that part. The darkness forces the eye to concentrate over here," she said, and pointed at the middle of the scene. "So, the whole thing seems . . . cramped."

She dropped her hand and looked beseechingly at Dorict and Marick. The larger boy nodded wisely, though Marick was sure he had no idea what was going on.

"Hah!" Sarth said and turned to look at the tall young man.

Marick was surprised to see him blushing as well, as if he had been caught out. That was a feeling Marick had suffered many times in his life, but he refused to feel any sympathy.

The old man chuckled. "She's got you, Chal-lat! You wouldn't believe me when I told you the same thing. Sea and sky, save me from stubborn students! Now what do you say?"

Chal-lat sighed. "I say I'll start fixing it right away, Master Sarth."

He took a small chisel from his belt and began prying away at the darkest part of the mosaic.

Sarth waved at the drawings and Dorict began to gather them up.

"Wait," the old man said, and he plucked out a portrait of Vinir's former banehall master, Relict, from the pile. The sketch showed a trim, bearded man in uniform and sash, sitting on a chair.

"This fellow looks like a pirate. We'll use him on the north wall," he said, and then turned to Vinir. "Chal-lat isn't as wretched as that scene makes him out to be. He'll show you how to take off the glass and then how to put it back on! When you know that, I'll find you something else to work on."

With that, he turned away and shuffled over to the north wall, waving Vinir's sketch at someone high on the scaffold.

"Pirate!" he warbled.

Vinir looked at the two younger banes and smiled. She was radiant, and Marick was pleased she was happy again, though he was less pleased at her instructions.

"I think I'll be here until the midday meal, and maybe later," she told them. "Dorict can continue at the bookshop, and Marick, I suppose you have to wait outside the tower until I'm done."

With that she turned away and was deep in conversation with Chal-lat before Dorict and Marick left the room.

"Look," Marick said, catching Dorict's arm, "the old man acted like he didn't know what a demon was, so can't we go home now?"

Dorict shrugged. "He may be lying, or afraid to talk about it. Or it could be that there are no demons around here, but that doesn't mean our searching won't turn up some useful hint about where they do come from. And there's still the silkstone – maybe I can find a reference to it in one of Bortor's books," he said, and looked down at the fuming Marick.

"As for you, patience – which is something you need to learn sooner or later. I'll come back at the midday meal."

Dorict waved farewell and hurried off towards his own investigations. Marick watched him go. His friend seemed more confident these days, more likely to choose his own course and less likely to rely on Marick for outrageous suggestions and dangerous plans. The abandoned bane sighed and found an out-of-the-way place next to a fountain where he could sit, safe from the rushing feet of industrious citizens. Or so he thought. He was dozing when a toe prodded him. He shifted aside without opening his eyes but was nudged again. He looked up to see the one-eyed man he had noticed days earlier standing over him.

He was squat, with a round belly pushing at his tunic's belt, in which two dirty thumbs were hooked. The rest of him was just as grimy, and he stank of sweat and sour wine. He leaned over and grinned, revealing very few teeth.

"Hey there, boy. You're a foreigner, aren't you."

Marick scrambled up and away, putting a bit of distance between him and the smell.

"No more than you," he said. While a small part of his mind was plotting an escape route, the larger part was calculating how much information, or at least fun, he might get out of this filthy fellow.

The one-eyed man laughed a bit at that and abruptly sat down on the curb of the fountain. He spread out his legs, causing some passers-by to trip and others to swerve around.

A middle-aged woman in a brown tunic and trousers stopped to glare down at him.

"You're in the way of everyone's business, including mine," she said, rebalancing a basket of bricks on her head.

"So go mind your own, hag," the dirty man shot back, and spat on the ground.

The woman's eyes narrowed, and she went into the tower.

"She'll have her friends on me in a minute, so I can't stay to chat. I only stopped 'cause you looked so out of sorts, bored it seemed like."

Marick shrugged. "I am bored. Maybe because this is the most boring place in the whole world!"

The man stood up and laughed. His one eye on the doors to the tower, he said, "I'll say yes to that! Maybe you should go to the Mother of Waters if you want fun. A day's travel on good roads to the east. That's where I camp. I'm just here scouting for goods to trade. Well, if you get tired of this place, seek me out there. I'll find something interesting for a likely lad such as yourself."

He twisted away into the crowd, disappearing just as the woman returned with a knot of followers. One brought a bucket and splashed water on where the man had spat. Some of that water hit Marick, and he swore.

"Watch your language, child," the woman said. She hoisted the heavy basket back onto her head. "Your two friends seem sensible enough, but you're looking for trouble talking with a man like that."

"Like what?" Marick demanded, but the woman only sniffed and stomped off, the bricks in her basket making little stone-bell sounds as they bounced.

Like me, she means, though I have two eyes, all my teeth, and a much more recent washing! So, the fine people of this town think I should stay clear of him? Why, when he's the only person in this place who wants to talk to me!

He pushed back into the corner between the fountain and the tower wall, trying to make himself invisible to the passing workers. Vinir and Dorict found him there, dozing again at midday, and they went back to the inn to eat. That afternoon meant more waiting outside the tower, and Marick saw a long line of such days stretching before him. He would have welcomed a demon attack at this point, or even another battle with the Masks. They might be allies of the Shirath banehall now, but he bet there were still some who bore him a grudge for revealing their training compound and the identity of their leader. That adventure had cost him an arrow in the leg.

That evening, while Vinir droned on about the harmony of colours and something called perspective, he rubbed the scar on his thigh and thought that another arrow would be a small price to pay for a bit of excitement.

CHAPTER 5
ARROWS IN THE WIND

Two rows of shifting dunes had formed a deep, narrow valley between them. It would not last, for the sand hills were always moving, some a few grains at a time, others in sudden avalanches that would bury those beneath. That explained why the slavers whipped their captives so vigorously, and why their leader, a thin man with a long, black whip, kept looking to the red walls towering above them.

The wretched prisoners, fixed by their iron collars to a long chain, stumbled and swayed, but the whips fell and the line moved on. The leader was almost clear of the valley. He took one last doubting look at the red slopes, and his gaze stopped on a patch where grains tumbled from a hump that broke the smooth face of the dune.

"Danger!" he said, and turned to run, but the first arrow took him in the neck, just above his shoulder. He fell to the ground and the sand above the rest of the slavers erupted. Archer after archer stood, shedding from their red cloaks the thin layer of sand that had hidden them until now. By the time the last grains had rejoined the dune, every slaver had at least one arrow in him, and more followed.

One tried to run, despite the point in his shoulder. He was fast, but no one is faster than a sandwalker's arrow.

Yala came upon her mother pulling shafts from the bodies on the sand. The older woman eyed the quiver on her daughter's back. It was still full. Yala had been one of those tasked with guarding the edges of the ambush, so that none might escape. That last slaver, a boy too young to grow a beard, had fallen just below her station.

"Look for a key," Tral ordered. She pointed to the line of ragged slaves cowering on the ground. Without uttering any words of comfort, sandwalkers moved among them, giving water and food. Some of the captives drank and ate ravenously. Others looked at the bread in their hands as if it were a mirage, or worse, a trap.

Yala began to search the bodies, her hands tentative until she grew used to the slick feeling of blood on skin. She found the key on the whip-wielder's body, tied by a cord around his scrawny neck and half hidden in his beard. She brought it, and a blue-shafted arrow, back to Tral.

"Yours," she said, and handed the arrow to her.

Tral grunted and examined the steel point for damage. Satisfied, she thrust it into the sand to clean it, then slid it back into her quiver.

"Free them," she said, and turned away.

Yala grit her teeth and obeyed. Her mother had avoided using her name for three days now, ever since she had returned with news of the slavers. That information caused much concern among the women of the well. After only a day's talk, the Old Carving Well joined with the Slow Sand Well to track the trespassers and plan the ambush. Soon, messengers would take the story of this slaughter back to their wells and then to all the other wells. Slavers had not been seen this far north for ten years, not since they came in force against both the towns and the wells. Many sand-walkers had been lost back then, and if they came again in great numbers, no well would be safe.

Yala moved down the line, unlocking each collar. The chain that joined them would be divided among the two wells, providing much metal for sand shovels, sled fittings, and tools. No one would take the collars, lest they bring a bad wind to trouble their lives. Besides, they would serve another use.

Tral came back to stand beside her daughter. She spoke to the freed slaves in the tongue of the town-dwellers.

"You are free. Free. Take what you need from them, from the bodies. Take clothes and coins. We will take the weapons. Yes? Take them and go now."

A man tried to stand, making it on his second try.

"Thank you, thank you from all of us! May you always find water!" He paused to steady himself against the shoulder of a young woman who rose beside him. "But we must have weapons too. Would you let us be taken again?" His voice quivered as much as his knees, but he stayed upright, a hand held out in supplication.

"No," Tral said. "Take the knives, but nothing else."

"Shall we die in the desert then?" he said. "We don't know this place. The slavers were taking us north, far from settled lands. Where are we? Are we near the coast?" the man asked, and many others rose from the sand, adding their pleas.

Tral shouted over all of them. "Where are you? You are in the desert. Look at your feet; that is sand! Look up. Can you not see the sun? Go to where it rises, and you will die in a few days. Go to where it sets, and you might live to see the coast. But you will die, most likely, and turn into spirit winds to trouble real people. Some of us will go with you to the Mother of Waters."

With that, she turned away, but Yala did not. The girl beside the talking man stared at her with burning eyes. Under that intense gaze, Yala bristled. It was her first battle, and she could still feel the dead flesh under her hands.

"You," she said, pointing at the woman with the tip of her bow. "Why do you stare at me so? What is it you want?"

The woman spoke in a tone as rough as blown sand. "I want every slaver in the world to die, sandwalker."

That voice, ruined and halting, came as true as any wind. Yala lowered her bow and nodded.

The woman coughed – a rasping sound – and added, "But I am weak, and crippled now by hardship and torment. Will you kill them for me?"

Her voice was cultured beneath the damage done by screaming, and there was a fineness to her manner that spoke of a very different life before the chains.

Tral stepped between them. She held out a long knife taken from one of the bodies.

"Brave words," she said, "but that is none of our concern. We only kill slavers that come into our land. Kill them yourself in your own lands, if you wish. Cheppo, lead these fools to the Mother of Waters, but look out for slavers on the way."

Yala followed her mother but looked back to see the woman sink back down to the sand, cradling the blade as if it were a child.

"Leave her," Tral said. "We have much to do back at the well."

Yala hurried to catch up. "Mother, I must go south and deliver the message Inla-phor gave me."

Tral did not slow down. "If your duties allow it," she said. When the others were out of earshot, she turned and hissed, "Dare you speak of this before the others? It was a promise you should not have made. Fool! Do you entangle us with the one-souled just to satisfy your own endless curiosity?"

Yala stopped short. Tral stood in her way, waiting for an answer, but Yala knew there was no answer she could give. It was more than curiosity that drove her to help Inla-phor. It was the bone-deep knowledge that the dying man deserved her help, because even the single-souled might suffer and grieve. Yes, sandwalkers were different, but if she and her people were twice-souled, shouldn't that make her more compassionate, more willing to help?

She did not say these things to Tral. Her mother waited until it was clear her questions would go unanswered, then turned and walked away. Yala set herself to the task of tying swords and spears to her sled, then taking up the harness and pulling away from the smell of blood. Soon, the sand-snakes and the hawks would come, maybe even a sandcat, to feast upon the bodies. In a few days, there would be little left, but if other slavers came first, they would find a grim message: their dead fellows collared in their own iron, with a long, leather whip threaded through each binding ring to tie them together in death.

CHAPTER 6
TOWN LESSONS

Marick shaded his eyes against the sun and peered up into the sky. As with yesterday and all the days before that, it was a weak, washed-out blue with not a single cloud to give it grace. The tower underneath that sky and the painted houses around it provided plenty to look at, but Marick wanted to ignore all that. He yawned and rubbed his eyes. Dreams kept interrupting his sleep, and for the hundredth time he wondered why he remembered them so clearly here, when in Shirath, if he dreamed at all, he forgot them on waking. He folded his arms across his chest and leaned against the well curb. Closing his eyes, he yawned again.

Maybe the lack of fun left a hole in my brains that the dreams are filling. Claws, what a thought. A whole month chained to this stupid town has driven me mad! I really will die of boredom if this...

He drifted off and was finally running and jumping over the rooftops. He looked down and saw the streets of Old Torrick, the city of his birth and where he first served as a bane. But in his dream, this was long before that. Here, he was just a hungry street-urchin, stealing to survive. He looked down and saw bread and cheese in his hands. It must have been a good night for thieving, but why was he running?

He paused in mid-flight. Something was on the roof with him. He tried to turn but could not. He could only listen. A quick, scrabbling sound came to him. He felt a claw of demon fear scratching along his spine. He ran, his legs now pushing against the stubbornness of the dream. The sound followed him, always a single step behind. Cries now rose from below, and he looked down to see the poor of Old Torrick chasing him, stones clutched in skeletal hands, calling to him in pitiful voices, "Feed us. Feed us." He pushed harder against the night. He couldn't feed them. There wasn't enough in his hands, and he must save that for his mother. She was hiding from the guards – no, she was hiding from what followed him, what had now caught up and was racing beside him effortlessly while he still struggled to move.

The dream demon spoke in the voice of his first training master, Corix. In harsh, dry tones, it said, "You cannot feed them all. Feed me, bane. Feed me."

Claws pressed into his back, and he leaped out into the darkness and landed, still dreaming, in the day.

He was on a rooftop in Shirath, the city he loved most. It was the same day he had found where the Masks were hiding. They had chased him through the fields surrounding the city and into its crowded wards. They were here now, blurred except for their stone masks and buzzing back and forth like bees.

Marick smiled. He had escaped before by his agility and wit, and now he would do it again. A board thrust out over the street below. He ran onto it, his legs as free and light as he remembered. A last jump from the springy wood and he was flying over the street, arms outstretched to grab onto the edge of the next roof and pull himself to freedom.

His fingers found no purchase. The roof retreated and shot up, became a multicoloured tower that pierced the sky. Flailing, he fell, and the Masks gathered below, eager for his death. He saw them clearly now, saw that they wore not one mask, but two. The outer one was the silkstone protection that gave them their name. The inner one was different. It was a human mask fixed over a demon face. The waiting figures bent and twisted into monstrous shapes. They howled for his blood, and the street rose up like a hammer.

A hand grabbed him. He pulled away, but the grip held, held and shook him until the last of the dream fell away. He opened his eyes to see Son-neen glaring down at him.

Marick started back but had nowhere to go, crouched in the angle of the well curb and the tower.

She poked him in the chest. "Northerner, you should be ashamed to sleep on duty."

"Duty?" Marick demanded. "Tell me, did the wall I was staring at run away?"

Son-neen half turned before swinging back to glare at the bane. "Very funny," she said. "Don't you have anything to do?"

Marick frowned. It was the same question he had been asking himself. Dorict was off buying paper to make more notes from his wretched books, and Vinir was inside with *him*, making a huge, useless picture.

"I'm supposed to wait until Vinir's done," he said, and sat back down.

"Whips and chains! Do you ever tire of resting?" Son-neen demanded. She put down the basket of food – she brought lunch for Chal-lat every day – and stared at Marick, hands on hips and shaking her head. "Enough! It hurts to look at you," she said, and grabbed his hand to pull him up.

"What? Let go." Marick squirmed but failed to free himself, a surprise to a practised troublemaker like himself. Son-neen was no taller than Marick but had long, strong limbs and shoulders that matched his own. She ran every-where, and Marick had never seen her without some burden to carry or push about.

Today, it seemed he was the burden, for she set her basket down on the fountain curb and pulled him back down the stairs.

"Wait," Marick said, setting his feet but only slowing, not stopping, his forward movement. "Someone will steal your basket! Look, I'll watch it if you have something to do."

Son-neen turned her head without lessening her pull. "Steal? Nobody steals, not if they're from here. 'Thieves only steal from their own names,' as my father said."

"Then he's crazy!" Marick protested. "You can't steal a name."

He grabbed the plastered pillar of a porch. Someone had pressed shells into the surface to make decorations, and he dug his fingers into a scallop-shaped depression. Using these hand-holds, he managed to free himself from Son-neen's grasp. She snatched at him again, but he jumped back out of reach.

"Wait!" he said from behind the pillar, hoping to distract her enough to escape. "Get your crazy father to help you, unless he's smarter than you and runs when he sees you coming."

That would be smarter than me too, come to think on it.

Son-neen stopped chasing him and shrugged.

"Smarter? Hard to say. He's been dead for ten years." She let out a long breath. "Look, you can't sit around doing nothing all day."

"That's what I tell Vinir—" Marick began, but Son-neen put a finger across his lips.

"Shhh! You're like a child. Fair trade, I'll take you around the town with me, teach you something, and you help me with my work. Deal?"

Marick pushed her hand away and glared, but any offer of movement was too tempting to refuse. The thought of returning to that little space between the well and the wall was like acid in his belly. After a moment, he nodded, and they were off.

They ran down the narrow street. Then Son-neen darted left into an alley and led Marick along it until they came out into a small courtyard. It had a fountain and three buildings forming the walls, identical except for colour: one was red, one was blue, and the last was yellow.

Marick pretended to look around while he caught his breath. He turned to see the girl looking at him.

"I'm sorry about your father," he said, nothing else coming to mind.

"Why?" Son-neen asked. "He died fighting the slavers when they came with a hundred ships to steal our city. He was a good carpenter who looked to the Red-Blue-Yellow Tower and died a hero on the docks. His name is safe enough."

Marick, who had never known his father and lost his mother when he was a small child, said nothing.

"Look," the girl said. "I've figured out that you're not dumb – well, not so much. More . . . uneducated. That's dangerous and really annoying. So, come over here. I want to show you something."

45

She took him over to the blue building. When he got closer, he saw that it wasn't a single shade of blue but a weaving of different shades, complex and subtle, that must have been the work of many days. The door was open to catch whatever breeze the morning offered. From inside came the voices of children chanting out a lesson. A stone pillar, head-high, stood beside the door. It bore a long list of symbols. Son-neen pointed out one set, which Marick could just make out as a name. He looked his question at her.

"Can't you read at all?" Son-neen asked, incredulous. "That's me! I worked for three years to make my name here. I sold bread on the docks, ran messages all over the city, and made paper flowers until my fingers ached."

"And that's all you got?" Marick asked. "Your name carved on a stone?"

Son-neen looked up at the sky as if that cloudless dome might lend her strength.

"Idiot! I helped build this school. I made my name worthy of carving. Storm and sloth! You say you come from Shirath like it's only a place. Well, I don't just live here; I *am* the City of Fountains, and so is everyone else whose name is on this stone and on all the other stones, fountains, steps, houses, towers, and ships! And that is forever! Do you see those names down there? They didn't help build this healers' school. They were on the building that stood here before this. We don't forget in the City of Fountains, and we build our names so we can always be part of it."

She waved at the wall, then twisted around to include the whole square, and perhaps the town beyond, in the motion.

"We're different from other people. I've met traders from Solantor and some from farther south than here. They come here every year or three and try to make as much coin as they can before they sail back home. They parade around with their sword-guards and mad clothes, and our towers have to check every deal, because foreigners cheat to make more profit."

Marick watched, eyes wide, as she stomped back and forth, waving her arms.

"They're idiots! What use is wealth if it's locked in a chest?" Son-neen demanded. "What use is a name if it isn't remembered?" she asked in her piping voice. She stopped her pacing to look at Marick.

"Enough," he said, one hand raised. "Do I have to pay for such foolish wisdom?"

"Yes," Son-neen said, "but I'll throw this in for free, since you're a beggar when it comes to sense. Tell me, Northerner, what will your name be if you just sit by a wall and complain?"

Marick started to laugh at her posturing, but he found he had no good answer to her question. Son-neen smiled, and they went on, picking up packages from one part of the town and taking them to another all morning. Marick marvelled at her energy. When there was room, she ran. When there wasn't, she strode. The beating sun seemed to have no effect on her, not even burning her pale skin. After much more running, Marick decided that it was possible that Son-neen moved too fast for the sun to scorch her. It seemed she did this every day, filling up the slow times when Chal-lat was making art.

"Usually, I only have to be there when he goes to his studies, comes home, or needs his lunch," she told Marick.

"Sometimes he sends me out to pick up his supplies, like the day you first came to the tower. Not today, though. That's good, since it's a busy time now with the festival coming up. Here, give me the cloth," she said, and handed the bolt over to a shop owner who gave her a coin. The coin went into a pouch with a clink that showed it wasn't alone.

Out in the open and hanging by a single cord! I could take that pouch in a trice and she'd never know it.

He didn't though, and no one else did, so he began to believe her tale of a town with no thieves.

"Why is it so busy?" he asked, taking a paper-wrapped package from her. It smelled of spice and berries, reminding him that he was getting hungry.

"The Tower Festival is in three nights," Son-neen said. She took back the package and checked the address written in ink on the surface.

"It's always a big party, so everyone is too tired to work the next day. That means they work extra-hard in the days leading up to it."

Then they were off again. Though Marick wanted to ask more about this Tower Festival, it was hard to converse at a dead run. When they returned to the Purple-Yellow-Green Tower at midday they found Chal-lat already eating his lunch, the contents of the basket laid out on the curb, and to Marick's dismay, he was not alone.

He was sitting very close to Vinir on the curb of the fountain. He offered her some dried fish, and Son-neen nudged Marick with an elbow.

"I never saw him stare at anything except murals and mosaics," she whispered. "But now he seems to have found something better to look at."

Marick held his answer behind his teeth. Vinir had been spending too much time with the young man, who was handsome, Marick supposed, in a useless sort of way. They were talking now, and he listened as closely as Son-neen did, though with much less enjoyment.

"You must work with dangerous materials in Shirath," Chal-lat said.

Vinir choked a bit on the piece of fish but managed to swallow it down.

"What do you mean by dangerous?" she asked. The bane shot a glance at Marick, but he shook his head.

"Your hands," Chal-lat said. "I can't help but notice the scars. I have some from working with glass, of course, but those – and the one on your neck by your right shoulder – seem too long to be caused by that."

At Vinir's arched eyebrows, the young man did a little choking and coughing of his own. Vinir pounded his back, and he managed to sputter out, "Not that it detracts from your . . . I mean they don't, well."

"Have you been examining me when I wasn't looking?" Vinir asked, smiling.

Marick ground his teeth until Son-neen looked at him in a very measuring way.

Chal-lat managed a weak chuckle. "See and remember, as Master Sarth always says. He claims that a true artist can take in an entire street scene at a glance."

"So, I was only worth a glance?" Vinir asked, tilting her head and looking at her fellow student.

Son-neen pulled Marick away from Vinir and the very flustered Chal-lat.

At the bottom of the steps, she said, "Let's leave them to work it out. Hanging around won't help them or you."

Marick stopped in his tracks and shook off her arm.

"What's that supposed to mean?" he asked.

Son-neen looked at him and shook her head. "You really are stupid as a stone," she said. "You're in love with Vinir. That's as plain as a storm and as clear as a blue sky."

Marick backed up, but Son-neen followed him, step for step.

"Hey, don't worry. I fell in love with Chal-lat for two whole ten-days when he hired me. Servants always fall in love with their employers, or the other way around. Songs and plays are full of such things."

She stopped and set her hands on her hips. "You'll get used to it. You'll just be love-smacked until you see its hopeless, or that she isn't what you thought she was, then you'll fall in love with someone else, though . . ." she said, crossing her arms and frowning, "you might have trouble finding someone who'll put up with you."

That was too much. Despite his aching legs, Marick turned and ran. He dodged around vendors' carts and knots of students listening to street teachers. He ran as if the demon from his dream had appeared and was close upon his heels. When he came to quieter streets, he did not slow down, dashing up the long flights of steps between the town's tiers and pounding down the garish streets until he came to the large park at the south end of the town.

There, he leaned against a tree and gasped for air. Even that angered him. This town had taken so much from him: Dorict, Vinir, and now even his strength. A morning running after Son-neen shouldn't have tired him so much. There had been so whole days in Shirath when he hadn't taken a step slower than a dash. Now, he could barely last a few hours at speed.

At last, his heartbeat slowed, and his chest stopped heaving. He even managed a half smile. He had forgotten how good it was to run all out, even if you were running away.

After he caught his breath, he looked around. The park was empty for the most part. A few elderly men and women took their exercise there, swinging arms and hopping about, and others fished at the edge of the salt-water lake, though he realized they must be using long lines indeed to reach the water below. Dorict had mentioned that such lakes were actually tunnels to the sea, and the level of the water came up and down with each tide. There were three such deep salt lakes in the town, the largest very near their inn.

It's a shame Son-neen didn't follow me. I could have thrown her in!

Hands on hips and wincing at the tightness in his legs, he shuffled down a tidy path between neatly shaped trees.

Everything in this town is planned, pruned, and cleaned to within an inch of its life, even the people. The whole place is like one of Andarack and Dasanat's machines. And everything fits into it, except me. Even Dorict and Vinir are becoming a part of it.

He didn't' understand how Dorict could bury himself in books and Vinir could, well, forget herself when they should be *doing* something. They had a mission. They were banes; they had always been banes.

He sat down on a stone bench, sighing a bit in relief. True, as his dream had reminded him, there had been a time when Marick was not a bane but a child-thief, running along the rooftops of Old Torrick, that ancient city set where the Midlands met the River Ar. The lords there didn't much care about parks or pruning, or even their citizens. They cared about money. In fact, they were exactly like Son-neen's description of all foreigners, squeezing every coin they could from their subjects. That wealth went to the comfort of the lords, not the support of their subjects.

Marick's mother had died from such neglect. Abandoned without help or hope, and with a small child to raise, she gave up. A long descent into illness and drink ended her life, and a very young Marick ran from the guards who would have sent him to work for the profit of the city's rulers. Instead, he had lived as he pleased, mocking everyone and everything, until the night he came face to face with a demon.

He had meant to raid a lord's house, a fancy mansion full of food and treasures, but a Rat demon had beaten him to it. He followed a trail of corpses to find it menacing a child, a mere infant in its crib. That was when he found out he was a demonbane, one who had tasted enough fear in his life to learn something about controlling it, and so able to blunt a demon's paralyzing power.

He had grabbed the baby and led the beast on a dizzying chase across the rooftops and along the top of the city's walls. At last, he crushed the creature beneath an avalanche of loose stone, in full sight of the banes of Old Torrick, who took him in and trained him for a year. After some misunderstandings about a series of pranks and who really owned what, Marick was sent with farewell curses to Shirath, and there he had stayed.

But as a bane. That's what I'm supposed to be. Vinir and Dorict have forgotten what they are. Thanks to all of Garet's high talk, they think the demons can be defeated for all time, so there'll be no more need for banes. She'll be an artist and he'll be a book reader of some kind, maybe even a steward, but what of me?

The leaves whispered in the fitful breeze, but they had no answer for him. He walked over to the salt pond and looked down, over the stone railing. The sun was just high enough to reach the water. It was low tide, he supposed, but even at the highest tide, the sea would stay well below the circular banks. If it ever did rise higher, this tier of the town and all below it might wash away.

Marick waited in hope for a while, but no such cataclysm occurred. The few people nearby threw long, weighted lines down into the shadows, hoping to hook any fish trapped there by the in-rushing current.

"Old codgers fishing!" he muttered under his breath.

This is what passes for fun in this town! Maybe I should go look for One-Eye or take his advice and go to that Mother of Waters on my own. Would Dorict even pull his nose out of his books and miss me? Would Vinir . . .

An old man in a faded grey tunic wedged his fishing pole between the stone bench and his thigh and turned to look at Marick.

Before he could turn away, the bane looked back into the man's eyes – a watery blue, deep, curious, forgiving – and the bane felt . . . smaller.

Marick had lived his life looking down on people. Even his friends provoked him into good-humoured scorn: Dorict with his eating and timidity, Garet with his boring dedication, Salick with her lack of humour, and even his beloved master, Tarix, who was limited to a limping walk while he could race across Shirath's rooftops. He soared above all of them. Even an arrow through his leg had failed to slow him down, though it left a scar that still itched.

In all his life, Vinir had been the only one to capture his unqualified affection, but now, Chal-lat hung over her shoulder and all she thought of was art.

Maybe I was wrong. Maybe she's like all the other clawed fools who crawl along the ground when they should be flying like birds. Why can I see this, and everyone else is blind?

But the eyes that looked back at him now were not blind.

They saw him. Marick felt the gaze held neither a contempt for his foreignness nor jealousy of his youth. With a slight nod, the old man turned back to his fishing, and Marick shook himself.

No. He backed away from the well. He rejected any kinship with the people of this town, or even with the people of Shirath and Old Torrick, with the whole world, if need be! He was alone in this world, walled off by his perfect understanding of its stupidity and pain.

The fisherman whistled a tune, practised notes trilling up and down in a haunting scale. It ran up Marick's back, and he shuddered. Turning away, he walked back towards the tower, thinking up excuses for his absence, but in the end, he didn't need to make any. Vinir had not noticed he was gone.

CHAPTER 7
NAME AND CHAINS

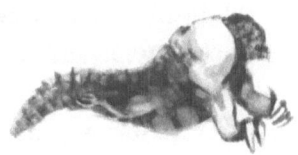

Yala watched her cousin, Sota, take her sled out along the path that pierced the rock wall. She was on her way to the Mother of Waters with a load of trade goods.

Journey carefully, Sota. I wish I was going with you, but will they ever allow me to take that road again?

She shrugged that thought away and returned to the trade-house. At the back, an old woman waited for her. Yala handed her Sota's reed-paper tally and waited for a grudging nod of approval.

Would it split their faces to smile? she wondered.

It had been a month since the attack on the slavers, and she had not set foot beyond the limits of the well. Every small task that came up in the trade-house found its way into her hands. Every request to leave so that she could fulfill her promise to Inla-phor was brushed aside. Her mother was behind this, of that Yala was sure.

She had tried to complain to her grandmother, Ke, but was cut off before she could finish.

"Are you Yalasana to whine like a baby?" Ke asked. "Earn your name, Yala, and do what is given you to do."

So Yala had done just that. She fixed holes in the roof a hundred days before the first rains would come. She arranged trading tallies, taking them off their shelves and then putting them back in the same place she had found them. She hunted for dust to wipe and sand to sweep, and there was always another job waiting.

As the time of the solstice neared, she worried that she would be chained by these tasks until after the spring rains. Every time she spoke of leaving, some old woman mocked her with her childhood name, as if "Yalasana" had never been shortened to "Yalasa" and then "Yala" by hard work and the slow growth of wisdom.

So, they would make me out to be a child? Enough of names and chains. I am Yala. Yalasa and Yalasana are gone, and I don't care if I ever become Yal or Ya. Let the future worry about itself; I am Yala, and I choose to stay or go.

Easy to think, but hard to say, as she found when she confronted her mother at the wind mandala. The older woman stood at the edge of the carving, pouring white sand onto the deeply gouged lines that quartered and re-quartered the circle.

"A change wind," Yala said. She stood behind her mother, her back touching one of the pillars that tracked time by the sun's shadow.

"But too close to full west," Tral said, not looking back. "Chaos, disruption. This is not change. It is disaster."

"Wind is not always a clear prophecy," Yala said, quoting Tral's own words. She swallowed before continuing. "Mother, I must go now, or I'll be false to my promise."

Tral did not turn but kept her eyes on the streaks of dropped sand.

"Go," she said, "and you come back as Yalasa, not as a sandwalker. Will you risk your name for this foolishness?"

Yala forced out an answer, pushing it past the fear and sorrow in her heart.

"If I break my promise to a dying man, what good is any name to me?"

When the last word left her lips, she felt as light as a hawk's feather floating on the wind. Her answer had set her free, and she knew this as both a joy and a terror. The next words were easier, though they bore great sadness.

"Whatever my name is, if I still have one when I return, I will always honour you, Mother," Yala said, and turned away.

She did not leave fast enough to miss Tral's last words, words that cut like a pit-killer's jaws.

"Whatever name you try to claim, it will not be 'daughter.'"

CHAPTER 8
THE FESTIVAL OF THE TOWERS

The longer he dawdled in this town, the more Marick felt alone, even abandoned. It sent his thoughts back again and again to that dark place in his childhood, when his mother died. Being so alone, it had been easy for Marick to hate everyone else. That heat in his heart had made the long nights easier to bear. In Shirath, surrounded by Dorict, Vinir, Salick, and all his other friends, he had almost forgotten those days. Now, he seemed Heaven-cursed to live them again.

Vinir spent her days with Sarth and that fool, Chal-lat, and her nights sketching and playing with bits of glass. As for his so-called friend Dorict, he spent all his days studying books and all his evenings "looking around the town." If Marick didn't have such a low opinion of Dorict's romantic abilities, he would have thought the bane was stepping out with a young woman.

That night, he looked across the table to where Dorict sat shovelling in food. The sound of his chewing and the scratch of Vinir's pen set hooks in his stretched nerves.

It was too much. They were all here on a fool's errand. None of Vinir's fellow students had heard of demons, though they said many horrible beasts lived in the deserts lying north and east of the town. As for Dorict, he had found nothing useful either. Yet, they both sat there, ignoring the plain fact that they should leave this clawed town and return to a normal life in Shirath. Had he not feared the dreams that waited, Marick would have left his dinner and gone straight to bed.

He managed to keep his tongue behind his teeth until he finished eating, a feat of willpower that turned the stew to acid in his stomach. At last, he could stand this noisy silence no longer. Since his supposed friend had failed to see how he was nobly ignoring the situation, he slapped his hand down on the table and demanded, "So, where do you go at night? Is she pretty enough to make you forget your duties?"

Dorict glanced up from his stew, startled, but his look quickly changed to one of anger.

"You're going to lecture me about duty?" he asked. "And what if I am seeing someone . . . I mean, I'm not 'seeing' her."

He pushed his bowl away, half-finished for once, and stood up.

"If you need to know, Bortor, the owner of the bookstore where I'm conducting my research, has a niece named Vella who's a bookbinder. She's showing me something of the work . . . and she's better company than you are these days – or any days, now that I think of it."

He left the room, closing the door with more force than was wise, for Marick heard the innkeeper chide him on the stairs and Dorict's brief apology.

"Why do you irritate your friends so much?" Vinir asked. She was sitting up on her bed, her meal forgotten on the table and her sketching pad in her hands.

Marick said nothing aloud.

Why do I? Why do you task your friends so much by taking up with a foreigner? Why do you keep me from doing what I can to help? And why are we still here when they know nothing of demons in this town?

That last part at least he could put into words, and he did.

"Why are we here, Vinir? There's still no trace of demons. Isn't it time to go home?"

Vinir put aside the pad and stood, stretching out her arms until the joints cracked.

"Ow! Art is harder than I thought. All day I've had to bend myself into a knot while hanging off a scaffold thirty feet above the ground, and just to make a seabird's feathers!"

She shook herself and her braids danced. Marick swallowed.

"Soon," Vinir said, sitting down in the chair Dorict had so quickly vacated. "I suppose we have some information to take back. You're right that there're no demons in this town, and none farther south that Sarth's students have heard of. Still, they might be found in the desert, where all manner of wonders exist, at least according to Chal-lat."

"And he knows everything," Marick said. He pushed the bowl from him as if it held poison.

Vinir regarded him for some time before answering. "No, he knows a lot about art, but maybe not about other things. He's not puffed up, Marick. He knows very little about the world outside of this town, but he's eager to learn. Listen, you can't be angry if I make other friends. You know I'll always care for you. And you have Dorict here as well. He can cheer you up."

"Cheer who up?" Dorict asked. He had just opened the door. "Forgot my notes," he said, and picked up a shoulder-strapped bag from the table.

Marick shrugged. Dorict had offered to take him to the bookshop, but Marick's reading skills were not the best, so he had sullenly refused. His demands that Dorict accompany him on explorations into the darker corners of the town, if there were any, had been dismissed with the wave of a hand.

"We were talking about the wonders of the desert," Marick said, and Vinir hid a smile behind her hand.

Dorict paused at the door. "There are wonders, or so Bortor's books say. Some of the beasts found there are savage enough to be demons, though they don't cast any fear. There is a mention in one book of something called a killing wind or a poison wind that the sandwalkers fear, but there was no more about it," he said. Rubbing his chin, which rasped from a recent growth of bristles, he added, "If we could find a sandwalker to ask, we might know more, but they don't come closer than a trading town called the Mother of Waters."

Vinir leaned back in her chair. "I've heard the name, but nothing else."

Marick sat up. "It's a day's ride to the east on good roads," he said.

Dorict raised his eyebrows. "So, you've learned something after all. I hope the source was reliable."

"Not likely," Marick said, remembering One-Eye and his smell.

Vinir laughed. "Good! Even if the source isn't reliable, I'm glad you're getting to know the people here."

Marick slouched again. "Not really. Nobody stops to talk. They're too busy making coin. I mean, Son-neen talks. She never shuts up! But she never says anything useful either."

"She's all right," Vinir said. "In fact, she reminds me a bit of you." She held up a hand at his protest. "Well, maybe not entirely, though you're both so full of energy and opinions! But I see what you mean about people being too busy to talk. They're so rushed, so . . . dedicated. Garet and Salick would do well here! I think you have to get inside their lives, like Dorict and I have. You could try that, at least with Son-neen."

She grabbed for Marick's tongue, which he had stuck out but quickly retracted.

"Hah!" she said, grinning. "And, even if there are no demons, we can tell our people how others in the world live, for this is a strange place, strange to a girl from Shirath anyway. They're always trying to chase profit, like you say, but they give away their coin as soon as they earn it! I ran into an old man today selling buttons. Chal-lat said he was once as rich as a king but used all his wealth to rebuild parts of the city after the slavers raided a decade ago. Now he pushes a button cart, but people still treat him like a king." She chuckled and added, "Our dear Lord Sacourat would die of shock if she saw him, and good riddance!"

Marick and Dorict both smiled at that. Sacourat was the miserly lord of Shirath's Fifth Ward. She was very rich and also very loyal to the banehall and the king, as long as people were looking.

Vinir stood up and stretched again. "Oh claws, my muscles are both overworked and underworked here. Tarix wouldn't be pleased!" she said, referring to the master who had trained them all. "Come on, you two. Let's go down into the kitchen yard and amuse our lady innkeeper by practising our banehall skills. You too, Dorict. Your book-making girl can wait a night to see you again, or is that too long for love to bear?"

Dorict reddened but picked up the staff from where it leaned in a corner. Marick retrieved his from under his cot, and Vinir removed a pair of long knives from her bag of brushes and pigments. They trained in the small courtyard, attacking and avoiding, each taking a turn in playing the demon. Their host was mightily impressed and gave them each a large slice of cake for the show.

Fair trade.

For that evening, at least, Marick felt something of home's peace come back into his heart. When he slept, his dreams slipped from memory like fish diving through deep waters.

TWO NIGHTS LATER, the town changed. From sober speed and courteous commerce, it fell into a mild riot of celebration and joy. Even before the towers rang evening on their bells, people came out onto the streets to drink and dance. They wore unexpectedly colourful cloaks over their sombre tunics, patchwork things with a front and back and a hole for one's head. Marick guessed that they represented individual towers, for each cloak – like those tall spires – bore only three colours. The dancers nearest to him were all in yellow, purple, and red. Behind them came a larger group in orange, blue, and yellow.

Not all were dressed so bravely. When Son-neen came

to the inn to collect Marick after supper, she wore a pure black robe that reached her ankles, black boots, and a dark blue mask chased with silver wire that dangled from one hand.

When the bane saw it, he stepped back.

"What's the matter with you?" Son-neen demanded. "Haven't you ever seen a mask before?"

"Lots," Marick replied, "but the people wearing them are usually trying to kill me."

Son-neen laughed. "I'm not surprised! Come on, your friend is already out there. I saw him with Vella, Bortor's niece, and I don't think they were talking about books. Where's your boss?"

Marick shrugged. "Vinir's up on the roof. She wants to make sketches of the festival, she said."

"I don't think anybody has ever done that. Everyone is always in the festival, not watching it, but you'll see it better than she does. I promise you that."

"Is this still part of our trade?" Marick asked. He slipped on his cleanest tunic, dark green with a short collar and wide sleeves, over his undershirt. Son-neen looked pointedly at his boots until he bent over to wipe them with a cloth from the washstand.

"That first trade? Not likely," she said, "so expect to run and carry for a few days more. Hey, why is there a bruise on your cheek?"

"Practising," he said, and straightened up.

Son-neen snorted. "What, practising walking into walls? You foreigners are funny. Come on then, or I'll be late!"

The length of her robe hampered her usual speed, until she hitched the fabric up under her belt and sprinted out of the inn and across the road to the festival grounds. Marick managed to keep up this time.

At least I'm getting back into demon-fighting shape!

The big field facing the inn was lit up by hundreds of oil lanterns, which seemed an incredible expense to Marick, though perhaps oil was cheaper here since the oil pools were closer. Under those lamps, the citizens of the City of Fountains laughed and danced, laying aside their serious nature for a night and drinking from some deep, shared reservoir of joy. One group of people didn't dance. They stood in the centre of the field and were noteworthy for having no colour at all, just black robes like Son-neen's. She led Marick straight to these people.

"Son-neen!" an old man called out. He pulled back his hood and removed the round, blue mask he had been wearing, revealing a white beard and anxious eyes. Marick thought he had seen him selling vegetables on the market level of the town.

"You're very late," the man said, "and who is this you bring? The foreigner? He should stand aside or he'll ruin the dancing."

"Tell that to your carrots!" Son-neen said, brushing down her robe. "He'll get out of the way when it starts, won't you?" she said, turning to Marick.

He shrugged, which she dangerously took as a yes. He helped her tie the ribbon of the mask, glad that these were made of some sort of stiff paper and not of silkstone with a murderous ex-Duellist behind it. He then found a spot at the edge of the field and squatted down to watch.

Nothing happened for a while, except the dancing, which seemed to be in pairs or groups of various sizes. There was no music to dance to, but lots of drumming. Marick sat beside one such player and was impressed with her energy. When the woman saw this interest, she nudged a smaller drum over to him with a foot, all the while keeping the beat. Marick shook his head, but she kept pushing it towards him until he picked it up. It seemed small enough to go unnoticed among all the larger drums, so he began tapping it, trying to copy the woman's rhythm. She smiled at him and he kept it up, feeling himself drawn into the spirit of the gathering, not entirely against his will.

At some signal he missed, the dancing stopped, and so did the drums, his hesitant strike being the last one heard. The woman said, "Wait a bit. It'll start again soon."

She drank from a flask and offered it to Marick, but he declined. Wine dulled the wits.

There was movement in the crowd; something was happening. People crowded against the edges of the field, and the drummers, including Marick, stood up to watch. He saw the group of black-clad men and women in the centre of the field spread out until they formed a circle. They linked arms at shoulder height and began to dance. Moving a few steps left and right, and then a step or two inwards and outwards, their feet scuffed the ground, making the only sound in the space left by the silenced drums.

A person near the rising tiers called out, then another. Soon everyone was pointing and calling, and Marick turned to see bright apparitions floating down the tiers of the city, all of them coming towards the festival ground.

Looking closer, he saw that they were platforms, lit up in some way, and carried on the shoulders of men and women. When they came into the field, he saw that each platform bore a model of a tower made of wood and glass, the panes coloured to reflect the colours of the city's real towers. Lights shone from inside them, making them giant lamps. They were all carried onto the festival ground through partings in the crowd, tipping back and forth under the enthusiastic steps of their bearers, each shining like captured daylight.

"Green! Yellow! Blue!" one part of the crowd shouted but were soon drowned out by those who wore the next tower's colours and yelled, "Yellow! Red! White!" in even louder voices.

Marick counted seventeen platforms as they came into the open spaces between the spectators and the circle of dancers in the centre of the field. The towers began to revolve around that circle, bouncing and wobbling until Marick feared they would topple onto the ground and spill their inner flames. By some magic or skill, they did not, and he let out a held breath when the platforms were carried to specific spots upon the field. Those wearing the same colours as the towers began to surround their corresponding model, dancing and chanting.

The woman beside Marick started drumming again, and he did as well, though he climbed up on the short retaining wall behind him to get a better look.

Nearby, two platforms were being pushing against each other, like two bulls put in the same pen. Many of those wearing their colours rushed in to add strength to the challenge, but the black-robes intervened, weaving their arms-linked dance between the two groups until they separated with a chorus of cheerful insults.

The black line danced away to another confrontation, then another, and Marick kept up his drumming, lost in the beat and the weaving, dancing throng until a familiar one-eyed face shook him from his trance.

The man was wrapped in one of the black robes, though not a well-fitting one, and he was helping a young man walk out of the grounds. His companion's legs wobbled at each step, and One-Eye's arm was more prison than support, pulling him away from the lights and prying eyes.

Marick gave the drum back to the woman and smiled his thanks. He wriggled through the crowd until he found the peacemakers dancing between another two bumping towers.

"Son-neen! Son-neen!" he called out, and one of the black-robes, a small one, ducked from the dance. Those on either side closed the gap with linked arms before anyone could break through their line.

"What?" Son-neen said, lifting her mask to peer at him. "I'm very busy here. You know, it's an honour to be a black-robe."

"Is it an honour to steal one of those robes and the person who wore it?" Marick asked. He grabbed her elbow and pulled her to where he had last seen the two leaving the festival grounds. As quickly as he could, he explained the situation.

"I'll get some help," Son-neen said. She made to run back to the crowd, but Marick held her arm tight.

"No! Trust me, for once. We can deal with this on our own. I've done this kind of thing before," he said.

She shook off his hand and looked at him. "Don't lie! You're a servant, like me, not a soldier or a port guard."

"I know what I'm doing!" he said. "Please!" he added, and the desperation in his voice, born of a bone-deep desire to *do something*, made her relent.

They ran up to the next tier, and the noise of the crowd lessened. Under a crossroad lamp, they paused and listened. Someone was talking further up, a drunk babble that was answered by a deeper, calming voice.

"I've got to . . . get back!" a man slurred. "I'm a black-robe. It's im-im-important. Where are we going?"

The deep voice replied, and Marick knew it was the one-eyed man who now answered the drunkard. "To get more wine, of course! Can't have a festival without wine, can we? Come on, then."

The other balked and said, "No, I-I shouldn't. Have to dance or they'll be . . . they'll be what? Fights, that's right. And your wine is too, too . . . very strong. The stuff you gave me before . . . before what? It's too strong. Let's go back."

There was a short, gurgling laugh before the other spoke. "We're going back now, so relax, friend," he said, but the voices were getting fainter, going farther up the town and away from the festival grounds.

Marick and Son-neen looked at each other. The girl twisted a lock of hair as she thought. "All right, we see where they're going, then we get help," she said, and they followed the voices.

Each corner was lit by a small oil lamp hung on a pole, and by that light they made their way up the streets from one tier to another. Once they were nearer the voices, they had to move as quietly as possible.

"He's wearing a black robe, but he wasn't chosen this year, though the drunk one was, I think. I don't even know who that other one is," Son-neen whispered in Marick's ear.

He turned his head and whispered back, "He spoke to me once. I don't know his name, but he's a horrible foreigner, like me."

Son-neen smothered a nervous giggle and pushed Marick forward. The voices stopped and then they heard the sound of a key in a lock. Marick glanced at his puzzled companion, understanding her confusion. There were few locks in this town. He had only seen them at their inn, probably for the benefit of foreign guests who were afraid to sleep without them.

69

They peered around the corner of a saddle-maker's shop in time to see a house door shut. After a shared, considering look, they slipped across the open space to press their ears against the closed door. The first thing they heard was the key again, then muffled voices. Listening as carefully as he could, Marick could make out only a few words, but Son-neen had better ears.

"I think he's telling him to stay there, maybe drink some more," she said. "That's disgraceful! He's a black-robe. He should be at the festival."

"Like you?" Marick asked, unable to resist the jibe. Son-neen glared and stepped back from the door.

"I'm going for help," she whispered. "You stay here and make sure they don't leave."

Marick began to argue, but there was a noise from within and the tip of a key appeared in the keyhole. He pulled Son-neen around the corner and behind a water cask. From their hiding place they saw the one-eyed man, still in the other's robe, lock the door and walk softly down the street.

"Don't go yet," Marick said. He pulled his lockpicks out of the top of his boot and went back to the door. Using a probe, he felt two pins that would have to be shifted to open the door. He was just inserting the proper probe when Son-neen grabbed his arm.

"What are you doing?" she demanded, not lowering her voice at all.

"Shhh!" Marick hissed. "We need to find out what he's up to before anyone else gets involved. Don't you want to save that man?"

Son-neen backed away, a strange look in her eyes, as if she was seeing Marick for the first time. She whirled and ran down the street.

Claws! She'll bring back her friends before I can search One-Eye's room, or worse, she'll run into him on the way down.

As quickly as he could, he worked the lock, twisting the picks, moving them according to the sensations of tension and release he felt in his fingertips. With a click, the lock turned, and he opened the door.

Stairs. He must live on the second floor. Heaven shield me from creaking treads.

He kept his weight near the walls, creating no noise. At the top of the stairs was another door, this one with no lock, and he pushed it open, a crack at first, then wide enough for him to slip through.

There was not much to see. There was a single window with a table pushed under it, and a stool pushed under that. Against the other wall was a cot. Splayed out on that was the robeless dancer, snoring like thunder and with a wineskin under one limp hand. Moving to the table, Marick scanned the papers spread over its top. Even with more light than the little that came in through the window, he doubted he would have been able to read much of it, so he thrust them under his tunic to save for Dorict to decipher. There was nothing else to look at. He found only dust beneath the bed and dirty clothes in a cloth bag keeping company with the stool.

He tried slapping the young man awake, but only got a curse and a shove for his trouble. Leaving him for Sonneen's friends, he took one more look around the room, checking for loose floorboards or cleverly covered holes in the wall.

Nothing. Best leave before I'm caught. At least I can show Vinir and Dorict that I'm still of some use.

He closed the door at the top of the stairs and came down as quietly as he'd gone up. He stood in front of the door for a moment, deciding whether or not to secure it from the outside when he left. It wasn't an easy choice. While it was always better to leave no sign of how you entered, he didn't want to leave the snoring man a prisoner.

He was still deciding when the door swung open. He leaped back, expecting the appearance of the one-eyed man, but it was Son-neen glaring at him, and she wasn't alone. Four black-robed figures stood behind her. She pointed a trembling finger at Marick, precisely where the sheaf of papers stuck out of his tunic.

"Take him," she said. "He's a house-breaker and a thief!"

There were several audible gasps.

"Son-neen, no!" Marick said, and turned to run back up the stairs, but many arms grabbed him and bound him with cords.

"What are you doing?" he yelled, as he tried to wriggle free. "I trusted you, and you betrayed me!"

Son-neen scooped up the lockpicks. "Search him," she said, spitting out the words. "A thief is tricky enough to hide a blade and cut his bonds."

Hands probed his clothes and soon found his hidden knife, climbing cord, and chalk. Two of the robed people remained at the house, and the others led him away, Son-neen following at a distance. The nearest tower was pink, orange, and white, and they left him there, still bound, in a high, bare room. Son-neen looked down at him, tears marking her cheeks, but when she spoke, her voice was steady.

"You say I betrayed you, but it was my name you risked," she said. "And after I gave you fair trade! Remember that. I will."

She left the room and pushed the thick door almost closed. "I'll tell Vinir what happened," she said.

"No, wait!" Marick called, but she shut the door. He had barely twisted upright from the floor when he heard a bar slide into place and Son-neen's retreating footsteps. He leaned against the wall and tried to curse, but what came out might have been a sob.

CHAPTER 9
THE WIND SPEAKS

"Whatever name you claim, it will not be 'daughter.'"

Her mother's words chased Yala out into the desert. She did not weep at this cold parting, but she cried later, in the shadow of a stone pile while she waited out the sun.

Fool! To lose water over something like this. You should have known you were breaking with her and leaving everyone you knew when you agreed to take Inla-phor's words to the Mother of Waters.

She looked out into the dying daylight and wiped her cheeks. The wind blew from the south, and then the southwest: sorrow and loss. She finished drying her tears and reset the goggles over her eyes. The glass holders were leather and let the sand in if they weren't tight enough, but that gave her a headache, so she had to choose between two types of pain.

All my life, the same choice.

The man she believed was her father had left these eye

shields on the wall separating the men and women's areas before she had left on her first solo trip.

"Someone might be able to use these, though they're badly made," he had said as she was passing. Then he walked away, and Yala, after checking that no one else was showing interest, picked them up. They were not badly made at all, of course – they were exquisite. The glass rounds were exactly the same size and lacked any bubbles or bumps. The leather was well-cured and oiled to prevent cracking in the dry air. On the straps, the maker had embossed a pattern of wheat stalks for strength, and an arrow's point for protection. She picked them up and said, as was the custom, "Someone left these old things here. I might as well use them, though they don't seem well-made."

When she left the well, her mother had even said they made her look like a sandwalker, the highest compliment she had ever given her daughter, and the last.

"Enough," Yala commanded her tears, though she spoke no louder than the whispering sand. She left the deep overhang that had guarded her day-sleep and climbed to the top of the natural shelter, feeling the heat of the falling sun still in the stone. On a flat space near the top, she crouched down and began drawing with a piece of ochre from her pouch.

First, the inner circle, then the quarters and the eighths. Now the next circle, and the next, then two more . . . and the final one.

She finished that last outer line and above each division drew the symbol of the animal: sandcat, locust, lizard, hawk, pit-killer, sandsnake, blue flier, and tocca. Inside that was the personal circle, left blank until the wind made its will known. Within those were the moon, season, and spirit circles. The innermost circle was that of male and female, old and young.

The mandala complete, she took a small bag from her pouch, untied it, and poured white sand into the palm of her hand. She held it for a long time, eyes closed, lips pursed. The sun was touching the horizon when she opened both eyes and fist at the same time.

The sand fell in long, white streams over the ochre circles. The wind caught some, moved it across the mandala, pooling it here and there until her hand was empty, save for the few grains that still stuck to her palm. She brushed these off against her red cloak and stared at the omens.

The first thing she saw was that most of the sand had fallen north. She swallowed. North usually meant death, but that tiny, white dune bent mostly to north-by-north-west, the spirit of the sandcat rather than the locust. Death by choices, then, not nature. It cut the season circle at spring, a male time, then the inner circle at a female eighth, but left a tiny pile sitting squarely beside that on a male space. Both read as young, which meant she could be the female, though she had no idea who could be the male. There were two other spots of white on the grey stone. One was on the spirit eighth of wisdom, almost edging into joy, and the other, twice as large, sat squarely in the middle of disruption.

Another breeze came up, whirling against the rocks and threatening to erase her mandala before she could meditate upon its meaning. She drew her cloak around it and waited until it stopped. Carefully, she uncovered the circles again, but stared in confusion. She had saved the white sand, but the passing wind had dropped red grains across it. To Yala's eyes, they bled streaks of red pointing both north and south.

She wiped away the sand with the empty bag, for the white grains were too mixed with the red to recover and use again. When she thrust the bag back inside her tunic, her fear lizard stuck out its nose from the leather tube tied to Yala's upper arm. She smiled and let Chit-chit creep about on her arm until a gust of wind drove it back into its sanctuary.

Yala climbed back down and checked the runners of her sled. The thin stone covering was well-set and polished, so there should be no problem pulling it through the dunes, and when she came to the hard lands nearer the Mother of Waters, she could use the wheels again. She picked up the harness then paused, thinking of the wind omens she had just seen.

Wisdom, disruption, and joy. Perhaps I'll learn everything in the world and change into a happy person. That would shock even Ke!

That brought a smile to her lips, and she set the harness around her shoulders in preparation for the long night of work.

CHAPTER 10

THE END OF DREAMS

The morning after the festival, Vinir didn't speak a word to Marick all the way from the tower to their room at the inn. The streets were nearly deserted, as Son-neen had predicted, but the few they did meet examined Marick as if he bore some dire, catching disease. To make it all the worse, Dorict was waiting for them in their room, though it was midday. He closed the door, and Vinir walked slowly over to the window and pulled it shut.

With a quick twist, she rounded on Marick and spoke.

"You clawed idiot! You've ruined everything. I don't know what you were thinking, or if you thought at all, but our mission is ruined because of you."

"Send me home, then!" Marick shouted back. "If you don't appreciate what I did . . . I found out something. That man is up to something, and it might have—"

"Nothing to do with demons," Dorict said. He didn't raise his voice, but his face was red with the effort of not shouting. "He told the tower people he was letting the other man sleep off too much wine, and that he was wearing the man's cloak so he wouldn't soil it if he was ill."

"A lie!" Marick said. "He's a villain of some kind. I know it because he's so sly. What about those papers?"

"If you could read as well as any Black Sash," Vinir said in a cold voice, "you would have known they were bills of sale for some animals. The man's a trader from the Far, Far South. He's bought exotic beasts before, to sell to the nobles there for their gardens. The tower people don't seem to like him much, but he's never broken any laws . . . unlike you. You broke into his house and stole those papers! Is it any wonder they believe his story and not yours?"

"But he was doing something!" Marick said, speaking to the floor.

Dorict slammed his hand on the table. "So were you!" he yelled, all restraint gone now. He backed Marick against the table and poked his chest with a stiff finger.

"Stealing here is as bad as, oh, I don't know, killing someone in Shirath! But I suppose you were so busy chasing shadows, you never found that out. Now, because of you, Vinir can't study art anymore, and I . . ."

Vinir turned away to look out the window. Her shoulders started to shake.

"You what?" Marick demanded, saying anything that would stop him from feeling so small. "You lost your new girlfriend because of me? Don't lie. She probably saw how much you eat and was too disgusted to stay!"

Suddenly, he was flying through the air.

"Dorict, no!" Vinir cried out, but the shock of hitting the wall took away any other words she might have been said.

When he came too, only a few breaths later, Dorict was still standing over him, chest heaving and fighting against Vinir's enveloping arms. Marick pushed himself into the corner by the window. He shook his head, trying to force his eyes to see clearly again.

"Enough, Dorict. Enough!" Vinir said and dragged the angry bane back to sit on his cot.

Still cowering, Marick turned his head to avoid his friend's angry eyes, but a firm hand grabbed his chin and pulled up his face so he could not do the same with Vinir's glare.

"You have betrayed the mission and your friends," she said. "You nearly ruined Son-neen's name as well, until I told them that you were known for such behaviour so it wasn't her fault. They wanted to throw us out of the city right away, so I had to tell them why we're here."

She let go and sat down heavily on a chair. "Claws! Everyone is talking about this, or soon will be. If there are agents of those Shirath traitors in this town," she said, "they'll know banes are here."

Dorict took a deep breath and let it out slowly. "What did the tower people say when you told them?" he asked.

Vinir frowned. "Believe me, they weren't happy at being fooled, but they are a sensible people, and I convinced them our mission was important. Heaven shield them for their understanding and mercy! They chewed on it all night, but in the end all the towers agreed. They will let us go to the Mother of Waters to ask the sandwalkers about demons before we are put on a ship and sent back home."

She turned back to the window. The hand on the sill was shaking, but her voice was steady.

"We leave tomorrow. You will continue as a servant, since you have failed at being a bane. When we return to Shirath, I will report your actions to Hallmaster Branet. You've been thrown out of one banehall already, so I suggest you plan a future as something other than a bane."

Neither spoke another word to him that day or night. They all packed their bags in silence. Vinir made a small stack of pigment bottles and brushes on the table and set a coin and a note beside it. It asked the innkeeper to return the materials to Master Sarth, with another note expressing her thanks and profound apologies to the art master. Dorict left his own note to the bookseller, then a second one, sealed in candle wax. Marick felt the heat of the others' anger on the back of his neck until Vinir blew out the candle.

All three tossed and turned that night, but it was Marick who woke up sweating and thrashing in the narrowest part of the night when the darkness left barely enough room to breathe. He clutched the bedframe and tried to make sense of what had happened, but all he could manage was one thought that came to him again and again.

What do I do now?

CHAPTER II
UNDER THE SUN

D*o not sleep under the sun, no matter how tired you feel. That is death. Do not sleep until you find shade. That is life. Do not sleep under the sun...*

Those words repeated in Yala's mind, over and over, while she sweated beneath her cloak, the red cloth blending with the sand and hiding her from the slaver camp. She had come upon them unawares, leaving her sled at dawn and climbing a dune to see if the next water refuge was near enough to risk pulling through a morning sun.

It was. It lay so close that if the breeze had been blowing towards her, she might have been warned by the voices of many men, but instead it blew the words away, and she had to drop to the sand and curl up under her cloak before a roving eye saw her. Forming a careful tunnel for her sight, she counted, then counted again. Ten in view and maybe more to come, for these ones seemed content to wait. They cooked meat, drank from skin flasks, and cursed as if they knew no other words. Two worked with hammers on a long chain, adding iron collars every three or four feet.

Their captives were kept under a rock overhang, too

much in shadow to be counted, but their presence made Yala curse under her breath.

"Death and deep water!" she whispered. "Did those fools learn nothing from the message we left them in the dunes?"

While the sun climbed, Yala watched and thought, pinching herself to stay awake under the smothering heat. None lived at this particular shelter. There was water enough for travellers but not enough for the population of a proper well. It should have been empty until the next trade moon, when sandwalkers pulling heavy sleds might stop to refill their waterskins before going on to the Mother of Waters. That had been Yala's plan, before she saw the slavers.

She needed the water. Sandstorms had kept her sheltering among an outcrop of dry rocks for days. Last night, she had drunk the last drop from her stores and made the decision to continue travelling, even after the sun rose if necessary, rather than wait till night and backtrack to the last cache of supplies.

A foolish choice. Fear drove me on when good sense should have stopped me.

A day's patience and the thirst that went with it would have been uncomfortable but travelling under the sun could kill the most experienced sandwalker. If you lost too much water to sweat, the heat could put false pictures in your thoughts, making you see vast fields of water where there was only sand. Go far enough, and some said the sand spoke to you in words, leading you farther into the desert until the sun shrivelled you up.

Tral would beat me for this if I were still her daughter, but even she must think it bad to find more slavers here.

Many years ago, when Yala's grandmother, Ke, was a

child, slavers attacked the Mother of Waters and pushed north, raiding the nearer wells. The nobles of the Far South had much wealth but no souls, as Ke told the tale. Gold and silver flowed through their hands, but they were evil and would not pay coin to their workers, like the towns did. Instead, they sent slavers, like the ones who killed Inlaphor, to steal men, women, and even children. Those raids had been met with arrows and sharpened shovels, but the slavers were many and the southern wells suffered greatly.

Then the raids stopped. Many said the sandwalkers had beaten the slavers on their own, but in Ke's version of the story, the fight only turned when town-dwellers from the City of Fountains came to save their people at the Mother of Waters. That gave the wells time to gather all their forces and join the attack. Between the two forces, the slavers were forced back to the Bay of Tears and those who did not escape by boat died at the water's edge.

After that, only one raid of any note had occurred. Ten years ago, a new band of slavers, raiding from islands offshore, again attacked the Mother of Waters and the City of Fountains. This time, the sandwalkers immediately came against them in great numbers, each well sending many women and even some men. Since then, none of the brutes had come into the desert to take real people captive. Yala's mother and grandmother believed that the slavers the wells most recently killed were not part of a new assault, since they were so few, but had merely been lost in the sand, like any other town-dweller, and had wandered north by mistake.

Lying motionless beneath her cloak, the image of that young woman cradling a knife rose in Yala's mind. What had become of her, of the angry old man, and of all the others? Tral and Ke would say it was none of their concern what happened to animals, especially after they led them safely out of the desert. Even that had been an act of necessity, not mercy, for when the one-souled died, their earth spirit, not held in check by a more noble sky spirit, clung to the desert, churning the sand and wind together in their pain. These whirling winds could travel for leagues and rip apart a camp or ruin huge swaths of planted crops. Despite the heat, Yala shivered. It had been unavoidable, but because of the sandwalkers' ambush, the ghosts of seven slavers now howled across the dunes, ready to trouble the living.

There were shouts from below. The men paused in their drinking and cursing to call greetings to a man guiding a cart up from the trail leading to the Mother of Waters. Below her perch on the crest of the dune, Yala saw the man, bald and single-eyed, yanking cruelly on the carthorse's halter. The poor beast drew a wagon made into a cage, such as the men of her well made to keep their chickens from running away, but this was much, much bigger.

Yala dared to widen the opening. She might as well have stood up and gotten a good look, for all the eyes below were on this new arrival and his captive.

It wasn't a slave, at least not a human one. The men gathered around the cage, poking sticks through the iron bars and laughing at the snarling reaction from within. It was a sandcat, a fierce and stealthy hunter whose kind ranged from the heights of the Fingers to the fog-covered western shore. Sometimes they killed the well's cows and horses, and a sandwalker who managed to set an arrow in one would be overwhelmed with trade goods every time she walked along the dividing wall.

Yala shook her head just a bit, fully alert now. Sandcats were swift and wary, so she could not imagine how this one came to be a growling captive in a cage, nor why stealers of people would also steal beasts.

While the slavers were distracted, she slowly crept back down the far side of the dune. At the bottom, she brushed the sand from her cloak and strung her bow, flinching when it creaked. She knew she could not stop them if they came after her in force, but a few well-placed arrows would slow them down. None came, and she sighed with relief. She would sneak away. Sneak and then sleep. She'd heard of a place farther on, though off the main trail to the town. Sandwalkers used it, which might mean water.

Don't sleep under the sun. Pull until you reach shelter.

She repeated those instructions to herself many times that morning. It was the only thing that kept her from collapsing beside her sled and letting the heat carry her off into the long sleep. When the sun climbed to its highest point, she reached a small stone ridge and crawled grate- fully into the meagre shade. She found the water sign on the wall and moved the concealing rocks until she found a full jar. At first she drank greedily, then, remembering her dignity, sipped. When she was done, she put a few trade goods in the hole as thanks. Lying on top of her cloak, against the hard rocks, she was asleep in a few breaths, and woke as the evening air cooled her skin.

While she waited for full dark, she checked the lashing of her cargo to the sled. It was a wonder she had anything to trade at all. She had expected to go empty handed except for Inla-phor's message, but when she pulled her sled past the low wall separating the women's and men's areas, she'd found a neat stack of trade goods wrapped in straw matting.

"These are poor goods," a quiet voice had said, and Yala saw Narrow Field Man sitting with his back against the men's side. "Not worthy of a sandwalker with such a long journey ahead of her," he'd added and got up. Without looking back, he walked down the hill towards the green of pasture and garden.

Yala had watched his straight back and long, black hair as he returned to the never-ending work of men.

"Perhaps these things are not as bad as they seem," she called after him.

He had paused for a moment, shrugged, then continued on his way. He was a young man, with only one scar, for he liked making things more than knife dancing, it was said. No woman had gone with him to the small houses at the end of the wall and, until now, he had favoured no particular person with his makings.

Shaking such memories from her thoughts, she picked up the harness. Whatever awaited at the Mother of Waters, she would have coin to deal with it, for Narrow Field Man had given her five packages of glass shards to trade and a sixth smaller box of copper and opals fashioned into ornaments loved by those in the South. That was as much as a seasoned trader like Tral might expect to carry. Narrow Field Man must have worked a whole season to acquire such wealth.

He waited to make sure I found these goods on the wall. He does not strut and preen like the one who is likely my father and most other men. He doesn't flaunt his scars or boast of his field, yet he trusts me with this. Why?

The wind spoke only to itself, and the stars spoke not at all, so she began another long pull, one that would last the night.

CHAPTER 12
ALONE

I've finally left that clawed town, and it feels as bad as staying.

So Marick thought over and over again on the wide road to the Mother of Waters. The view did not improve his mood. The surrounding dry land, a pan of baked soil and scrubby bushes, stretched as far as he could see. There was supposed to be a highland of dry rock ahead to the west and even drier desert to the north, but for now all there was to see were grey-green bushes that smelled like medicine and the swaying bottoms of the horses in front of him, which smelled worse.

He brought up the rear, riding a pony and leading another on a rope. That animal was foul-tempered, stubborn, and laden with all their baggage and supplies. If not for the food it bore, he would have turned the nag loose the first time it had tried to bite him. Now he must watch both ahead and behind, not that those riding in front him were likely to bite. Well, not too likely.

"Keep up," Dorict shouted, barely bothering to turn his head. Two words might count as an improvement after a morning of single-word commands like "mount," "hurry," and "quiet." Vinir had said nothing to him all day, and little to the others, even Chal-lat, who seemed to understand her mood and rode beside her silently. Marick could not even see her face, shaded as it was below a new broad-brimmed hat, a soon-to-be-parting gift from Chal-lat.

The only one who would talk to him was Son-neen. Every league or so, she dropped back to lecture him on his sins and promise an expensive retribution.

"You're going to pay for the damage to my name," she said for the hundredth time, or so Marick imagined. "I'm still calculating the cost, and you're lucky Vinir spoke up for me and Chal-lat convinced our tower to let me carry some letters of trade. That gives back some of what you took."

"Leave me alone," Marick growled, irritated out of his sullen silence. "I took nothing from you. I'm the one who got locked up. I'm the one they won't even talk to now, and I'm the one who'll be kicked out of the banehall when we get back home."

His pony flicked an ear at this, but the two banes riding ahead ignored him. Chal-lat gave Son-neen a warning look, but she was still glaring at Marick.

"Took nothing? I spent years making my name bigger. I told you what I went through to help build that healers' school. Even before that, I saved small-coin just to pay for street teachers. I learned fair trade and the rules of commerce from them when most were still playing with toys," she said, then stopped to breathe, but only for a moment. "In the last year, I'd gathered enough capital for a one-thousandth share of a trade ship that'll go next season to buy and sell along the Fog Coast. After your crimes, I was told to take my coin somewhere else, lest I taint the journey. What do you think of that?"

She managed to look indignant astride her pony, a placid beast that plodded on regardless of her moods. Marick frowned.

"I can't think at all," he replied, "or so I've been told, so I don't think much of your complaints! Find another ship or save for the next ten years and buy your own. Now, get away from me or I'll sic the pack horse on you."

At that, Vinir turned and gave him a cold, quelling stare. Marick's heart sank down to the bottom of his stomach and stayed there for the rest of the morning.

At noon, they stopped to eat in the shade of what Chal-lat claimed was one of the greatest building feats of the world. It was made of two parts. The first, a wide curb of cut stone that rose from the hard ground, circling a hole that stretched a good thirty yards across; the second, a series of connected arches that towered over them and stretched east to the limits of sight. The two were connected by an immense stream of falling water, a wondrous thing to see in this hard, dry land.

"It's the aqueduct," Chal-lat said. He pointed to the top, an unbroken run of stone held several stories above the ground, and launched into a detailed explanation that Marick ignored.

The noise was harder to keep out. It reminded Marick of a trip he'd taken long ago, down a spray-soaked road beside the Falls of the River Ar near Old Torrick. While that had been impressive, he decided this display was only annoying. He stepped back and glared as the water thundered off the end of the aqueduct and down into the deep hole to flow – he supposed – to the town they had just left, probably to feed its hundred fountains. He shrugged. It was an answer to a question he had never cared to ask.

"A river in the sky!" Vinir said, shocked for the moment out of her anger.

"That has to be forty feet high," Dorict said, shading his eyes. "I bet Dasanat and Lord Mandarack would like to get a look at this. How did your people make it?"

Vinir was already going back to the pack horse to get her sketching paper and charcoal. Chal-lat shook his head and said, "No, it wasn't us, though we repaired it when the city was founded. The aqueduct, the Mouth of the Mother of Waters, even parts of our city were made long ago, and by a people who are a mystery to us." He put a hand on the nearest pillar and looked up into the shadows below the high waterway. "But they built wonderful things."

Marick said, "It's not as impressive as the Falls at Old Torrick."

"Quiet," said Dorict, and Son-neen smirked.

Marick turned away.

I won't be quiet or anything else if this goes on.

He could feel old sensations rising up in him, a powerful mix of anger and contempt that had fuelled his thieving in Old Torrick and most of his dangerous escapades in Shirath.

If I'm not one of them anymore, then I don't have to jump when they call.

He had no wish to eat, so he drank some water and then gave the horses their share before spreading grain along their picket line in the shade of the aqueduct. Son-neen made a great show of taking out the leather folder of trade papers and going through their contents, exclaiming now and then how valuable they were and how much she was trusted. The others tolerated her with nods and grunts, but none noticed Marick, his back against a pillar, looking at those papers and scowling.

CHAPTER 13
THE ONE-SOULED WORLD

Yala looked in horror at the torrent gushing out of the cliff face. Green, foamy water splashed everywhere, more than she had ever seen at one time in one place. This was the Mouth of the Mother she had heard about all her life. It was beyond excessive. The most detailed reports had failed to match this lavish reality. It was ... frightening, for water was both life and death.

So much must be lost to the air and the rocks. How can the people here be so wasteful?

She eased her sled down one of the two roads that came from the dryland above, across the face of the town, and down into the shadow of the aqueduct. A few people passed her, quickly going down or more slowly going up, but she had eyes only for the roaring Mouth. As she came level with the torrent, she saw that less water was lost than she had first thought.

The water shot out from beneath the feet of a tremendous statue, a standing figure that was so worn it couldn't be called man or woman. From there, it crashed down on other carved images, these smaller and likely men, bent down under the burden of the great cauldrons they bore on their shoulders. Those slanted vessels tipped their contents into a grander pool, which in turn fed the great aqueduct. Yala followed that waterway with shaded eyes but could not see the end of it. Ke once told her that it ran west from this cliff all the way to the City of Fountains before all that water was lost in the sea. It was only in seeing it that Yala could now believe such a tale.

"It's big, isn't it?" a man said beside her.

Yala started and her hand went to the shovel hanging at her waist.

"Careful there!" the man said. He was sun-baked, stout and bald. One eye was missing, leaving only an empty socket to stare out at the world.

The one who met the slavers! Should I kill him? Do I have the right to do so in this place?

"See you're packing trade goods," he said, ignoring her silence and prodding the packages on her sled with a grimy finger. "Well, young sandwalker, I know the best places to trade. Why don't you come with me, and I'll show you where to get the most coin?"

He kept talking and moving until she was nearly pinned against the sled. One hand was suddenly on her shoulder, and the man grinned at her, revealing a half-toothed mouth.

Yala flicked her shovel free of its loop and pressed it against the man's throat. He froze, then lifted his hand and backed away.

"Easy there, desert girl," he said. "I've got friends, men who'd gobble you up if I told them to, so . . ."

A woman spoke from below them on the road. "I doubt you'll ever have any friends, at least until you bathe."

Yala slipped to one side so that she could see who had

spoken and still protect herself from the slaver. The woman was dressed in a grey tunic and pants, both bearing black stripes down the arms and legs. She tapped a short, knotted club against her palm. A man dressed the same way stood behind her, shaking his head and tapping his own club against a leg.

"We wouldn't be your friends even then," the man said. They were both brown-haired and slightly darker-complexioned than Yala. "I think we've already told you to mind your own business here, haven't we?"

"Or you could go back to the City of Fountains," the woman suggested. She had a slightly upturned nose that gave her an air of continual judgment.

Her companion's nose was bent in a different direction, but he seemed in complete agreement with the woman when it came to the one-eyed man.

"Probably don't like him any better there," he said, and stepped up to prod the one-eyed man with his club. "Go away, and don't bother other people. If you have trade, do it and get out. We find you sticking your nose in again, we'll put you in a cell underneath the Mouth, understand?"

"You won't like it," the woman added, getting in a prod of her own. "Water drips all the time. Drives prisoners mad."

The one-eyed man needed no more convincing. With a sour look at Yala, he scurried down the road as if a ghost wind were at his heels.

"Wrong sort to have around," the woman said. "I'll talk to the commander." She turned to Yala and put a hand in front of her heart, a sandwalker greeting.

"May I know your well?" she said, courteously avoiding asking her name.

Yala returned the gesture. "Old Carving Well," she said.

The woman nodded. "I haven't seen you before. Is this your first time at the Mother of Waters?"

Yala nodded. She had not expected to find anyone here who knew how to act like real people.

The man raised his eyebrows and turned down the corners of his mouth, making his face look even longer. "The thing is," he said, "there are some here who might harm you. We try to keep them under watch, but . . ."

The woman interrupted. "There's only so much we can do, see? Such people keep to the shadows. We've had our eye on that one for two days, but we have no cause to take him yet."

When she frowned, it made her round face look wider.

Yala thought about this. "Can't you kill him?" she asked.

He was a slaver, after all, though maybe they didn't kill such here.

The man and woman shot each other another look. "Well, we don't kill people just because we don't like them," the man began.

"Or you'd be dead long ago," the woman told him. She turned back to Yala. "Look, sandwalker. No killing – or even wounding – unless your life is threatened, see? It's the way of this town. If you trade here, you have to follow that rule."

Yala nodded. The foolishness of town-dwellers was well known.

"I'm Mor-ra," the woman said, "and this is Stetta," she added, pointing her club at her companion. "We're with the Watch. We guard this town like you sandwalkers guard your wells, understand?"

Yala nodded. This made more sense, though she wondered why they didn't carry bows.

Stetta looked down the road. "Mor-ra, I want to follow that man, and we should inform the commander."

Mor-ra raised her eyes to the flat, blue sky. "Are you a baby? Find some patience in that big empty head of yours."

Stetta frowned. "I use up all my patience on you," he said. "Goodbye, sandwalker of Old Carving Well. May the wind favour you!"

Yala made the gesture of parting, one palm facing out from the heart. "May you always find water," she said.

"Or wine," Mor-ra replied, and followed Stetta down the road.

At the last moment, Yala remembered the letter in her pouch, and chased after the two guards, her wheels rattling on the paved road. After explaining her need, Mor-ra took Inla-phor's note and promised to deliver it to the chief trader of the Far South.

"Slavers going north, hmmm?" she said, folding up the letter and sliding it into the top of her boot. "One more bit of trouble for the commander."

Stetta shook his head at the bad news before smiling at Yala. "Be easy," he said. "I'll make sure she deliver's this. A profitable day's trade to you."

Yala's trade was very profitable. Merchants from the City of Fountains exclaimed over the colour of the glass shards. It seemed that Narrow Field Man's work was known to them, at least by reputation.

"Old Carving Well, I think," a town woman said, examining a mass of red glass spread out for inspection. She picked up one piece and stepped away to hold it in the light.

The market was in the shadow of the aqueduct and bore no permanent structures, just tents, movable carts, and soft rugs that could be pulled away from the sun as it crept across the foundation stones. This cart bore flags of orange, red, and purple, and the grey-haired woman was ready to outbid anyone else for Yala's goods.

"Someone in your well makes the best glass I've yet seen," the merchant said. She pulled her hand back from the heat and put the piece with the others on the cloth.

"Fifty in coin or trade for each box, and another hundred for the worked goods," she said.

Yala considered. Before her first, interrupted journey, Ke and Tral had coached her on the current prices of everything from ground grain to beaten iron. The price was high, though perhaps not enough for the quality.

"Sixty for each glass box," she said.

The older woman frowned. "Fifty-two," she said, and sat back cross-legged on the rug.

"Fifty-nine," Yala said, after a long time pretending to consider.

"You call that fair trade?" the woman said. "Fifty-three, and not a coin more!"

Yala began gathering up the glass, careful of sharp edges.

The woman brought her hand down on a corner of the cloth. She smiled and shook her head.

"For one so young, you could trade sand for water! All right, fifty-five, and that's the best price you'll get in this place. And if I didn't have urgent orders to fill for my tower, I wouldn't pay so much."

Yala dropped the three corners of the cloth she had already gathered and held out her hand, palm down. The merchant placed her own hand, palm up, beneath it.

"It is done," they both said, and slid apart their palms.

"The woman called a boy over to carefully gather up the

glass. "Check the ground," she cautioned him before turning back to Yala. "Coin or trade?" she asked.

"Trade," Yala said, after a rapid calculation on fingers hidden under her robe. Thankfully, Ke and Tral had also taught her how to convert useless coin into useful trade goods. "Half as twelve metal ingots, and the rest in three measures of spice and a bolt of good quality cloth."

"As you wish," the woman said. "It will take all of this day to gather it. Will you take these tokens for now? It is how we do it here."

She handed Yala small wooden plaques, each thick with writing.

The merchant, who knew that sandwalkers did not read but used only a few symbols and numbers to record their trades, pointed to the top slip.

"This one says 'a standard ingot of iron' and this one is 'a large bolt of linen, red in colour.' The others add up to the amount I promised. The watch commander will tell you the truth of this, if you wish."

Yala shook her head. Ke had told her to trust the cart merchants with the coloured flags. They had a spell on them that made them trade fairly, she said, some magic of the one-souled.

With her wooden tokens placed carefully in her pouch, she pulled her sled back up the ramped road to the level of the aqueduct. It was hard work in the sun, even with the sled emptied, but she had no wish to linger in the bustle of the market. Nor could she wait in the shade of some nearby rock below, for the sun would soon bake the cliff face. Luckily, the town provided a refuge of sorts for sandwalkers. Yala searched for the right symbol above the many openings carved in the rock along the cliff-road wall.

Although these dwellings were dug-out caves, their

fronts were fashioned to look like two-storey buildings, with doors, windows, and the simulation of a roofline, but each room within was bored, not built. The sand-house, for so it was called, was one such a place. She found it near the top of the road on the far side of the Mouth, the wind mandala carved above the door. Two other sleds were left outside, tipped up against the wall. She placed hers beside them and entered the shadows within.

"Come inside and away from the animals," a woman called from the darkness.

Yala's eyes slowly adjusted to the dim illumination given by the opened door. Two sandwalkers sat on benches set behind a table. The one who had spoken was of middle age. She worked on a bowstring, stretching it out from a peg thrust into a crack between the table planks. Her fear lizard clung upside down on the line, unconcerned by the twisting and tightening of the fibres. The other was Yala's age, sleepy-eyed and nodding over a plate of stew.

"Old Carving Well," Yala said. "Yala, daughter of Tral and granddaughter of Ke."

"Red Rock Well," the woman replied. "Shen, daughter of Sil and granddaughter of Se, who's gone to the wind."

She pointed at the other. "She's Long Valley Well. It's her first journey, so she's worn out by all these animals." She tied off the cord and coaxed her lizard back into its stone tube by offering it a small bug plucked from the floor.

Yala set her pack against the wall and sat down on a bench opposite the two. The interior of the rock-cut house was pleasantly cool. She accepted the water flask offered by the Red Rock Well.

"Your first time too?" the woman asked. They both glanced at the young woman dozing with her head pillowed on her arms and her stew forgotten on the table in front of her.

"Second," Yala said. She pulled out a round of travel bread and bit into it, wishing she had sharper teeth.

"Here," the older woman said. She took the bowl from the table and slid it to Yala. A delicious aroma of lamb rose from it, but Yala shook her head.

"Go on! They bring it three times a day, as if we were their guests. I suppose they value our trade so much they act like humans, at least to us. Dip that bread in there and you might be able to chew it. Long Valley here can wait until sun-height to eat again."

Snores from the table joined with the wonderful smell of the stew to overcome any reservations Yala might have had about taking another's meal. She dipped the bread and began to eat.

"Good trade?" she asked after her third swallow.

"Good enough," the woman said. "Our well has a big source of alum. They want lots of it here to make paper, though why they need so much paper I don't know. Wind shreds it, water eats it. Seems useless to me."

"They write on it," Yala said, remembering Inla-phor's letter to his kin, though that had been written on reed strips. She had a momentary image of someone – a woman perhaps – reading that note and weeping. She blinked the image away and bit into the softened bread.

"Reed works for trade symbols," Red Rock Well said. "But these ones seem to have a thousand symbols and no sense. Can't expect much from animals, I suppose."

She got up and pulled a bedroll from her pack, unrolling it on the floor beside the table.

"Worse luck, I have to stay in this sun-blasted place for another two days to collect my return trade. You?"

Yala laid out her own blanket. There was little to do until the evening, when her goods should be ready. She took out the wooden tokens and stared at them but found no symbols she could understand.

"Only this day," she said, and put them back in her pack.

"Wouldn't put those where they might be taken," Red Rock said. She nodded towards the sleeping woman at the table.

"I'm all right, but everybody knows Long Valley people are all thieves and raiders," she said.

Yala took the slips back and put them in her pouch, then twisted her belt until it lay lumpily underneath her. She had heard such stories of Long Valley people, but then she had heard the same story about Red Rock people. Cloak wrapped around her and her trade slips, she wondered what tales they told about Old Carving Well.

Probably nothing good. Maybe every well says, "We are honest and everyone else is a thief!"

She smiled and drifted off into sleep.

CHAPTER 14
THE STOLEN THIEF

With his plans made, Marick found it easier to ignore the disdain of his companions, though, if he'd been more reasonable, he might have accepted some sympathy from an unexpected quarter.

"Here," Chal-lat said. "This is water mixed with juice from desert plants that grow along the aqueduct. It's a bit sour, but it kills the thirst."

Marick took a small sip and handed the cup back.

"I'm sorry you and your friends are fighting," Chal-lat said. "It's hard to be cut off from those you care about."

Marick shrugged. He had no interest in this fool's thoughts. He turned away and began to break up sticks for the fire. The night was cold, and they had only tents to keep out the chill, for the Mother of Waters was crowded. Traders from the Far, Far South were here in abundance, come up the trail from the Bay of Tears. The cliff-face inns were full, and these tents were all that remained to be rented – at a high price – for a night's rest.

Chal-lat ignored Marick's ignoring and kept talking.

"Vinir will forgive you," he said. "It's just that leaving the town is hard on her."

"Leaving the town or leaving you?" Marick said, breaking a branch over his knee and wishing it were Chal-lat's neck.

"Both, I hope," Chal-lat replied, smiling. "But more the town, I'm sure. She is one of the best artists I've seen, and to think she was untrained! She has a grasp of colour and form that amazes even Sarth, though he'd never admit it. And her passion for creating such images of beauty . . ."

Marick paused at that, the two halves of the branch squeezed in each hand.

Playing with pictures is not my concern.

Chal-lat shrugged. "Well, I only wanted to say that maybe she's madder about leaving her lessons than about you, that's all."

He stood up and walked back to the small fire where Vinir, Dorict, and Son-neen ate bread dipped in a selection of sauces, Son-neen giving a detailed commentary on each taste.

He looked down at the cup Chal-lat had left by the fire and poured out its contents into the sand. He dropped the branches and took his bedroll to a pillar some distance from the tents. Vinir seemed about to call him back, but Son-neen pulled down her hand.

"Leave him be. If he's fool enough to freeze, it'll teach him not to betray his friends," she said.

Chal-lat's half-heard warning to Son-neen did little to cool Marick's anger, a rage that had been building with every league battered by either silence or the girl's nattering. That fury kept him warm until the others were deep in sleep, and then it was time to act.

The stars were crystal clear, blocked only by the narrow

slice of the aqueduct that cut above their camp. First, he went to the tent shared by Chal-lat and Son-neen. He listened to their deep breathing long enough to be sure of their sleep, then he slit the fabric of the tent with his belt knife and reached in to open the girl's bag and remove the trade papers she was so proud of.

Maybe this will shut your mouth!

He stuffed the papers into the secret pocket sewn inside his trouser leg and went to Vinir and Dorict's tent next. He hesitated before cutting the fabric. Trained as demonbanes, they might wake unless he was extremely careful, but there was another reason that held back his hand. They had been his friends.

Had been.

He slid the blade into the canvas. It parted the cloth with the merest whisper of a sound.

Not anymore. They betrayed me too. I tried to help them. They weren't getting anywhere, and I did the right thing – the right thing as a bane and a friend. Now Dorict hates me, and Vinir . . . Vinir wants me kicked out of the banehall. They deserve this.

That last thought gave him the will to continue his thieving. If he were to be on his own again, he'd need coin, and plenty of that lay in Vinir's pouch. It sat on a thick rug that formed the floor of the night-tent. He reached over Vinir, pausing when she murmured in her sleep. Slowly, so that the coins slid rather than clinked, he lifted the bag over her and out through the hole in the side of the tent. Cradling this treasure, he backed up until he was out of earshot.

The stars still shone, the wind still blew, but everything was different. Now, he felt the cold. Shivering, he shoved the papers into the secret pocket in his pants leg and hung the bag of coins on the end his staff. Finally, he tied his blanket in a loop that went diagonally across his chest in a mockery of the bane's sash he would never wear again, and he was ready to go.

So, where to now?

It came to him that he had planned no further than this: to get revenge upon the others and leave them to regret their treatment of him. He looked along the length of the aqueduct, back towards the distant City of Fountains. He couldn't go there, not alone and not without answers to the questions those busybodies would ask. To the north was desert, or so everyone said, empty except for the sand-walkers Vinir had been so keen to find. He turned to the south. It had a bad reputation. All the people he'd met so far called it a land of feuding nobles, slavers, mercenaries and thieves.

That's settled then. Now I just have to find the road south. Maybe a merchant caravan would take me for a few coins, though I'll have to get out quick before they raise the alarm. As for that fool's papers, I'm sure they'll be good for starting fires when it gets cold at night.

A chill went down his back and he wished for a good cloak over him. No sooner had he thought this when he was indeed covered. A rough bag slid over his head and he was wrestled to the ground.

Marick started to yell, then snapped his mouth shut. If this was the Watch, he'd best save his breath for later excuses. The thought of waking Dorict and Vinir so they could look down at him, to hear Son-neen laughing at him, or worse, bear Chal-lat's sympathy kept him quiet, and he twisted fiercely but silently against the hands that held the bag, trying his best to silently escape his captors.

A cuff to the side of his head rang like thunder in his skull, and he stopped moving.

"That's better," a low, male voice said on the other side of the canvas, close to his covered ear.

"Now let's see what you've stolen, eh, thief?"

There was a rustling beside him, and Marick realized that there must be two of them, one holding him and one searching his makeshift pack.

There was a sharp intake of breath, then a low chuckle. Marick's ears pricked. He had heard that laugh before.

"Oh, I knew you were a rare one when I first set my good eye on you, I did!" the man said. "Now look at the profit you brought me. Didn't I tell you about him, Goz? How he ruined my chances in the City of Fountains when I had that drunk on the hook? I was mad enough then to skin you, little one, but I pardon you everything for the gift of these coins, and of course the gift of yourself."

That one-eyed rogue! Claws, he said to meet him here, but I'd forgotten.

He was lifted over a broad shoulder and cuffed again to encourage silence. It was some time before he could think straight, let alone yell for help. When he could string words together in his mind, he realized his predicament. His only help lay back in the tents he had just robbed, and that was no help at all. Even if Vinir and Dorict rescued him, he'd be no better off – worse now, for his sins were compounded. It seemed better to play out this rogue's game for a while. He was supposed to be an animal trader, and Marick did feel like a sheep trussed up for slaughter, but within the black and stifling bag, he grinned. One-Eye had never caught an animal like Marick before.

I've escaped guards, assassins, and demons, you clawed fools. I'll wait for my chance, and then you'll pay!

They went uphill, his bearer – Goz, he guessed – huffing and puffing like a blown horse. The noise of their footsteps suddenly echoed, and Marick guessed they were in the tunnel that climbed from the cliff-face road to the drylands above. This drilled and dug exit was the only way out of the Mother of Waters save for another tunnel on the south side of the town, and the path below the aqueduct.

They stopped and waited for many breaths. Marick willed himself to hang limply over the brute's shoulder.

"Boys did their job," One-Eye said, and Goz nodded enough to rock his cargo.

"Come on," the other commanded.

They made their way up and down obstacles and brushed past sharp rocks until Marick lost all sense of direction. When he did escape, he'd need to get his bearings back, and his coin, for he still meant to head to the Far, Far South, despite whatever plans these brainless kidnappers had for him.

"Get the rope around his ankles," One-Eye said.

Marick's legs were secured by a loop tied tight. He was lifted into the air and then lowered, bumping and scraping against a rough surface on his way down. When his head connected painfully with a hard floor, eager hands grabbed him and rolled him against a wall. There was grunting and cursing as his captors climbed down to join him, and the canvas bag was finally pulled off his head.

Marick blinked, then blinked again. He was in a small cave, or maybe a hole, for the light of the one dim lantern showed a reed mat blocking out the stars above. A dozen figures surrounded him, filthy men, scarred men, leering men, and One-Eye crouched beside them, pulling Marick up by his hair.

"This is the one I told you about," he said to the others, displaying his prize.

A low, mocking laugh went through the cave. Hands probed his pouch and pulled off his boots, but there was nothing to be found. Vinir had all his lockpicks and other secret tools, and his belt knife had fallen somewhere when he was taken. The papers in the secret pocket went unnoticed in their rough handling.

"Give him back those boots, Goz," One-Eye said. "You can't wear 'em with those ox-hooves you've got, and our new friend'll need them for the trek."

Marick pulled his boots back on, pretending to concentrate on the task while looking for a way to dart out between the legs of his captors.

"Don't try it," warned One-Eye. "There's a drop that would smash you like a bug, and if it didn't, we'd put an arrow in your guts before you could crawl away."

Marick leaned back against the rock wall, avoiding the man's singular gaze.

Wait for a chance. This fool thinks he knows everything, but he doesn't know me.

He folded his arms and nodded.

"Good," his captor said. "Now, let me tell you, friend, there's nothing mean in this; it's all trade, a bit of hard business, you might say. I'll admit though, I had different plans for you. Watching you in the city, I saw how sly you were, and I thought, there's a good lad to take as an apprentice, but then you got me into a bit of trouble back there. After all those questions, I couldn't do any kind of sharp trade without those cursed tower-rats following me around, so I came back here, and who do I find? You, that's who. Come to make amends!"

He looked around to see if his gang appreciated the

irony of the situation but was disappointed by their slack-jawed regard. He turned back to Marick.

"Well, I'm afraid the job of apprentice ain't available anymore. But you'll still serve a use. Since you kept me from getting my catch in the city, you'll take his place."

He turned to the big one named Goz. "Get some chains there, man! Don't laze about."

Marick soon had a collar locked around his neck and manacles on his wrists. All three were joined by a single circle of chain, giving him very limited freedom to move, and even that was lost when Goz fixed that to a ring hammered into the wall.

"Rest now, little one," One-Eye said. "You'll need it, for we'll have to scamper soon, before your friends wake and give the alarm."

"Where are we—" Marick began, but Goz cuffed him.

"Slaves don't talk," he said, and left Marick to spit blood from a cut lip onto the floor.

CHAPTER 15
A SECRET PURSUIT

Yala waited until most of the town had quieted into sleep before packing up her sled. She had no wish for further confusing conversations until she had time to think. All that long day, she had talked and listened to people she didn't know and only half trusted. When Long Valley woke up at midday to eat, she told Yala much of the wells to the north. The girl was a talker, driving Red Rock out into the heat.

"I'll go through the tunnel and up onto the scrubland," the older woman had said. "By sandstorm and drought, I'd rather walk back without any goods than listen to this chatter."

After she left, Yala let Long Valley ramble on, saying only a word or two to show she still listened. She sifted the chatter for some justification of her own well's distrust of Long Valley sandwalkers.

She found none. Long Valley was much like other girls at her own well: cheerful, anxious, and likely to smother her fears with a sandstorm of words that buried any listener. If she was a thief and raider by virtue of her birth, it was well hidden.

Or maybe false. We say so many things are like this or like that, but do we really know?

Red Rock came back in the late afternoon, weaving a bit, and Long Valley whispered that an inn was near the entrance to the tunnel and she doubted the woman had gotten farther than a table and a wine jug. Red Rock ignored them both and lay down upon her blankets. Long Valley shook her head and took up again her numbering of the men in her well that seemed to favour her with their trade goods.

After dusk, Yala left them both sleeping and went back down the steep road, holding the harness in her hands and letting her sled roll before her. Lights shone from the windows of the cliff-carved houses, and only a few men and women still lingered outside. Those who did chatted quietly, following her with their eyes as she passed. One, an old man sitting beside his door and weaving a basket by lamplight, sang a reedy love song. Since he kept his eyes on his quick fingers and careful work, Yala supposed the song was not for her but for someone long ago.

Near the bottom of the hill, she saw the woman guard, Mor-ra, and nodded. The woman smiled back.

"Your sled is empty," she called out. "I hope you got a good price."

Yala shrugged, for it was not anyone's business except for hers, and continued on. She found the orange, red, and purple flags again. The old woman was waiting for her.

"Good" she said. "I was about to climb that wretched hill to find you! If you could give me those tokens, please."

Yala handed them over, and the woman explained how

each one matched a package of silk, worked iron, or spices to liven up the food grown in the well. The sandwalker tried to appear knowledgeable about the process, but in the end, she had to rely once again on the fabled honesty of the tower merchants. Using her own symbols, she recorded the goods on her reeds. When she was done, they both stood up.

"There," the woman said, and brushed back a strand of grey hair. "Fair trade for both of us, I'd say. Well, safe journey to you, sandwalker. I know you don't talk much to the men in your well, but if you get a chance and it breaks no rules, tell that glass-maker that his goods are valued in my city."

Yala thought this over. She supposed she could find a way to get the message across the wall if Narrow Field Man was nearby. So she nodded, and both made the sign of leaving, palm outwards from the heart. It was a long haul up the left-hand road to the tunnel, but there was no other way out of the cliffs that cradled the Mother of Waters, save by the aqueduct path, and that went the wrong way.

At the top, where a guard had come out of his little stone house to question her that morning, there was only silence and the flickering of an oil lamp set beside the door. She hesitated, then looked inside the hut. The guard's eyes were closed, and his head slumped down. Yala lifted the lamp and looked at the trickle of blood on the grey collar. She bit her lip, then put the lamp down and went back to her sled.

Animal business. Town troubles, not mine. Others will come soon to find him. He's not alone like Inla-phor.

But she went back into the guardhouse and made sure the old man was still breathing. His wound was slight, but she bound it with a strip cut from his tunic. If she went back for help, wouldn't they blame her, a stranger and a sandwalker? At a loss for what else to do, Yala took up the harness again and pulled her sled away from the tunnel entrance, glad that she had oiled the axles and wheel hubs before leaving the sand-house, though she winced at each click of a wheel rim against stone.

The land ahead was as she remembered, a dry plain, broken and confused by upthrust ridges and sudden, sharp drops. It took a moment to find the trail north, and she had barely started on it when she heard steps behind her, hollow and magnified by the tunnel's mouth.

Yala concealed herself and loosed the shovel from her belt, thumbing the sharp edge and hoping that whoever had caught the old guard would not snare her as well.

It was two men, clear enough in the lamp light, and one of them was the one-eyed man who had bothered her that morning. His companion was a powerfully built brute who carried a sack over his shoulder. Both were breathing hard after the climb, and One-Eye took a quick look into the guardhouse and came out smiling.

"Boys did their job," he said, not bothering to whisper. "Come on."

As quietly as she could, Yala set down her shovel and slid her unstrung bow from its place on the sled. She took the string from her pouch and bent the stave, slowly, over her leg. They might not kill slavers in the town, but . . .

I'm not in the town anymore.

The bow strung, she set an arrow on the string and peeked around the rocks concealing her. The two slavers were gone, but she heard them talking as they moved off towards the cliff edge. She made ready to follow when she heard another set of steps, quieter but again amplified by the tunnel mouth. It was a young man, by his height and the width of his shoulders. He had a pack on his back and a stick of some kind in his hand. Moving quickly, he kept to the shadows, as far away from the lamp hanging outside the guardhouse as possible. He stopped to listen, then crept along after the two slavers and their burden, who could still be heard cursing at the darkness.

Yala drew back the bow string and centred the arrow's point on the young man's back. Was it his club that had knocked out the old guard, and was he chasing these slavers or joining them?

She eased the tension from the bow. This puzzle was too hard to solve with a single arrow. Tral and even Ke would tell her to leave now, to flee from this trap into the welcoming desert, a place where a sandwalker was always at an advantage. She laid her bow, still strung, on top of the sled and picked up her shovel.

Ke and Tral would tell me to leave this alone. One truth for them, harder than stone, but not for me. Not anymore!

She bit her lip, looped the shovel back onto her belt and again picked up the bow. Three arrows in hand and one on the string, she stepped out from her hiding place. Yala didn't know exactly what she was searching for, but she had been seeking it ever since she was a child. At that point in her life, she had looked behind the words of her people and seen nothing but a dry, windless void. Yala had torn those words from her souls, leaving behind an aching emptiness. Now, she needed her own truth to fill that space.

The wind has driven me to this place, to these others. I will not turn away.

The young man crept towards the cliff, and Yala crept after him.

CHAPTER 16
LEFT BEHIND

Vinir woke to a hot breeze playing over her face. She stretched, then grimaced, as if she remembered some great trouble. Sighing, she opened her eyes and found herself staring at a long, vertical cut in the wall of their tent.

"Dorict?" she said but turned to find the young man's blankets empty and his staff and pack missing as well. That was not all that was gone; the pouch holding the rest of the coins given to her for this journey had also vanished.

Nearby, a desolate wailing rose into the morning air. She grabbed her knives and crawled from the tent though the cut, rather than pausing to untie the door flap.

Chal-lat was standing in the morning sun, blinking and rubbing his face. He was orbited by Son-neen, who was whirling in a state of utter panic.

"He did it! I know he did!" she said, dancing around her employer.

Chal-lat woke up enough to grab her in the middle of a revolution and hold her still. "Son-neen! Who did what?"

he demanded. He glanced up as Vinir came running, daggers in hand.

"What's wrong . . ." he began, but Son-neen drowned him out with another fit of wailing.

"Marick, he's stole the papers! He took them just to ruin my name, I know it. Oh, I'll never get over this! I'll . . ." She collapsed on the ground in a ball of woe.

"Did he? Are you sure? Marick really stole your trade papers?" Chal-lat asked. He knelt down beside Son-neen and clumsily patted her head, which only made her moans louder.

Vinir walked to where Marick had spent the night. His blanket was gone, and the layer of loose sand found everywhere under the aqueduct showed the traces of many feet, and perhaps a struggle. Something shone in the dirt. She picked up a short-bladed knife and saw that it was Marick's. Holding her breath, she examined the blade but breathed out in relief when she saw the metal was free of blood. Had Dorict followed him here and disarmed him, maybe fought with him over the coins and the paper, or had he been a partner in the crime?

No, Dorict at least I have faith in, but Marick . . .

She shook her head and looked back at Chal-lat and Son-neen. Her commotions had brought the Watch, a man and woman in grey and black uniforms. The woman was kneeling beside Son-neen, trying to get some sense out of the girl.

"Come on now," the guard said. She was a short, round-faced woman with an easy way about her.

"My name's Mor-ra, and this tall lump is Stetta. We're the Watch, so we can help you get your papers back, but you have to tell us what happened. You're not afraid, are you?"

At that, Son-neen's head came up and her eyes flashed.

"Afraid? Of that thieving fool?" she said, and stood up, rubbing the tears off her cheeks with a sleeve. She pointed to the nearest tent.

"Look there. He cut the back of the tent and took the papers," she said, then pointed at Vinir. "Ask her what kind of criminal he is. He's already been kicked out of the City of Fountains!"

Vinir came up and handed Stetta the knife. She looked down at Son-neen's tearful face.

"It might well have been my . . . servant, Marick, though the other one, Dorict, is gone as well. I think he might have chased after Marick, for some money is gone from our tent. Marick . . . probably stole both the coin and the papers."

She swayed a bit but took a deep breath and steadied herself. It was just as well, for Son-neen leaped at her, wrapped her arms around her ribs and cried into her shirt.

"Thank you, Vinir," she sobbed. "I knew you wouldn't betray me! What are you going to do to get my papers back?"

She was saved from answering by the male guard.

"Whose knife is this?" Stetta asked.

"Marick's," Vinir said. "Of that I'm sure. Maybe Dorict tried to catch him and they fought."

"Maybe," Mor-ra said, her eyes betraying her doubts. "Though the two of them could be in it together."

"No!" Son-neen said. "Dorict's sensible. He'd never do something like this. It's Marick's fault. I know it is."

"Why was he banned from the city?" Stetta asked Vinir. He flipped the knife up and down, catching it by the point in a way that was both amusing and threatening.

Vinir nodded. "There was a . . . misunderstanding. We were asked to leave, but the towers gave us given permission to talk to any sandwalkers we could find here about a matter of great importance to our city, Shirath."

Stetta shook his head and handed her the knife. As Marick's employer, it belonged to her.

"Shirath, hmmm?" Mor-ra said. She scratched at her cheek. "Then it's true about Northerners being mad, is it? Well, we'll start looking. The commander will make a search of the town and the aqueduct trail, but if he's already banned from the City of Fountains, he's more likely to go through the tunnel and maybe join a caravan to the Far South, the gods help him!"

She gave Son-neen a supportive pat on the back. "Chin up, girl. Stetta will report to the commander and I'll go up that cursed cliff road to the guardhouse and check with old Fan-col, if he hasn't been relieved yet. There'll be traffic there soon enough, and we can question those coming in from the horse pickets."

Vinir went back to her tent, put on her boots, and threw on a tunic over her shirt. She still had a few coins in her belt pouch, and she added her daggers and a full waterskin to hang beside them. The hat Chal-lat had given her seemed a frivolous addition to a grim mission, but the sun was beginning to bake the air, so she slapped it on her head before meeting Mor-ra, Chal-lat, and Son-neen where the aqueduct trail divided into two climbing cliff-face roads.

They went left, for Mor-ra had already sent others to the right and the southern exit from the town. Even this early, the heat slowed their steps and used up half of Vinir's waterskin.

"Fill it at the inn," Mor-ra told her. "Tell them I said so and they won't charge you."

The inside of the inn was cooled by thick rock walls, and

her companions waited while she filled up. Mor-ra got the rest full skins as well.

"Oh, shut up, Brast," Mor-ra shouted over the innkeeper's complaints. "You shouldn't charge for water anyway, and as for the skins, tell it to the commander if you want a lecture about civic duty."

At the top of the tunnel, they found two Southern traders in the guardhouse bending over the old guard. One was patting his forehead with a wet cloth, and the other was rubbing his wrists.

"Fan-col!" Mor-ra shouted and ran over to the man.

His eyelids fluttered, but he did not speak. Blood seeped from under a strip of cloth binding his skull. She turned to the two traders, who made gestures of innocence and explanation.

"Not us," said one in a thick accent. He pointed at the guardhouse.

"Come from tents," the other said. "Look. Find."

They both pointed at the guard. Mor-ra examined the still-burning lamp and nodded.

"All right," she said. "This happened in the night, or so the lamp tells me."

She pointed to the unconscious man and, in a loud voice accompanied by many gestures, directed the two to carry the injured man down to the inn.

Vinir motioned the others back while she examined the ground. The hard pan of the soil showed little, and it was only after circling out past the first piles of loose stone that she found signs of definite travel.

"What is it?" Mor-ra said, after Vinir called her over. "Tracks towards the cliff face? Nothing much there except a fatal drop, but let's take a look." She hefted the club in her hand and eyed Vinir's long, slender daggers. "Mind who you prick with those things," she said, and followed the tracks.

"I'd expect him to go the other way," the guard continued. "There're water wells up there, and it's where traders from the Far South camp and picket their horses so they don't have to bring them up and down the cliff road. But this way, there's nothing but . . ." She held up a hand to stop Vinir.

The guard pointed to the edge of the cliff. They crept forward, and Vinir felt her stomach sink at the sight of the desert hundreds of feet below.

"Careful," Mor-ra said, perhaps unnecessarily. "The edge crumbles sometimes, but look here."

She picked up a coil of rope and pointed to where it was secured to a wooden peg jammed into a crack in the stone. Looking down, warily, they saw a woven mat that, when pulled aside, revealed a deep cleft in the rocks.

"Maybe we should wait for Stetta and the others," Mor-ra began, but stopped when she saw Vinir sheathe one dagger, put the other between her teeth, and shimmy down the rope as quick as a sailor in a storm.

At the bottom, dagger once again in hand, Vinir waited for her eyes to adjust, using her other senses to search for danger, but all she heard was the whine of the hot wind and the beating of her own heart. As for what she smelled, it was disgusting, but not an immediate threat.

As her eyes began to pierce the shadows, she realized she was alone. The cleft became cave-like at the back. By the refuse and the smell, it was used as both a storage room and a privy. Cut links of chain littered the floor, and patches of darkened rock here and there could have been blood.

Mor-ra slid down the rope with less grace but no less

speed. She tumbled to the floor and jumped up, club at the ready.

"Gods, what a stench. Is this some animal's den?"

After prodding each shadow with her club, she went over to the wall and fingered an iron ring hammered into the stone.

"Worse than animals. I thought we cleared out those cursed slavers years ago."

Vinir paused in her inspection and removed a pinching hand from her nose.

"Do you mean when they attacked the City of Fountains?"

Mor-ra nodded. "We got them here too. Fought them with sandwalker help, all of us chasing them back to the Bay of Tears. Before that, they used to snatch traders and even townspeople, selling them to the Far South to work on those big farms their nobles have. It got worse until ten years ago, when they attacked in force, coming off islands in the Bay of Tears, but we blocked the tunnels and shot them with arrows when they tried to lower themselves down on ropes. Then the sandwalkers – it must have been twenty wells joined together – swept down on them. I doubt a single rogue got back to his ship. You see, they'd raided the sandwalker wells too, and there's little mercy in those women at the best of times."

Back at the top, Mor-ra cut the rope from its anchor and slung it over her shoulder.

"No use making it easy for them," she said, and looked at Vinir. "You're strong. You'd make a good guard, better than Stetta, I'd bet. The commander had a letter about you, said you were banes looking for monsters."

"Demons," Vinir said. She looked down into the slaver's hideout. "But not the human kind."

"Well, nothing like that here, unless the sandwalkers know of them. There's much in the desert that we never see, and I thank my name and tower for that."

"You have towers out here?" Vinir asked. She had seen nothing like the colourful structures in this town.

Mor-ra shrugged. "Not as such, but most here look to a tower back in the City of Fountains. Mine's the Purple-White-Green Tower, same as Stetta's. But we came here a long time ago, and I doubt we'll go back. You can move slower here, and it's peaceful, except for the occasional drunken brawl or a knife-fight over trade, so some find it a better life."

Vinir shook her head.

Not peaceful enough. Not with Marick here. Oh, you imp! You clawed fool! You could have stayed, said you were sorry. That's all it would have taken for me to forgive you. Even Dorict would have come around, if you'd given him a good reason. Where are you now, both of you?

Back at the guardhouse, an old man in the uniform of the Watch was questioning a group of traders in their own language. They touched their hearts with their fingertips, and the guard did the same. He saw Mor-ra and waved her over.

"Commander," she said, and touched her right hand to the opposing shoulder.

"No sign of the boys going out the southern tunnel," the commander said. "Nor were they seen near the traders' tents." He stroked a rather glorious grey moustache and looked to the north. "By sand and storm, Mor-ra, were those boys taken or were they running away? They wouldn't be mad enough to go into sandwalker territory, would they?"

The woman shrugged. "It's where they come from, the

North, I mean. And you know what they say about North-erners." She pulled Vinir forward. "Commander Norn-i, this is Vinir, the boys' employer. We found a slaver's hideout by the cliff. It's possible the missing ones were in league with them," she said, and held up a hand at Vinir's protest. "But not likely. We found signs of a struggle near where the robbery took place."

The commander stroked his moustache again. "Slavers have been reported in the desert, didn't a sandwalker tell you so?"

Mor-ra nodded. "That's what she said, though where they'd be going, especially if they already had slaves, is a mystery. They could try to sneak past the wells by avoiding trade routes, but then what? You can't sell slaves to sandcats."

"Maybe they mean to sell them to the river cities," Stetta said. He had come up very quietly for such a tall man.

"We don't have slaves in the Five Cities," Vinir said, in a voice so cold that it seemed to settle the matter.

"A mystery then," Mor-ra said. "How do we solve it?"

"Can't have slavers camping on our doorstep," the commander said, stroking his moustache. "Get horses. Stetta, you go north. Mor-ra, south. Talk to everyone you meet and don't get killed, or your children will surely blame me. I'll send two guards up here to replace poor Fan-col."

"What about me?" Vinir asked. She couldn't just stand there and let her charges vanish into the desert air.

"Stay at the inn for now," the commander said, an order rather than a request. "Give us a chance to search first, then we'll decide what you can do to help."

CHAPTER 17
WATCHING THE WATCHER

The slavers went north, and a cruel wind followed them, kicking up clouds of dust from the hard ground and letting it find every eye, every inward breath. What was already miserable became unbearable, but they didn't stop. Nor did two others: the red-cloaked figure that followed at a distance, and the other, who crept as close as he dared.

That one was clever, Yala decided, for a town-dwelling fool. He had no skills in desert travel, but he had managed to keep up with the slavers as they drove their captives, both animal and human, through half the previous day and all of the night. The boy, for so Yala had decided after creeping up to his camp the day before and looking at him while he slept, had taken water and supplies hidden by the slavers, first at their lair a day's walk north of the Mother of Waters, then after seeing them dig jars up at stone-marked points on the high hardpan. The raiding party kept to the heights, wisely perhaps, for by avoiding the sand they also avoided sandwalkers, except for a single unlucky woman.

The slave convoy had come upon her suddenly at dusk

as she pulled her sled up over a rise in the ground. She'd shot an arrow into one of them but had not escaped several shafts fired in return. The slavers broke the sled into firewood and buried the woman in the softer earth under a spike tree. Yala barely kept her own arrows in her quiver when she witnessed this desecration. The slavers then quickly left, throwing the wounded man on a cart stacked with animal cages.

She had watched the boy creep to the grave and dig the body out with his bare hands. He crouched there for a long time, head bowed, unaware of the arrow trained on his back. The dead sandwalker's shovel had been buried with her, for keeping it would be proof of guilt. The boy picked it up and held it between himself and the dead woman. He pulled down the strip of cloth that covered his lower face. His lips moved, and he wiped at his eyes, leaving smeared streaks of dust. When he was done, he looked up to the sky, raised his arms, and spoke again, long and passionately. Yala lowered her bow. She watched him fold the dead woman's arms across her chest and leave her there, the red cloak draped over her face.

He frees her souls from the ground? Why would a town-dweller, a one-souled animal care?

She had no answer save the one she had always feared, the one that had driven her from her own people.

He does it because we are the same, and all I have known is false.

The void between Yala and her people felt very wide that night, and she looked to the slavers' guttering fires with relief. Even the presence of enemies was a comfort when the darkness pushed in and every wind whispered dread in her ears. The boy lay hidden between Yala and the camp. She wondered how he felt about those fires.

The wind strengthened and kept the slavers huddled against their wagons the next day, for the horses were driven half mad by the torment of the blown grit. Before they left in the long-shadowed evening, they took all their cached water with them, leaving only a few sips at the bottom of the hollowed stone they used as a horse trough. She watched the boy try to drink those dregs, going so far as to soak a cloth in the last drops and try to chew the moisture out. The next morning, while the slavers hugged the shade of an outcrop and he slept, Yala crept up and refilled his water flask from her own, knowing she could find more in caches left by sand-walkers who came to this high ground to hunt blue fliers, dawn bugs, and other medicinal creatures. These caches were not marked, but they were buried in the most reasonable places – for a sandwalker. It didn't take long to find the first, which was empty, and the second, which was full.

She returned at dusk to watch both the slavers and the boy. The brutes whipped awake their captives but treated the caged animals with greater care – mostly.

"I told you, Goz, no whips on the sandcats!" One-Eye said. "And give the beasts water! You want to haul them all the way to Dry Hills just to see them die before we're paid? One more lash and I'll cut your tongue out."

The answer was profane, but the torment stopped at once. Not so for the slaves, who were whipped to start, to stop, to go faster, to slow down, even to sing, if a slaver was bored.

"You there, grey-beard!" called the pace-keeper. "Sing us a song, Grandpa, or I'll whip those bristles off your face."

The old man stumbled and tried to cough out a song, but nothing came except wheezes. The slaver grinned and raised his hand, but a boy, small but absurdly brave, jumped between the two.

"Hold on their, my friend," the little one piped up. "I'll sing for you. I've been making up a song on this pleasant stroll anyway, and now's the time to sing it."

The whip-wielder, the big brute One-Eye had named Goz, rubbed the leather handle against the stubble on his face and decided to let the old man off with a single lick of the lash.

"Go on then, but if it stinks, I'll leave no skin on your back!"

The boy helped the old man back up and took back his place behind him on the chain line. With a deep bow, much embellished by waving his manacled arms, he began to caper about and sing:

"See old One-Eye with a whip in his hand,
Handsome leader of the slaver band,
He'll stand up to anyone as long as they're tied,
But if they're free he'll run and hide!

HE'LL DIG a big hole and hide in the sand,
The ugly leader of the slaver band!"

"More! More!" the slavers shouted, clapping and stomping in the flickering light, but a shout silenced them. One-Eye came roaring up, torch in one hand and a knife in the other. He jabbed the blade into the dancer's calf, piercing his boot and drawing blood when he pulled it free.

"There, now you've something to think about beside song-singing when you walk, don't you, you piece of dung?" he yelled.

The boy fell to the ground, screaming and holding his leg. Goz pulled One-Eye back, to save the merchandise, no doubt, but the leader swung the torch at his lieutenant's face and the larger man backed off in a shower of sparks and curses. One-Eye glared at them all, slavers and slaves – and animals too, perhaps. He held up the dripping knife and very deliberately placed the blade in the torch's flame.

Yala did not know if she heard the sizzling of the boy's blood or just imagined it. She swallowed and watched the slaver stomp back to the head of the convoy, while Goz stood and snapped his whip. The chain line shuffled forward, pulling the boy until the old man helped the lad up and tore a bit of cloth from his own coat to stuff down the boot and staunch the flow of blood. He gave a stooped shoulder to support him, and the line followed One-Eye's torch. The last she saw was the whip cracking, and the boy grimacing at each step.

Yala shook her head. She lowered a finger to the sand and Chit-chit, who had been loosed to hunt for insects, scrambled up, a larval dawn beetle in its mouth. She lifted her hand up to her neck and the fear lizard found its own way back into the tube.

A brave fool, and not long for this world if he keeps this up. That wound will slow him for weeks, and the winds alone know how long before they kill him.

She dabbed oil on the wheel hubs of the sled, waiting for the slavers to pull out of hearing as well as sight. They still went north, as if they hoped to climb higher up to the Fingers and keep off the sand altogether.

Dry Hills, that filth said. That's their goal, though I've never heard of such a place.

She glanced down to where the boy waited behind a stand of oil brush and saw a strange thing. He was hugging himself with both arms, shovel and club dropped in front of him. He rocked back and forth until he was once again in control. After a moment of absolute stillness, he picked up his weapons and set off for the next piece of cover, another stand of oil brush a hundred feet away.

Yala watched him for a while and then went to where he had hidden to watch the slavers stab that foolish boy. Clods of dirt ripped from the hard ground by pure rage lay scattered about.

It's that boy he's after, not just the slavers, and I think he'll do anything to get him back.

She knelt there for a while, tracing the gouges with her finger while she thought. It was best that she turn west now, off this wide ramp of land before it reached the Fingers. She could cut across to Seven Rock Well or maybe Sandcat Well and they would send messages to Old Carving and all the others. Sandwalkers could be gathered and this band ambushed as the other had been.

She brushed the dry dirt from her fingers.

Only, the wells might not spare anyone. With alarms now running from one settlement to another, a sandwalker party might decide to kill all: slavers, slaves, even the animals, as a warning to those who would trespass on our lands.

She should tell Ke and let it happen as it would, but instead she waited until the noise of her sled's wheels could not be heard by those ahead of her and pulled north.

CHAPTER 18
BITTER TEA

"Another cup of wine, miss?" the innkeeper asked.

The crowd swelled as workers, traders, and others came in for the second meal of the day. A large pot of stew sat upon a hearth whose chimney, cut up into the stone, let smoke exit through a carved grill on the face of the inn. The fire made the inn hot, but not as hot as outside.

Vinir shook her head and pushed the empty goblet away. It wouldn't do to drown her fears when she might need a clear head at any moment. Besides, she felt unsettled enough already, for she had spent the last two days chewing on anger, sometimes at Marick but often at herself.

This is my fault. If only I'd found some way to use him, so he didn't get bored. He's so dangerous when he's bored. If only . . .

If. That was the word that first brought the wine. Now she asked for a cup of bitter tea, a desert brew the innkeeper said would clear the head even as it scoured the mouth.

She grimaced through the first sip and was braving

another when Mor-ra and Stetta came through the door. Mor-ra picked up the empty wine goblet and tossed it to a server.

"Wine won't bring them back, will it? And about that, we have news now, or more like no news, which still means something."

"What this empty-head means," Stetta said, "is that she checked the south road all the way to the Bay of Tears. They weren't seen, even where the road is the only way through, so your lads haven't gone south."

"And they haven't gone west, or they'd have been spotted in the City of Fountains," Mor-ra added.

"Nor east," Stetta said, sitting down on the bench opposite, taking off his reed hat, then the helmet underneath. "For there's nothing east but . . . nothing."

Mor-ra sat beside Vinir. She sniffed at the tea and grimaced. "That brew will clear your head, though it might turn your stomach. So, what's left is the north, and Stetta here found a camp that slavers might have used less than a day's easy ride in that direction."

Stetta nodded and signalled to the innkeeper for two mugs of ale.

"The ground there is hard to read, but I saw the ruts of wheeled carts going north, so I came back to report."

"You didn't follow them?" Vinir asked. She took a big gulp of the tea and started coughing.

Mor-ra helped her swallow with a pounding fist. "Careful there," she said. "Now listen, Stetta may be a big oaf, but even he can't take on a whole slaver band. There're sandwalkers to think of as well. If we go there, we have to take treaty gifts to make them less murderous. We'll track them all right. It's just . . ."

The mugs arrived and Vinir grimly kept to her tea while the others gulped down their ale and smacked their lips.

"Just what?" the bane asked. She spat a residue of leaves back into the cup and put it down in front of her with entirely necessary force.

Mor-ra frowned. "Easy now! No need to break the poor thing. It's just that we might track them on the hard ground, but if they go off into the sand, well, there's no trace. If we knew where they were going, we might have a chance."

"There's one that probably knows," Stetta said. He waved for two more ales.

The hum of the crowd was a hammer in Vinir's head, but she reached out to grab the man and pull him closer. "Who knows, and why haven't you asked them?" she demanded.

Stetta shrugged the shoulder that wasn't clamped in Vinir's grip.

"Trader by the name of Toosha-lun. Born on the islands in the Bay of Tears. Those bits of rock are old slaver bases, but he swears he left that all behind to trade silk and fine leather. By our reckoning, Old Toosh has his thumb in every dirty deal that goes on around here. Might have got his hooks into slaving again. He might even have your thieving servants."

Mor-ra gently pried Vinir's fingers off of her partner's shoulder. Stetta nodded his thanks and rubbed the bruised muscle.

"Problem is," the round-faced guard told the bane, "we've never enough proof to arrest him, for he's slippery as boiled grey-grass. So, forget about *us* asking Old Toosh hard questions. By our trade treaties with the Far South, *we* can't touch him."

The tea must have worked, for Vinir heard the slight emphasis in Mor-ra's voice. "What if a mad Northerner had a question for him?" she asked.

Stetta examined his arm. Finger marks were still visible on his dark skin. "I think she might just get an answer," he said, but when Vinir jumped up, he held up his other hand. "Tonight," he said. "Dark deeds don't like the sun."

"And wise sayings don't like your mouth," Mor-ra said. "Balt, where are those ales?"

Vinir sat back and cradled her head in her hands. No more wine, and soon no more waiting. By tomorrow, she must be on her way to find them. She must forget about Chal-lat, the unfinished mural in the City of Fountains, and everything else except getting Marick and Dorict back and returning to Shirath. They had found trouble here, but no demons, and that was that.

She ordered another cup of the horrible tea and suffered while Mor-ra and Stetta bickered over who would pay for the ale.

Marick, Dorict, keep alive, you two. Keep safe until I find you. Claws and teeth, I will find you and take you home. And Heaven shield anyone who tries to stop me!

Such brave thoughts could not dispel a horrible premonition that at least one of the two she loved like brothers was already in desperate need of saving.

CHAPTER 19
BAIT

A pale blob of light, its white surface brushed with red blowing sand, came in and out of sight. Darkness surrounded that tainted sphere, grew inwards, gnawed at it, turned its curved face into the colour of old, dried blood.

A very small part of him that could still laugh thought, *We have that in common. We both bleed.* A larger part that was his fear screamed, *I'm dying!* And the biggest part, the part that was pain, whispered, *Good*.

The last pinpoint of shrinking light shuddered as he fell onto hard ground, but an explosion of pain blasted away the darkness, for now. With sight came hearing, and a voice full of malicious cheer.

"There you are, free of your chains, just like you wanted! I saw you picking at them with a bit of twig, but all you needed were these."

A metal moon that resolved into a ring of keys swung through his sight.

"Suppose I might have been too hasty before, cutting

you like that. Well, what's done is done, eh? Brought it on yourself though, didn't you?" The key ring disappeared, and something else took its place, a round face, one-eyed and grinning. It wavered and spoke. "Now listen to me, lad, that leg's gone sour. You'll never live to see Dry Hills, though maybe you should thank me for that! Would have been worth some coin there, but I'm not going to carry you all the way north as freight, not when you're like to die on me anyway and be worth nothing."

A hand grabbed Marick's arm and pulled him along, his wounded leg scraping on the uneven, rocky ground.

"Saw a pit here when we first scouted out this campsite," the voice said.

Marick recognized the deep, mocking tones. It was the one-eyed rogue who had captured him . . . when was it? Days ago? Hours?

"Cheer up now, lad, you're still useful," the man said. "Our Northern friends want slaves right enough, but they want other things too, animals and such, especially fierce ones, and there's nothing worse in this cursed desert than what lives in that pit."

He was dropped again, this time onto a softer surface of banked sand, though his leg still screamed at the shock.

"Don't sing yet," the one-eyed man said. "Good bait shouldn't fuss till it's on the hook."

Marick could see the man's head now, bent over some work, but he couldn't see what, for his eyes shut of their own accord. The world swayed as hands tied a rope around his waist. He was lifted to stand on his good leg, and he forced his eyes open again. He was teetering on the edge of a pit at least twenty feet across and nearly as deep. The moonlight let him pick out every water-like ripple in the sand, though it might have been his wound fever that made it all seem to move. At the very bottom was the reflection of water, a small circle of impossible comfort in this dry, dry land. He tried to find hope in this, but his spirit felt as dead as the sand.

"Here we go, little scum," the man said, and laughed. "I've got a net ready for whatever takes you, and my men are fixing a stout cage for it while I go fishing. Now, over you—"

Whatever held Marick was gone, and he folded down onto the slope, sliding halfway to the bottom of the pit before he stopped. There was sudden noise above him, a mix of grunts and the smack of fist on flesh. He tried to turn towards it, but the walls of the pit heaved and gouts of sand showered him from below, knocking him loose and making him slide farther down.

"Marick!" a voice cried. There was a familiarity to it, but he could not recall a matching name. The sand roiled around him. Something was worrying the boot on his uninjured leg. He slid down another few feet.

"Marick!" the voice called again, louder, more insistent. The sounds of a struggle returned. Someone cursed then cried out, and a dark mass tumbled by. The thing biting at his boot let go, and whatever had fallen past him screamed, a horrible wail that was quickly smothered and lost. The rope around his waist went tight, and he began to rise back up the slope. Below him the sand boiled and pulsed around the body of the slaver. Two long black blades scissored out of the sand and pulled man below the surface. Marick twisted away from the sight as he slid over the rim, where arms caught and held him.

"Marick, Marick!" a voice said, and he knew it was Dorict, and he had overslept again and missed his training session in the banehall. Tarix would be mad at him, and Salick would scold him, but he didn't think he could get up. He was dying, after all.

The air cleared and the moon swung back into view, still red, a drop of new blood staining the pure black sky.

CHAPTER 20
HARD QUESTIONS

The tents on the plateau above the Mother of Waters were set far apart, one sign of the lack of trust the merchants from the Far, Far South felt for each other, and for all others. Each large felt dome boasted strings of horses, piles of packaged goods, and dozens of carts pulled tight against the cloth walls. Sleepy servants kept watch on each other across the bare ground in-between. Mor-ra pointed to the easternmost structure. It was the largest and had the most horses around it. In front of the draped door, three rough-looking men leaned against their spears and passed a wineskin back and forth.

"That's Toosha-lun's tent," Mor-ra whispered. Vinir crouched beside her. Stetta had gone around to the other side in case the trader wished to escape the bane's questions.

"You might want to wait a while until we're sure he's asleep and sneak . . ." Mor-ra began, but realized she was talking to herself. Vinir was walking briskly towards the tent, pausing only to pull a picket post from the ground.

"This will not go well," the guard said, and hurried after the bane. By the time she got to the tent's opening flap, she had to hop over the prone bodies of Toosha-lun's servants, big men from the Far, Far South who lay on the ground, unconscious.

Stetta came running around the tent, squeezing between the prancing, bucking horses. His club was in his hand, but he shook his head when Mor-ra frowned at it.

"No, it was all her, Mor-ra. I don't know what these 'banes' do in the North, but this one's got an arm like a blacksmith and a tongue like a sailor," he said.

Mor-ra grunted. "Just your type of woman," she said. "With luck, she'll take you off my hands."

From within the tent came the sound of furniture breaking, a man whimpering, and a low-pitched growl. The two guards looked at each other and Mor-ra pulled back the door flap just enough for them to see inside.

Vinir stood over a man lying on the ground. He was dressed in beautiful silks, perhaps a little less beautiful now that the bright yellow robes were torn and splattered with blood from his broken nose. There was no one else present, though a flapping panel at the back of the tent showed someone had made a hasty exit.

The bane tapped the picket post against Toosha-lun's forehead.

"You know," she said, calmly, as if speaking to an acquaintance on the street, "I'm known in the banehall as a quiet, reasonable woman."

She squatted down beside the cowering man and tapped his head again, harder. "Not tonight, though. Tonight, I'm more like my friend Salick. You don't know her, but she's a fierce woman who's not afraid to break a few bones to get what she needs."

The man kneeling on the expensive carpets wrenched a ring off his finger.

"Here," he rasped. "Take it! Gold!"

Vinir knocked it aside with her free hand. She stood back up and raised the post over her head.

"Not gold," she said, hissing out the words. "Nor clawed jewels or anything else you have . . . just information. Tell me, Toosha-lun, about the slavers that were hiding near the cliff above the tunnel. Do they work for you?"

Outside, Mor-ra and Stetta held their breath. When Toosha-lun shook his head, they both let out a disappointed sigh.

"Then who do they work for, and where are they going?" Vinir demanded.

"I don't know," Toosha-lun said, and wailed when the post swished down to strike the floor beside his skull. "I swear it on my sons' lives! That one-eyed thief would not say. But listen, please! He is a fool, for my men followed him the last time he came to this town. He went north, taking slaves and animals together, which is bad business, for one will always end up eating the other, but it does not matter because there are no buyers in the North! He will die in the desert, and all his merchandise with him!"

"Merchandise?" Vinir said. "I think you mean people." The coldness of her tone made Toosha-lun cower.

Outside, Mor-ra let the tent flap fall. At Stetta's questioning look, she drew him back and whispered, "Best not to look. We can't arrest her for a crime we didn't see, can we?"

Stetta shook his head. "Even if we know what happened?" he asked.

Mor-ra looked to the tent. Toosha-lun's screams were

not entirely muffled by the heavy felt walls. "There's know-ing, and *knowing*," she said.

They retreated until the cries were more easily ignored. No one left their own goods unprotected to investigate, no light showed from a raised door in any of the other tents dotting the field.

~

AFTER SOME TIME, Vinir emerged from the tent and threw down the picket post. She was breathing heavily but seemed unharmed.

Mor-ra calculated the amount of blood on the bane's tunic and said, "Toosha-lun's still alive then?"

"Bent, but not broken," Vinir said. "Well, a little broken. 'Merchandise!'" She stomped back through the scattered tents. Mor-ra and Stetta followed at a safe distance.

Back at the tavern, they took a corner table and whis-pered over their ales.

"According to the trader, those were slavers hiding out in that cliff hole," Vinir said.

Mor-ra and Stetta nodded.

"We heard most of what he said, but not all," Mor-ra said. "We missed the last part of your conversation. Dust and wind! It's a shame Toosha-lun didn't buy those slaves, because if he had we could have arrested him, or whatev-er's left of him."

Vinir shook her head. "Sorry," she said. "But you didn't hear what he said at the end. He did try to buy them. Seems the leader, a one-eyed man that we had dealings with in the City of Fountains, had a better price promised in the North. All he knows is that One-Eye took them in that direction, into sandwalker territory."

"We heard about the North," Stetta said, "but why there? Or wasn't Toosha-lun talking by then?"

Vinir smiled and the guard shuddered politely.

"Oh, he could still talk, and he wanted to," the bane said. "Anything to get me out of that tent. I think the women he's used to are more . . . forgiving. The last thing he remembered – after some persuasion – was some information he bought from the slaver's second in command, a big brute named Goz. Seems One-Eye has a rich buyer waiting for them at a place called Dry Hills, not too far from my city of Shirath, it seems."

Mor-ra shook her head, shedding a few drops of ale. "Sold out his own lieutenant? No loyalty among slavers, which is no surprise, but was that the truth or just a lie to get you gone? Hmm, I wonder. You said the Five Cities don't have slaves, so why take them there?"

"Trade them to the Midlands, maybe," Stetta said.

Vinir dipped a finger in her tankard and drew a rough map on the tabletop. She pointed to where the River Ar divided into north and south branches, enclosing the fertile Midlands between them.

"No slaves there either. Never have been, and with demons in the Midlands now, the amount of land they can farm barely feeds the people they already have," she said, and put a liquid "X" a hand's breadth south of the Ar's main flow. "Here's where the Dry Hill trading post is, according to Toosha-lun's map, which he gave me as a parting gift. You can copy it if you like. I've never heard of the place before. All our trade is supposed to go through either Solantor or the city of Old Torrick so banes can protect the carters and barge men from demons. How can they survive there without banes, I wonder?"

Mor-ra put down her mug. "Maybe they have that silkstone you told us about," she said. "All of it we have here comes from sandwalker lands, though the towers in the City of Fountains intend to ship their own stores to your people up north, or so the letter they sent the commander said." Mor-ra looked up at Vinir and frowned. "What puzzles me is the animals, see?"

She dipped a finger in Stetta's brew and drew a wavy line from the "X" of Dry Hills to her side of the table. "Here are the Fingers, the high ground east of the desert. That one-eyed son of a dog will probably keep them up there, or a sandwalker's arrow will soon put out his last light."

She recharged her fingertip before Stetta could move his mug and let it drip in a wandering manner across the scarred wood planks.

"These dots, and many more besides, are the sand-walker wells in the desert. You see they're all on a line? Some say the Mother's gift of water is really a river that lives under the sand, feeding all those wells, though that seems mad. Well, whatever fills their wells keeps them out in that desert, thank the Mother! So none live on the Fingers, though they hunt there at times. That means with any luck, we'll only have the slavers to worry about in our pursuit."

"*Our* pursuit?" Vinir said. "As much as I want it, I can't ask for your help. Marick and Dorict are banes, and this is banehall business," she said, frowning. "And it's my fault in the first place."

Stetta laughed, a low chuckle that Mor-ra copied in a higher key.

"Be reasonable, Vinir," Stetta said. "The theft of your coin and the girl's papers happened here, and so did the theft of the thief!" He wiped away the ale map with his sleeve. "Those slavers took your friends from our town.

143

That's guard business, and we have our names to protect. Besides, the commander will have our heads if we don't clean up this mess."

Mor-ra nodded. "He'd skin us for sure, and then what would our children do?"

"Starve," Stetta said.

"Pine away," Mor-ra added.

They looked so sad that Vinir laughed.

"All right, all right. I welcome your help, if only for the sake of your children, who I don't believe exist! When can we leave?"

Stetta shrugged. "By the night's second watch. Pack your belongings and meet us at the tunnel when the moon is touching the cliff wall. We'll see to supplies and horses. Will the others be joining us?"

Vinir considered, then nodded. They must, she supposed. Son-neen would not rest until she regained those papers and her tower's trust, and Chal-lat would not leave Son-neen's side – nor Vinir's – until both were safe again. She calculated the chances of sneaking off and leaving them but dismissed them as poor, since they would be waiting when she returned to the tents to collect her gear.

"Here's to dead slavers, rescued fools, and no angry sandwalkers," Mor-ra said.

Stetta raised his tanker in enthusiastic agreement. "Let the sand and those who dwell in it live in peace and keep far from our path," he said, but lowered his ale when Vinir shook her head.

"I wish that were true, but after giving up the map, Toosha-lun told me more of the slavers' plans."

As the two guards listened to Vinir speak, they paled. Mor-ra took a large swig of ale, choked a bit, then muttered,

"Husband, our children really are in danger of losing us, aren't they?"

For once, Stetta could manage no wise response, and the three sat, looking into their tankards and trying not to see dread futures in the foam lapping at the rims.

CHAPTER 21
UNEASY ALLIES

The shadow hiding in the rocks saw it all. One of the slavers had come close to her hiding place, dragging a boy to the pit-killer's lair. She had crawled there, closer to the camp than she cared to be, in part to find answers to a very troubling question. Instead of continuing up to the Fingers, halfway through the night, the slavers had come off the high ground, carefully bringing their carts down steep hills and into the desert. This seemed mad to Yala, as it put them at the mercy of the nearest wells, though not hers, for they were already far past Old Carving.

They move without fear, yet a single well could kill them all. Why are they so confident?

Her question was answered, but in a disturbing way. At the edge of the sand, several red-robed figures waited for the slavers. They were not alone; a line of men lay tied hand and foot on the ground. Although she had to stay far above that meeting to keep safe, she saw a chest passed from the slavers to the sandwalkers, and lengths of chain were added to the slave-line to accommodate the new captives.

Even at this distance, Yala could see the new slaves were dark-skinned. Men of the wells. One sandwalker stayed with the slavers, but the others left with the chest strapped to a long sled.

The convoy continued along that division between sand and hard ground for most of the night, finding easy paths for the carts when they could but forcing the slaves to pull through the sand when necessary. The one-eyed leader held up a hand to stop while the moon still hung high overhead. The sandwalker argued with him, their words echoing off the cliffs again and again until they were unintelligible. They could have travelled leagues before the sun struck them down, but One-Eye had his way. Yala found a cleft in the rocks near a pit-killer's lair, a safe enough place if you knew the water you saw at the bottom of the trap was just a dream made by the beast below the sand. A sandwalker would ignore that promise, even if she was close to death. Better to die on the sand than be dragged below it and eaten by the scissor-jawed creature hiding there. She fixed the stopper on Chit-chit's tube. This was no time for her fear lizard to run off chasing beetles

She had not been waiting long when she heard someone coming, footsteps and a child-like moaning. She pulled her cloak over everything but her eyes, becoming just another stone under the moonlight.

It was the one-eyed man dragging a boy by his arm. He spoke rapidly to his captive and tied a rope around the small one's waist. In the pale light, Yala could see it was the same one who had danced and sung his way into trouble. The slaver stood the boy upright, and Yala guessed his plan. He had a net ready, but he'd might as well try and catch the wind, for the jaws of a pit-killer would shred anything short of iron.

One-Eye was taunting the boy and so didn't see her slip closer. Within the folds of her cloak, Yala quietly strung her bow. Should she try to save the boy? She hesitated, bow strung but no arrow at the ready. Then she remembered his foolish courage in saving the old man and set the arrow. Parting the folds of her cloak, she raised her bow and pulled the nocked shaft back to her cheek. Before she could loose the arrow, the other boy, the one that followed the slavers, attacked.

He wielded his cudgel, not the shovel he had taken from the dead, and Yala saw that he had some skill with the heavy stick. The slaver jumped back and his captive fell, tumbling into the pit in a loose, unhurried way as if he welcomed death.

In the midst of all this tumult, that caught at her, his surrender. Often, in these last years, she had wondered if she should let go, simply give up her search for the truth of her life and act as others wished she would. If she just gave in to the way her people pushed on her, whether it would bring some kind of peace – but she would not surrender. In this struggle with life, she meant to win.

So did the charging boy. He swung his staff again and again, forcing the slaver to jump farther back from the pit. One-Eye's only weapon was the net slung over his arm, but he had his own skills to bring to this battle. He dodged to the side and swept out the net, entangling the boy's staff and wrenching it from his grip. Before the boy could pull the shovel from his belt, the slaver kicked him backwards, almost to the rim of the pit. Gouts of sand shot up from below.

The pit-killer is trying to knock the little one down to the bottom and drag him under the sand! That other won't be able to save him.

Yala half drew the arrow again, then stopped, for she had no clear shot. The boy had scrambled to his feet and was pummelling the slaver with flailing arms. He might have won, for he was tall and wide-shouldered, but the toll of days in the desert with little food and water weighed against him. In a last effort, he wrapped his arms around the slaver and tried to pull him down to the ground. It was no use. The man kicked him off and stood, spitting blood and drawing a long, curved knife from his belt. With his free hand, he grabbed the boy's hair and pulled back his head, exposing his throat.

The knife rose.

Yala dammed all doubts and let her hands move by their own will. The arrow took the slaver high in his back, knocking him forward to fall onto the boy, who pushed the brute into the pit. He then grabbed the end of the rope and pulled up the smaller one who, to Yala's surprise, was in no worse condition than when he went in. A scream pierced the cold air and ended mid-note.

The pit-killer gets to eat after all, and a more fitting meal.

The trussed-up boy lay unmoving while his rescuer called out some foreign name. From her position in the rocks, she could not see any answering movement.

The bigger boy looked around, then fixed his eyes on the cleft where she crouched. He lifted the other boy to his shoulder and stumbled towards her, the rope trailing behind them.

She fit another arrow to the string of her bow. All her training told her to flee or fire, but her doubting mind said to wait. He was a stranger, inhuman to her people, yet he had treated the dead with respect. He was also brave; they both were, as brave as any knife-dancing man of her well, yet they were . . . foreign. While her souls fought, the larger boy reached the rocks.

"Hello?" he said. "Are you there? I saw your arrow. We're friends. Please, we need your help. Please."

He spoke in the common language of the Mother of Waters and the City of Fountains, but in a strange, unlovely accent. She said nothing.

"Please, show yourself. We won't hurt you. Marick's badly wounded, and I can barely stand. We need your help."

Won't hurt me?

She grimaced. By all she knew, she should have left them to die, or killed them herself to avoid discovery. The other slavers – and that traitorous sandwalker – would come when the bald one was missed, and soon, even if they took his scream for the boy's. She must be far away and hidden by the time the sun came up.

But the wind had brought her here and guided her arrow. Right or wrong, she had shed blood for these two, and blood was bond. She stepped out into the moonlight.

"Thank you," the boy said. "Marick and I – I'm Dorict – we're from the river cities in the North. He was taken from the Mother of Waters days ago." He paused to cough out some of the dust of that journey. "He's wounded. He needs bandages and water. Please, will you help us?"

Yala nodded, slipped the arrow from the bow and pushed it back into the quiver at her waist. The boy's staff was nowhere to be seen, so she unstrung the bow over a bent leg and handed one end of it to Dorict.

He looked at it, then at her. She began to mime what she wanted then gave up trying to preserve her silence.

"Sit him on the bow. Put his arm over your shoulder

and your hand behind his back. I'll do the same, and we'll carry him to a safe place. Quickly, or we're dead."

Dorict did as she bid, and Marick was soon supported between them. His eyes were open and rolling, but he made no sound as they set off into the desert.

"Thank you," Dorict repeated. "What is your name? I don't know how to repay you, but . . ."

"Be quiet," she said. "Your voice hurts my ears. I am Yala. We have a long way to go before we are safe."

She did not add her mother's name – if she could still call Tral her mother – or the location of her well, things she would have told another sandwalker. A part of her, the part that was causing her stomach to churn, regretted her actions, but the wind of her will had been clear.

Her sled was where she had left it hidden, in a dip of the land a league farther on. She made a rough job of rearranging her trade goods so that the boy could fit between them.

It's a good thing the one riding is so small and the one pulling is so big!

Yala doubled the harness and showed Dorict how to set it across his shoulders, hands grabbing the front to keep it from rising and choking him. They pulled most of the night, Dorict struggling more and more as the moon dropped in the sky. In the pale light, his face was haggard, and he stumbled more than once as they climbed dune faces. At one point, Yana looked back and saw that Marick's eyes closed and his body had relaxed into sleep.

The wind rose and fell, spawning small whirlwinds that caught them unawares. They stopped so that Dorict, squinting against the grit assaulting his eyes, could tie a ragged piece of cloth around his face and then Marick's to keep their throats clear. Her own mask fit too well to share, and she needed the glass eye shields to look for danger both ahead and behind. Twice, Yala left Dorict to rest with the unconscious Marick while she ran back along their trail to check for pursuers.

"We are safe, for now," she said after returning the second time.

Dorict pulled the wrapping from his mouth but said nothing.

"Speak if you must," Yala said. She pulled a waterskin from her pack and squeezed a small stream into Marick's mouth, then her own. The boy roused enough to swallow his share, which was a hopeful sign. She handed the skin to Dorict and was glad to see how little he took. This would be even worse if they were both fools.

He handed it back and coughed. "Thank you. I'm saying that a lot, but I mean it. I've been following those clawed brutes for days, waiting for a chance to help him."

She looked at him. He wore rags that once were fine clothes, boots that were now sprung at the heels, and he was covered in dirt and sweat.

Here is one of them, not dying like Inla-phor, but alive, real.

The thought made her afraid and angry.

"Why just him? Are the others worth less? Are they . . . just animals to you?" she asked. She felt a stirring under her tunic, just below her shoulder, but in her anger ignored it.

The boy glared at her, "pretending to be human," as her mother might say.

"He was hurt, and I saw he wouldn't last. Besides, he's my friend, or at least he was, once. As for the others, I was waiting until we got to a town or way station where I could get help."

His voice rose as he spoke. Yala remembered how he had charged the bigger man, and she slid a hand to the shovel at her waist. Her sister, Brada, had sharpened it for her before she set out from their well and its edge was keen.

Dorict spoke again, quietly this time. "I'm sorry. You saved us and now I'm yelling at you. Heaven shield you and teach me manners." He sat back on the dune and tried to wipe the sand off his face. In the end, he only smudged it.

"Why did he sing that song?" Yala asked. Marick lay on his side between them.

"You saw that too? Why did you follow them?" Dorict asked, but he waved away any need for an answer. "Sorry, your business, not mine," he said, then grimaced. "As for why he provoked them. He can't help it. It's his nature. Believe me, he makes even his friends angry."

Under her mask, Yala bit her lip. That sounded like something her mother, Tral, would say about her wayward daughter.

While they rested, the dune spoke its own story of slow collapse, red grains piling against the unconscious boy's back. Once, they heard the low, thrumming sound of a slide to the east. It might have been caused by many feet crossing a dune face – or by nothing save the shifting weight of the sand.

She took off her cloak and wrapped it around the boy. The night-cold of the desert was still pinching at them all, and she hoped the renewed movement under her shirt was just Chit-chit searching for a warmer spot to sleep, and not because of the reason all sandwalkers travelled with fear lizards. She had enough trouble without such ancient horrors appearing.

"Not far now," she said. "Pick up the rope."

The wind dropped, as it often did before dawn, returning the silver to the low-hanging moon, a lamp that now lit the crests of the dunes and left crisp shadows in the troughs between them. The ruins were no farther than she remembered, and they made the shelter before the moon set. The refuge was small, but its walls still stood against the dunes. There was no door, only a wide entrance, and the sand was a foot deep inside.

Yala unhooked the shovel from her belt. She quickly cleared a space in one corner for Marick to lie, then continued shovelling out the small room, catching and tossing the sand far outside the fallen stones.

Dorict watched her work. "I'll help with that," he offered, holding up his borrowed shovel, but he received no answer. He set to work on the other corner of the floor, as far away from Yala as possible.

Hard work from both of them brought a clear floor by the first grey hint of daylight. Yala counted the flagstones from the sides and back until she found the ones that pulled up. There was more sand to dig out, but soon she had several jars of water and food, and two cloth-wrapped packages.

"Sandwalkers leave supplies here," she said. "The nearest well will replace them, but we should leave a gift." Searching through her pack, she found a spare eye shield glass and placed it on one of the jars. She looked at the shovel lying beside the town-dweller and said, "And that is not yours."

Taking the hint, Dorict handed it to her. Yala took it without comment and dropped it into the hole.

He puts himself at my mercy, or he's wise enough to know he always was.

They drank and ate enough to feel refreshed, and Dorict dipped a corner of his scarf in the water to work again at his face.

"Sorry," he said, when he saw Yala looking at him. "I know it shouldn't be wasted, but I never liked being dirty."

Strange, for an animal.

She looked to Marick's wound, a deep cut below the knee. The edges of the cut were swollen and red, a bad sign, she thought. After using more precious water to clean it, she prepared a bandage from cloth left in one of the wrapped packages.

Dorict paled as he looked over her shoulder.

"Do you have a needle and thread?" he asked.

She searched the supplies and found what he wanted, then watched as he used them to draw the edges of the gash together. That he would do this was not surprising; the men of the well often used threads to sew up the cuts gained in knife dancing. It was a man's skill. He took the bandage from her and tied it carefully around Marick's leg. The boy didn't wake but moaned softly.

After that, Dorict lay down beside him, both under Yala's cloak, to keep Marick warm, for the cold was at its worst. Yala took a blanket from the supplies and went outside. Away from the others, she could at last give in to cursing the mess she had walked into. It was light enough now to see her angry breaths.

She knew it would be better to keep the wounded boy – Marick – warmer until the sun rose, and there were branches of oil brush in the cache, but the smoke would be seen for many leagues. Even though the slavers might be poor trackers, they had a sandwalker with them. Yala pulled the blanket tighter. Chit-chit poked out its nose and received a crumb of travel bread. It turned the morsel over and over again in its tiny claws without eating it. Finally, it dropped the crumb and retreated into its silkstone tube.

I hope that these are only my fears you're feeling, Chit-chit.

Has a spirit wind taken over me? Maybe that is why my thoughts whirl, but how do I free myself? Enough. When the little one can travel, we have to go south, to Old Carving Well, to tell everyone of sandwalkers and slavers working together. Perhaps that is enough to keep me as Yala to my mother.

She shivered again and pulled the blanket tighter. It might be some time before they could leave. The boy's wound looked angry. If the flesh rotted, they must wait until he healed or died, and both would take time they did not have.

After much watching and listening, Yala felt a warmth on her cheek as the sun, lifted by the eight winds, broke free of the dead waters in the east. Soon cold would not be a problem.

CHAPTER 22
REST BY DAY, TRAVEL BY NIGHT

Dorict woke in a sweat. He wiped his face and looked to where Marick still shivered in sleep, wrapped in the sandwalker's cloak. Always a slow riser, Dorict scratched at his tangled hair and looked around. Yala was nowhere to be seen, and though her sled still sat across the opening of the refuge, her bow and quiver were gone.

He took stock of their situation as he checked under Marick's bandage. The threads were holding, but the wound itself was worrying. Banerict, the banehall physician, might have the skill to ease the wound rot, but all Dorict could do was hope his own rough tending and Marick's vigour would save the leg and his friend's life. He let out a long breath and sat back down. Whatever the state of his leg, Marick was still alive, and that was only the first of Heaven's blessings. He was free of the slavers, and they had the help of someone who knew this brutal country. If Yala's people were as kind as she, they had a good chance of getting back to the Mother of Waters and rejoining Vinir.

And what then? How can Marick be forgiven for what he did, and why under Heaven did he do it?

Dorict shifted a bit to get out of the sun. It was low, but fierce. He debated moving Marick, but the wounded boy was still shivering, so he placed a cloth loosely over his face to keep the light from his eyes and left him in the rising heat.

There was no warning noise, but Yala was back, climbing over the fallen stones. She pulled the cloth mask from her face. Without speaking, she drank deeply from the second jar and sat beside him in the shade.

Dorict searched for something to say, other than "thank you" or '"sorry."

"Are we being chased?" he asked.

Yala looked at him. Without her cloak, Dorict could finally see more of her than her hands and shadowed eyes. Uncovered, those eyes were a light grey, as if living under this sun had drained them of any stronger colour. In contrast, her hair was black, a mass of curls that fell to her shoulders, and her skin was dark. Dorict and Marick were both fair-haired and fair-skinned, as were almost all of the people of Shirath and the other river cities. He felt no strangeness at the differences between them, for he had travelled more than most and met people of many shades and tongues. Some in Shirath had other views, and his friend Garet, who was almost as dark as the sandwalker, had been called "crow" by many.

But to Dorict's mind, a crow was a crow and a person was a person, and this was a person sitting beside him.

"No," Yala replied. "We are safe for now." She studied him as he studied her, taking in his blond hair, sunburned skin, and blue eyes.

"You look sick," she said. "Why are you so pale, even your hair?"

Dorict swallowed. The sun had shifted enough to brush his face, but he was sure the heat he felt was from embarrassment.

"Almost all my people look like this," he said. "We live in the North, along the River Ar. It's colder, and the sun isn't so bad. It doesn't burn like this, anyway."

He touched his chapped lips and smiled.

Yala shrugged. "Cover yourself like I do; there's a spare cloak in that hole. Even sandwalkers burn on a day like this." She cocked her head to continue her examination. "You don't look like a human being, even though you act like one."

"Thank you?" Dorict said and frowned. "Do I seem like an animal to you?"

Her answer was a long time in coming. While he waited, a small, whirling wind hit the roofless walls and showered them with sand. Yala stood up and brushed the grains from her tunic and pants.

"It's just what my people say. Go to sleep," she said, catching her bottom lip between her teeth. She released it quickly and added, "We will travel at night to the next refuge. Two days if your strength holds out. One if the other dies and we don't have to haul him."

She showed him how to rig a blanket as a shade, using her bow and several long arrows as supports. When it was ready, they moved Marick inside and lay down on either side of the still-sleeping boy.

"He'll live," Dorict said. "He'd better, after all the trouble he's caused. And we're not animals, only clawed fools to get into such a mess."

He took the spare cloak and wrapped himself against the burning light.

~

WHEN NIGHT FELL AGAIN, they drank sparingly and set off under a wash of stars. Even at sea, Dorict had never seen so many. Rivers of them twisted above the travellers, and parts of the sky were so bright that he and Yala cast a faint shadow on the ground as they walked. For Dorict, it was like being under an immense temple dome, if enough bright jewels could ever be found to mimic this night sky. The blowing sand rose and hid it all for a moment, but only a moment, and the stars appeared again, harrying the dark.

He looked for familiar shapes, the Plowman or the Swallows, but the constellations were different here, save for the Southern Swan, which flew in a different part of the sky than it did above Shirath. Under such unfamiliar lamps, Dorict knew he would have been lost without his guide.

"Please, wait a moment," he said, and Yala paused to look back at him.

Dorict knelt beside the sled to check Marick's bandages. There was no fresh blood to his touch. He wondered if he should change the bandage again, but even with all this starlight he would have to wait until the moon rose before he could see well enough to do a decent job.

"Have we far to go?" he asked.

Yala looked at the dunes falling away behind them. If the slavers were still following, they must be far off, and perhaps lost in the sand hills if the sandwalker wasn't with them.

"Yes, far. One sip, and then we pull again," she told the

strange one. When they had drunk, she lifted the harness and motioned Dorict to do likewise.

"You don't have to pull this time," Dorict said. "I can manage it alone." He made a great show of leaping up off the ground and swinging his arms.

Yala didn't answer, just picked up her half of the harness. By sunrise, they must be at the rocks. She had thought to go back scouting as she had before, but speed served them better than caution. She raised her eyes and silently asked the north-west wind to cover their tracks. Settling the harness securely, she began a diagonal scramble up the hill. Dorict struggled to keep up before he matched her speed.

All night they pulled the sled until they both stumbled, their strength failing against the terrible effort of trudging through loose sand. Dawn was touching the sky when they crested a dune and saw a jumble of red rocks a league off. Dorict was too tired to ask the question, but Yala nodded in encouragement. They reached it just as their strength failed.

This was a more substantial shelter than the ruined hut of the day before. Here, the rocks were large and leaned against each other in an ancient partnership, bearing the slow erosion of the wind and raising a droning, whispering chorus as each gust made music in the clefts and crevices between them. Those spaces might have given the travellers shade during the fast-approaching day, but Yala passed them by. They circled the stones until they came to flat section where the rock thrust out over the sand. There was a pit gouged there, deep and wide.

Dorict tried to swallow. This looked too much like that other hole, and he remembered the boiling sand and the long-jawed thing that tried to pull Marick down to join the one-eyed slaver in death. He leaned over the rim. The growing light gave him some certainty that this hole was empty. There was no sheen of water at the bottom, and very little sand. Yala motioned him to bring Marick down into it. He followed her, using the roughness of the sloping sides to slow his descent.

Yala laid down a blanket on the small patch of sand, and Dorict arranged Marick as best he could.

"Are there any of those things . . . ?" he began, but Yala quickly shook her head.

She pulled back her hood and sat down across from him. The soft light at the bottom of the pit gave some peace to her tired features.

"No, not like you saw," she said. She eased a gloved hand into the sand and pulled up several small creatures, none bigger than a finger.

Dorict looked closer and then recoiled, more at their shape than at any danger they might have represented. Black-armoured, legged and jointed in too many places, and with scissor-jaws forming half their length, they snapped at the light and twisted off Yala's glove to land back on the thin layer of sand. Once there, they flung their heads back and forth, showering sand in all directions and burying themselves in the process. In a few breaths, none could be seen, though the thought of them underfoot was enough to make him shudder.

"Don't worry," Yala said. "These won't bite you, and it will be a long time before they are large enough to attack anything bigger than each other."

She smoothed the sand and put down her own blanket. Setting her pack on top of it, she motioned Dorict to attend to his friend. While he uncovered Marick's wound, she removed fresh bandages and water from her pack and continued talking.

"In another two or three years, one will have eaten the rest to claim this pit for her own. Then, even a sandcat won't take it on. The pit-killer that slaver found was an old one. It had already made its dream of water – the sheen at the bottom that draws anything foolish to its death. Why was One-Eye trying to catch it?"

Dorict looked up at the interest in her tone, a change from what had been an indifference towards him and Marick that bordered on contempt.

"They wanted animals as well as slaves," he said. "Those cages were full of all sorts: big hunting cats, a type of wild pig, and some lizards – the biggest I've ever seen."

"Not for food then," Yala said. "The pigs and lizards taste good, but not the sandcats. Why were they taking them north?"

She handed a wet cloth to Dorict, and he began wiping the dried blood from Marick's leg. The boy's hand trembled and flicked a finger, but that was all.

"Another mystery, at least to me," Dorict said. "From what I heard in the City of Fountains, slavers take their captives south across the Bay of Tears to the farms of the Exalted Nobles."

Yala laughed a little. She took back the dirty bandage and gave him a clean one to wrap the wound. "Hah! 'Exalted Nobles.' So they call themselves, though they buy others like bolts of cloth and work them to death. Years ago, they hunted sandwalkers, and they paid for it in 'exalted' blood. I've heard the town-dwellers fight them. Is that true?"

Dorict answered after he set the new bandage. The wound was still an angry colour and he feared corruption had truly set in, but without medicine there was little he could do except try to keep it clean.

"They do fight them," he said. "Ten years ago, there was a great battle."

Yala nodded and edged closer, clearly interested in what Dorict had to say.

"I knew a man in the City of Fountains who fought in that battle. He's a bookseller, a very educated man. Ten years ago, the slavers came in force from those islands in the bay. That man, and everyone else who could, took up arms and fought them. They killed hundreds of slavers and burned their ships, but the bookseller was struck on the head with a club and lost most of his sight. Now, his niece reads to him, and he still sells books! Let me think about what he said . . . Two years after that fight, the towers built a fleet of boats to chase the remaining slavers from the Bay of Tears and drive them farther south. There are still some slavers, as you've seen, but only because the Exalted Nobles protect them."

Yala pushed a fist into the sand. She snatched it back, sucking at a punctured knuckle.

"I thought they didn't bite," Dorict said. He passed over the water bottle.

Yala sucked the blood from the wound and spat it out at some distance on the sand. The ground boiled as the many inhabitants of the pit fought over the sudden moisture.

"They only bite fools who punch them," she said. "I'm glad the town-dwellers bite too. Some of my people say that they are as bad as the slavers, but I don't think that can be true."

"It isn't!" Dorict said. He pulled a blanket over his friend and leaned back against the stone slope. "Marick and I, with our friend Vinir, lived among them for a season, and they are a kind people, though different from our own."

Yala looked at him for a long time, biting at her lip as if weighing some crucial decision. At last, she took six arrows from her quiver and a coil of rope and climbed to the top of the pit. She pushed the shafts into cracks in the rock and tied the rope between them, back and forth, until the web gave enough support for her to lay her cloak over top. She motioned to Dorict, and he handed up the last blanket. The sun touched the top of the rocks and began burning its way down, bringing more haste to her actions. When she was done, she eased between the lines and slid back down.

"This should keep us cool enough, and no one will see us if they don't climb up. My people leave supplies nearby that can keep us for a few days. I think we have lost the slavers, may the sand take them, so rest here and let your friend regain his strength, if he can."

They slept, and then Yala woke and tended Marick while Dorict stumbled off behind the rocks to tend to his own needs. When he returned, Yala had retrieved her cloak and settled the wounded boy under the remaining shade.

"I must go. Will you be all right if I leave you?" she asked.

"As long as you come back," Dorict said, trying to make a joke of his fear.

"I will," Yala said. "We aren't done yet."

CHAPTER 23
PURSUIT

"Here, fresh traces of those carts again, even though someone's done a bad job of brushing them over." Stetta stood up and wiped his brow. The sun was still high enough to bring sweat to the mildest effort, and the guard had been walking beside his horse for a league, searching the ground for the slavers' tracks.

Mor-ra handed him down a skin of water. "Don't drink too much! We've a long way to go before we can beg water from anyone who doesn't want to kill us."

Stetta took a careful sip and handed it back. He looked to where Vinir rode up to join them. Chal-lat and Son-neen trailed far behind, so the three waited there for the stragglers.

Vinir took off her hat and shook out her damp hair. Shading her eyes, she looked north and saw nothing but more hard, rippled ground. Here and there eruptions of rock thrust up, leftovers from some cataclysm, she assumed, that gave welcome shade during parts of the day. They had been travelling in the morning and evening, as well as at night, hoping to catch up to the slavers before they used up half their water and were forced to turn back.

"I don't understand," Vinir said. She dismounted and took the skin from Mor-ra. "They're pulling carts and we're not. Why haven't we caught up by now?"

"We will," Mor-ra said. She slid down off her horse and made to spit, thought better of it, and swallowed. "Remember, we were three days behind, and we can't travel too fast, see, or the horses will die, and then we'll die, for we can't walk all the way back to the Mother of Waters."

Stetta nodded. "Only sandwalkers have the knowledge of such travel, and they're no kinder than the sun or the sand when it comes to sharing."

Vinir smiled at the guard's way of speaking, but Mor-ra scowled.

"Ten years I've had to listen to your high talk. I hope a sandwalker does get you! At least I'd have a chance at a normal husband."

Vinir let them argue. After three days, she knew it meant little and wouldn't interfere with their duties. So far, aside from the arguing, the pursuit had been uneventful. The only dangers they faced were the stifling heat of the day and the biting cold of the night. After starting out north, as the battered Toosha-lun had suggested, Stetta soon found the half-hidden tracks of horses, carts, and a shuffling line of many feet. Vinir's heart had skipped at that sight. Was Marick really with them, and was he a willing partner, adding slave-taking to thievery and betrayal? And what of Dorict? Was he trying to save his friend, or did he need to be saved from him?

No, I won't believe that of Marick. Not yet. Not until I've shaken the truth out of him!

Before anyone was rescued – or shaken – they would have

to deal with the slavers. Chal-lat and the girl both carried bows, though only Chal-lat had any training in archery. He had been teaching Son-neen, but with few positive results and many near-disasters. Vinir had a borrowed horn-tipped heavy bow strapped to her own saddle. Though she could use it, it felt odd for a bane to carry such a weapon. Before the discovery of silkstone as a way to blunt demon fear, bows had been of no use against their ancient enemies, since their terror marred even a bane's aim. Now, with silkstone masks and practice, even the archers in the king's guard could assist banes in protecting the city, raining down arrows from a safe distance.

Despite her recent practice, Vinir did not count herself an expert. She reached back and touched the upthrust haft of the axe sheathed at her back. The guard commander had given her a choice of weapons stored in a room carved into the back of the Watch's barracks. When she picked this axe, the commander had pulled at the long tips of his moustaches and questioned her ability to wield such a heavy two-bladed weapon, but Stetta and Mor-ra had both vouched for her strength.

The bane let go of the wrapped handle. It sat snugly in a stiff leather pouch held by straps to her shoulders, awkward, but ready to be pulled free. No, if it came down to a fight, she trusted her skill with this over a bow.

The guards bore swords but were more comfortable shooting arrows. Though they rarely carried bows on patrol, archery was still a major part of their training in case the Far Southern raiders ever returned. It was a useful skill. At the beginning of their chase, Mor-ra had often angled off from their small party to range the higher ground, joining them later to display a brace of skinny rabbits or a fat rock lizard. "Success!" she'd say each time.

"Hot food tonight! Enjoy it while you can, because we'll need to keep a cold camp soon enough."

With the slavers' tracks now so fresh, that time had come. Tonight, they would have no fire to cook their meat, warm their bones, or cheer them in the dark watches of the night.

Mor-ra kicked dust into a particularly deep wagon track. "They're too cocky," she said. The round-faced woman squatted down to look at these latest traces. "Before they made a better job of hiding their tracks, but now they don't seem to care if they're followed, do they? Why not?"

"They're fools," Stetta said.

"Or because they're joining with a bigger band," Vinir said.

"That's what that rogue Toosha-lun said, wasn't it?" Stetta asked.

The bane nodded. "Before he passed out, he told me the slavers would turn west into the desert at some point. They'd meet their friends and go to a vast ruin near the Fingers where they'd re-supply and rest before continuing north. It's on the map I showed you."

Mor-ra and Stetta looked at each other.

The woman shrugged. "I know, but I've never heard of a 'vast' ruin out there, though the sand sometimes uncovers things long hidden or smothers something you saw only yesterday. Well, if it is big, there'll be places to hide, and we can sneak up on those storm-wracked brutes to ruin their plans."

Chal-lat stopped his mare beside them and eased off it, groaning a bit. As a citizen of the City of Fountains, he was more used to stairs and a ship's deck than a horse's back.

He reached up to help Son-neen, who was even less used to horses, off her own mount.

"I'm going to walk for a while," the girl said. She rubbed her bottom and looked down at the ground, noticing the re-appeared wagon tracks. "That's them, isn't it?" she shrieked, and grabbed her unstrung bow and a fistful of arrows.

Chal-lat jumped back as the shafts scattered over the ground. "Easy," he said, and helped her pick them up. "We don't need them yet, and I'm not sure you should use them at all!"

Son-neen bristled. "I can too! How else am I going to get those papers back? I can't go back to our city without them, can I?" She struggled with the bow and string, wrapping both awkwardly around her legs. Vinir took the bow from her and strung it easily. This was a light stave, unstrength-ened by sinew or horn. She doubted it would be effective beyond forty yards.

"We should all walk," Vinir said. "To save the horses' strength. But at a quick pace, for I want to catch them before they get into the desert."

Son-neen was trying to fix an arrow on her string when Mor-ra came up and put an arm around her shoulders.

"You come with me, girl, and we'll pretend bushes are slavers as we walk. You can practise sneaking up on them and improve your bow skills, though, by the Mother's Mouth, I'll stand behind you and pray that's safe enough."

They travelled through the night, and by the end of it, Son-neen had only killed a single bush.

CHAPTER 24
NIGHT ARROWS

The hours were long until Yala returned, but when she did, her pack was bulging. She handed it down to Dorict and motioned him to climb up out of the pit. He did so and together they moved the sled into the space between two tall, leaning stones, hiding it from view. Yala made sure her trade goods were still secured to the frame.

"I didn't touch them," Dorict said. "I wouldn't steal from you."

Yala nodded, still running her fingers over the ropes and tugging at the knots.

Dorict stood there, shifting from foot to foot on the hot rock.

"Do all sandwalkers use sleds?" Dorict asked. His own family were loggers in Shirath, and most of their work was done in the winter, when loads of firewood and timber could be pulled over the snow on much larger versions of this frame. "How do you take it over hard ground?"

Yala pointed to the axles sticking out from the sides of

the sled, and then pulled out one of the wheels stuck between the packages.

"Over sand or rock," she told him. "Sandwalkers must haul their trade goods. We go all the way to the fog-dwellers on the coast and the town-dwellers in the South."

Back in the pit, she opened her pack and brought out heavy jars. Dorict shook one and heard the sloshing of liquid within.

"Water and food for days, if we are careful," Yala said. "This came from another sandwalker well's cache. Now, let us get out of this heat," she said.

At the bottom of the pit, under the makeshift awning, the temperature was much cooler. Yala laid her cloak over the rope web above, adding to the blankets and throwing the sand floor into a welcome shade.

"I have nothing to give this time," Dorict said. "Unless there is some task I could . . ."

Yala shook her head, her grey eyes lowered.

"I left something, since I too will drink. As for tasks," she said, and paused. For a moment her gaze came up, settled on him, then dropped again. "Leave that for now," she said. Chit-chit had been restless all day, turning again and again in its stone tube. She could barely coax it out with a stroking finger or a morsel of food. If this behaviour continued, they would have to leave soon, even if the journey killed the wounded one.

"Is that a pet?" Dorict asked. He watched the fretful lizard retreat into its tiny house.

"No," Yala said, and added nothing more.

To speak too much of a poison wind is to call it, or so Ke says.

They drank – more than a sip this time – and ate a dried biscuit that was filling, though no more could be said in praise of it. Marick took more water than usual, and Yala was sure she saw the flicking of eyes under his lids. Was he waking? Was he dreaming? What nightmares had his ordeal given him to relive in his wounded sleep?

When they had settled, Yala held out a hand, palm up in a curiously formal expression, or so it seemed to Dorict.

"You are from those who dwell in the North and have lived among those who dwell in the South. Dorict, can you tell me more of your journey?"

Dorict nodded. Was this what she fretted over, biting her lip? It seemed important to her, so maybe he had something to give after all. He took a deep breath. His work with the historian of his own city, Barick, had taught him something of tale-telling.

"It will be a long story," he warned.

Yala dropped her hand and leaned forward.

"Those are the ones that matter," she said.

Dorict smiled at that, for it sounded like something Barick would say.

"Yala, have you ever been on the sea?" he asked. Her reaction surprised him. Her reserved expression changed to one of panic, and she scrambled back.

"No! Do not say such a thing!" she said, her voice rising with each word. The sand trembled as the tiny pit-killers reacted to her sudden movement.

"Forgive me," Dorict said. He waited until she calmed down before he continued.

"This is part of our story, so I must tell you something of it. The water is bigger than this desert – I'm sorry if that upsets you – but it explains why it took us weeks to travel from the river cities to the City of Fountains. The wind you feel here is also out there, but it doesn't always push you where you want to go. A sea also has hills and valleys like this sand, but they are made of water and move faster than you could run. Our boat was tossed up and down so much that I thought we would die. Then I was so sick, I wanted to."

Yala flinched but didn't stop him from talking. Instead, she made a great business of pulling Marick's blanket to keep him away from the sunlight lancing between the hanging cover and the pit wall.

"Well, enough about the water then," Dorict said. "Though I bet you'd laugh at some of the pranks Marick played on the sailors. By the end of the journey, they wanted to throw him overboard!"

Yala's hand shot up, palm towards Dorict. "Water is life," she said, "but too much is death! It is no matter for laughing."

"All right! All right! Then I'll tell you about Shirath, my city. There is no ocean, only a river, and there are three bridges that save you from getting wet!"

He spoke long and proudly of Shirath's beauty, of its high, white walls, its sixteen wards and the breadth of its fields and orchards. He told her of the grand palace that sat in the same plaza as the temple, and of the banehall in a different plaza across the river. He told her of markets, Masks, Duellists, banes, kings and lords until Yala looked as though her head would burst and she would never be curious again, but there was one thing strange enough to her to bring forth a question.

"You speak of demons. What are these things, and why do you seek them here?" Yala asked. "Especially if they always want to kill you?"

She spoke to him from the rim of their refuge, pulling the blankets from one side of her web to the other and so preserving the shade at the bottom of the pit. That done, she slid back down to the sand floor beside Dorict.

The young man looked at her and sighed, but he set his shoulders and answered her question.

"I've already told you things that I swore to keep secret on this trip. Without Vinir here, it's hard to know what to do, Yala, but we owe you our lives, so I won't hide anything from you. We seek them because we are demonbanes, those who can fight these creatures. I told you of the banehall, yes? That is where the three of us live. It is a great house ruled by the hallmaster and the other masters, each of whom take apprentices to help them fight demons."

"These demons, are they fierce, like sandcats or pit-killers?" Yala asked. She touched the shoulder of her tunic. *Or the thing Chit-chit might be feeling?*

Dorict considered his answer before replying. At first, Yala had thought this was a sign of deceit, that he sifted what to say to suit his own advantage, but now she saw that this was his way, to think before speaking, not to hide the truth but to put it more clearly.

"Fierce? Yes, demons are cruel killers. There are different types though: some very large, some small, some can run fast, others can glide like a bird. One can even force other demons to do its bidding, but all of them have a terrible power to strike you with a fear that holds you help-less when they attack."

He looked up to see the sun had shifted another hand's breadth in the sky. The heat was merciless, and he pulled off his jacket to reveal a fine network of scars on his arms and shoulders.

Yala gave him water and a cloth. He wiped down his upper body and nodded thanks.

"Ahh, we really have no heat like this in my home, though I once I thought the summers there unbearable!"

She took the jar back when he was done. "Those are the

marks of wounds. Were you whipped by your masters or by these demons? Is that what you meant by 'striking with fear?'"

Dorict shook his head. "No, some masters can be harsh but they rarely harm a student on purpose. The other masters would not allow it. These scars come from training injuries, though this one," he said and traced at a long line on his arm, "came from a Shrieker demon that wasn't as dead as I thought it was, and as for ordinary fears like whips or deadly animals, it isn't the same. The fear a demon casts is like nothing else. It pierces to your bones. Most people can't move, not even a finger! That is when the demon strikes. If you're lucky, you heart stops from it, or else the clawed beasts will eat you while you're still alive."

He helped Yala move Marick another foot, then shifted after him to stay in the shade.

"Do you have nothing like that here?" he asked.

"There are many creatures in the desert that can kill," Yala said. Her hand dropped from her shoulder, and Dorict saw that she had touched again where her little lizard hid beneath her shirt.

Her voice had become distant, and Dorict was reluctant to ask more. For now.

"Shall I continue my story?" he said.

Yala gave the smallest of nods.

"Well, a demonbane is one who can bear that fear and kill the demon."

"Once you bear this fear, are they hard to kill?" Yala asked. Her voice still had that remote tone, and Dorict wondered what he had done to offend her.

"Yes, though we train and train until we are very good at it. The trick is to catch them before they can kill ordinary people – I mean non-banes. That's where the fear they cast helps us. We can feel them coming from, oh, say half a league off, so we attack them first. That's why more banes die than anyone else in my city."

"And he is a bane too?" Yala asked, pointing at Marick. "He's so small."

Dorict shrugged. "We don't look like fierce warriors, do we?" He leaned forward. "Think of it this way: living with fear as a child, learning how to act in spite of it, is what makes you a bane. Marick and I, we found our own defences against terror a long time ago. Not many can. And those that do are often small and weak, at least until we start to train them!"

He looked down at the unconscious boy.

"Yes, he was a bane and a good one, with many kills to his credit, though now . . ."

"He is no longer a bane?"

Dorict suddenly stood, and the sand boiled for a moment before quieting. "I don't know. Lately, things have changed a lot in Shirath. Instead of seeing demons as a Heaven-sent curse, most of us now think they are a weapon someone else is using against us, though we don't know who would do it or why. That's why we're down here in the Far South, Yala. We're trying to find out where the demons come from so we can stop them for all time."

He looked down at Marick, shaking his head. "But he stole from us, his fellow banes! We grew up together in the hall. We trained and fought together, and he . . . the Marick I knew would never do that, not even as a joke, but now . . . he's been so angry lately, so mad at the world, as if nothing fit him anymore, not even our friendship."

"It's hard not to fit," Yala said.

She looked up at the sky. The sun had dropped during

their talk, and it was a good time to eat and think upon what had been said.

~

THAT EVENING, Dorict volunteered for the first watch, and Yala showed him where he should hide among the rocks above the pit and how to keep the moonlight from revealing his presence.

"I will come for you at the top of the moon's journey," she told him, and returned to the pit.

She lay down on her blanket and turned one last time to check on the injured boy. His eyes were open and looking at her.

"Yala," he said, or rather whispered, for his voice was as low and hoarse as a branch scraped over hard ground.

"You have heard us?" Yala asked. She considered calling Dorict, but decided against it, lest she reveal him to any pursuers. She had not forgotten the sandwalker who still travelled with the slavers.

Marick nodded, then coughed. Yala sat him up and helped him sip some water. After that, he lay back, looking up at the stars.

"I thought I was dead," he whispered. "I think I wanted to be dead."

Though it was not her place to ask, she could not help herself.

"When you have a friend who will dare death to save you? Why go to your death?"

"Because," Marick answered, "I didn't have anywhere else to go. My city is . . . changed. I'm not needed anymore. Even my friends hate me."

Yala shook her head. This boy was as foolish as she first

thought when she saw him singing insults to his captors. But he didn't have to remain so.

"He came across the hard land for three days to save you," she said, "and did, though he almost died doing it. I saved him, and you too."

Marick gave her the ghost of a grin. "I'll let him thank you for it, then. Since I didn't ask for your help. Is he here? No, don't get him. I . . . we have nothing to say to each other."

His voice trailed off. Yala saw his closed eyes and regular breathing and leaned back against the wall of the pit. She was glad he hadn't asked about his wound. Even in the cold air, she could smell the rot. She thought of Inlaphor and his corrupted whip cuts. If she got the boy back to her well, the men might save his life, but she doubted they could save his leg.

At moon's height, she took her bow and quiver and crawled back up the rock jumble to relieve Dorict. He hissed a warning as she came near, and she saw he had already left his hiding place.

"Something moving past the rock ledge, a shadow that moves and then goes still, then moves again," he said. "I was coming to get you."

Yala looked where he pointed. The moon showed enough detail to soon see the shadow he spoke of, a shade darker than the surrounding sand and one that moved not with the wind like a scud of red grains but against it, pausing here and there, ever closer to their hiding place.

"I'll go around to the left and you . . ." Dorict began, but Yala held up a warning hand.

"She'll kill you if you show yourself. Stay here," she said, and slipped back down the rocks to the sand below. There, she crouched against the stone and strung her bow, her fingers slipping on the stave.

Curse you for following! Wasn't trading slaves shameful enough for you? Now must one of us die?

She waited until the shadow appeared in her field of vision. In a fluid movement, it neared the rim of the pit – and the wounded boy. Slowly, wincing at each small creak, she pulled back the string until her left hand brushed her cheek.

The shadow dodged, and Yala's arrow – loosed as much by surprise as intent – went wide. She threw herself onto the sand as a returning shaft cut the air above her head. The bow was in a tangle now, wrapped in the folds of her cloak, and she dropped it to scramble back up the rocks, hoping to avoid the next arrow and live another few breaths.

Something dropped from above and to her right, a heavy weight that knocked down the pursuing sandwalker's arm, snapping the string as the arrow buried itself to the fletches in the sand. Yala turned to see the woman sweep out her sand shovel. Dorict, for it was he who had jumped from the platform above, dodged back as well he could over the soft ground as his adversary slashed again and again.

Yala dropped back down and ran at the sandwalker, ignoring her own still-tangled bow. She stooped in mid-stride and pulled the arrow from the sand and jumped upon the woman from behind, plunging the point into her right shoulder.

For that, she took the woman's elbow in her cheek and might have died there, save for Dorict grabbing her attacker's other arm and twisting it until the shovel dropped from her hand. The woman punched the bane in the side of his neck and pulled free. She ran off to the south, leaving her bow and shovel, taking only the arrow that Yala had so painfully returned to her.

Yala sat down beside Dorict and unwound the cloak from her bow. She set another arrow on the string and stared off to where the other sandwalker, now a moon-lit dot against the sand, still managed a stumbling run.

She looked at Dorict. The bane was rubbing the side of his neck and moving his jaw as if it needed some adjustment to work properly again.

"You didn't stay where I told you to," Yala said.

Dorict gave his chin one last wag and answered, "The bad influence of Marick on my life, I guess, but you seemed overmatched. I meant no offence."

Yala spoke without taking her eyes from where the sandwalker had faded into shadow and distance.

"Truth will not offend," she said. "Or at least that's what the women of my well say when I do something they don't approve of. It is as you said; if you hadn't helped me, I would be dead. We might yet die, for she will go back for help, if she doesn't bleed out her life in the sand, curse her."

She re-tied her cloak and slung the bow over her shoulder. Reaching out a hand, she helped Dorict up off the ground and said, "She meant to silence us, so we could not tell the other wells of her crimes. Sandwalkers helping slavers! This is a wicked wind for the rest of us."

Yala shook herself and looked at the bane. He was scanning the darkness, ready for another attack. She nodded. *He is a good person to fight beside, even if he is a town-dweller and a man.*

"Take her bow," she said. "I have an extra string – and the shovel. We'll share arrows. You can shoot, I hope?" she asked.

Dorict nodded. He gathered the other sandwalker's

weapons and began the climb back up to the pit-killer's nest.

"I had a season's practice while we prepared for this trip. I've no great skill at distance, but I can hit a close target."

Marick woke enough to turn his face away from Dorict when they readied him for another night of travel.

"My well is to the south now. We'll go back up on the Fingers and travel faster that way, even though it's longer than hauling over the sand. Let's hope our enemies look for us out here until they're turned to sand themselves!"

They tied Marick to the sled and went east, skirting the rock wall of the Fingers until they found a collapsed cliff they could drag and lift the sled over. On top, Dorict pointed to the south-west. Points of light shone in the distance, like stars fallen to the earth.

"It seems you were right," he said. "They do wait for us on the sand."

Yala smiled.

Even Tral must say I have done well in this.

The smile faded.

But what will she do with these two? We take neither slaves nor captives. At best, they'll be fed and rested and sent back to the Mother of Waters. At worst . . .

She reached up to her shoulder and felt the small movement of the lizard that hid there.

"Why do you carry that lizard?" Dorict said. "If I'm allowed to ask."

Yala hesitated for a moment, then remembered her debt to him. She took the tube from its lashing on her shoulder and tipped Chit-chit out onto her palm. The small red lizard blinked in the moonlight and tried to scramble to the underside of Yala's hand.

"A pet?" Dorict asked, then smiled. "Sorry, I asked that before, didn't I?" He put out a finger, but Chit-chit climbed inside Yala's sleeve.

"No, I do not know that word. Chit-chit is a . . . companion," she said. After some gyrations, she retrieved the lizard and put it back in its tube.

"Not very friendly," Dorict said, then stopped. "Sorry. Maybe it's just afraid of strangers."

"No," Yala said. "Most times, Chit-chit is very good. Like you say, friendly. Maybe . . . never mind. We should pull again, if you are ready."

Dorict stretched his arms and looked down at the boy on the sled.

"If you have a burden, you have to pull it whether you're ready or not," he said.

CHAPTER 25
A SINGLE PURPOSE

"Thank the names of all our people for this cache," Chal-lat said. "Another day and we'd have been dead."

The young man sat beside Vinir and leaned back against the standing stones. Vinir handed him the water jar.

"It was already too late for Son-neen's horse," Vinir said, "and I didn't ask you to come with me."

She regretted the sharpness of her tone, but the two days since they came down from the Fingers and gave themselves to the sand had been a nightmare of heat, thirst, and, above all, doubt. Were they going in the right direction, or was this a fool's bet, taken on the word of a known criminal?

Chal-lat placed the jar between them, pushing the pointed bottom into the sand to keep it upright. He stole a glance at her profile, her sun-reddened and chapped lips not reducing her beauty, to his mind at least.

"No, you didn't ask me, but you know why I'm here. Son-neen is my employee. I'm responsible for her, and she needs to get those papers back or she'll never have a place in the City of Fountains. There's another reason, though you seem to not want to speak of it, at least, not since the Mother of Waters."

Vinir stood up. Her legs trembled a bit, for they rarely rode their exhausted horses and a night of ankle-deep slogging had sapped her strength, but she did not lean against the rocks. Unsteadily, she turned to Chal-lat and spoke.

"I cannot speak, not now, and maybe not ever! You don't understand. How could you. Your city doesn't have demons!"

Chal-lat got to his feet as well, slowly, and put his hands on her shoulders.

"We have slavers, and even crazy Northerners to worry about, so try and explain it to me," he said, smiling.

Vinir shook her head. "No, you can't understand. How could anyone who hasn't seen monster after monster invade their city? Have you watched as your friends were torn apart? Have you been soaked in blood while you killed nightmares?"

She fell to her knees, and Chal-lat followed.

"I have seen blood," he said. "Ten years ago, when my city was attacked by raiders from the Bay of Tears. They were nightmares, though they wore the skins of men. I remember the blood and the screams. I should have been too young to fight, but anyone who could hold a spear did so that day. I saw my friends fall beside me, Vinir, and I saw my share of blood."

The bane looked up. There were tears in her eyes, but her voice was cold.

"Once, Chal-lat. Once, you saw that. I have fought demons over a hundred times. I have faced an army of creatures who make these slavers look like tabby cats! The only way a bane survives in Shirath is by training, fighting, then training again. There can be nothing else in my life."

Chal-lat paled but did not let go of her. "Maybe I don't understand all of that, but what about your art, Vinir? Master Sarth knows your talent, and so do I! You can't give that up, can you?"

Vinir brushed away his hands and spoke down into the sand.

"If I hadn't pretended to have another life, Marick wouldn't have turned against me. Dorict would be safe, and I'd be on my way back with the knowledge that no demons come from the south. I'd be back home, Chal-lat, fighting as a bane. That is my duty, not pretending about art or peace . . . or love."

Mor-ra passed Chal-lat as he walked back to the horses.

"You've broken his heart then?" she asked Vinir, who was sitting again beside the water jar.

"Did you know I would?" Vinir asked. She shifted sand through her fingers, letting the red grains fall.

Mor-ra clicked her tongue. "Tchh! Had to happen, see? You're like me. You've got a job to do. When the job's over, then you can play, but not till then."

"What if the job's never over?" Vinir asked, her voice tired, but she didn't wait for an answer. The bane leaned back against the rocks and closed her eyes. Within a few breaths, she was asleep.

Mor-ra looked down at her with a mixture of amusement and sympathy. "Poor thing," she said softly. "The world's got you tight in its grip, doesn't it? As for Stetta and me, it's the same job, girl, or it wouldn't work at all."

Stetta came up behind her. He was wiping blood from his hands, having cut up the haunch of Son-neen's horse, much to the young girl's disgust.

"Did you tell her about the smoke I saw?" he asked. "And what were you saying about me?"

Mor-ra knelt down and brushed a strand of hair from Vinir's face.

"No, I didn't tell her," she whispered. "Let her rest, Stetta. The weight she carries would kill a weakling like you, and even bend me." She stood back up and rounded on her husband and hissed, "And as for what I said about you, it's none of your business! Why don't you go bury yourself in the sand until you're needed, which'll be never."

They whispered insults at each other for some time, standing there next to the sleeping bane, but none of their words pierced Vinir's heavy, troubled sleep.

CHAPTER 26
THE HOSPITALITY OF THE WELL

Yala stopped pulling when the entrance to Old Carving Well came into sight. The sled teetered for a moment on the top of the dune before Dorict, coming up behind her, reached out to steady it. Marick made no sound. As his wound worsened, he had slipped into an uneasy sleep, thrashing and moaning but not waking.

"Is this another refuge?" Dorict asked. He wiped the grit from his face and studied the tall rock walls and the gap that promised entry. He shaded his eyes and added, "I see some smoke beyond that rock."

"Cooking fires," Yala said. "The home fires of my well. The entrance is there. It leads to . . . well, I hope you will see."

Dorict turned to look at her. "Hope? Is something wrong, Yala?"

The sandwalker shrugged. "When I left, some called me . . . I don't know the word. One who doesn't listen when she should."

"Disobedient," Dorict ventured, and Yala nodded.

188

"Yes," she said. "Disobedient. Let us see if our news of sandwalker treachery makes them forget my sins and yours." At Dorict's confused look, she added, "You are not of our well. You are not of our people. And you are not human in their eyes."

The bane swore under his breath. "Claws, I hope they'll still help Marick. Should we leave?"

Yala shook her head. "No, the guards have already told the old women with short names. See, they gather outside the entrance. I think . . . I think my mother is there as well. Come. Waiting will not make this better."

"THEY CANNOT ENTER," Tral said. She stood, arms folded between Yala and the well's entrance. "Even Yalasa should know this," she added.

There were small noises from the women ranged behind her, all cloaked, all armed with bows. Yala did not know if those were murmurs of agreement or gasps of surprise, but it did not matter now.

"The wounded one was a slave and the other rescued him," she said in a loud and, she hoped, confident voice. "I helped them both, just as we helped those others, Tral. Did you forget that?"

She pointed to the bow slung over Dorict's shoulder. "Look at what he carries. It came from a sandwalker, a sandwalker in league with the slavers!"

Now the shock was unmistakable. The arrows lowered, and the women looked at each other. Ke stepped forward to stand beside her daughter and stare at her grand-daughter.

"Hard to believe," she said, peering up into Yala's eyes.

"But this needs talking. Send these two to the fields and come tell us your story."

Tral held up a hand. "Yalasa has no place in our counsels," she said.

There was a stillness among those gathered there, but Ke waved away the objection.

"We will see if she is Yala or Yalasa after she speaks. Sometimes, daughter, I wonder if you fear she will become Yal too soon!"

There were smiles at this among the guards, though hidden behind hands and folds of their red cloaks. While Tral fumed silently, a child was sent to bring some men to take Dorict and Marick away. Before he left, Yala took the borrowed bow and arrows from the bane.

"Don't worry," she said. "They will do what they can for his leg and look after you."

Dorict shrugged. "It seems we have to depend on your people, just as we depended on you. I hope we will talk again soon," he said.

Even Ke shook her head at that.

Yala bit her lip. "No, that is not our way, not here, Dorict of Shirath. Tell your tale to the men and be well."

Marick was laid beside him, and Yala nodded once before turning and pulling her sled behind Tral and Ke.

It may be that I will never see them again, but I know one thing now: sandwalkers can be animals and animals can be human.

"How could you stand travelling with such creatures?" Brada asked. Yala's older sister wrinkled her nose and put an arm around Yala's shoulders.

"Mother is madder than a sandsnake tied in a knot, and even Ke wonders if you went wind-crazy on your first trip, all those months ago. Best you keep your tongue still for a year if you want to keep your name short," she added and grabbed the harness. She helped Yala pull it after the retreating knot of muttering sandwalkers. Tral was first among them, silent, back straight, cloak pulled tight over her shoulders, and not once looking back at where her two daughters pulled a sled full of good trading.

Yala bristled. *I'll get no credit for this! And I'll not keep my tongue still in the face of insult and contempt. "Fair trade," as that town-dweller said. My truth for yours, Mother, and let's see who bargains better.*

Brada nudged her with a shoulder, almost knocking her into the wall of the cleft.

"Hey!" Yala said. "I'm not a child anymore. You can't bully me."

Brada laughed. She had a big laugh, for she was a big woman, broad-shouldered and long-legged, one who could pull a loaded sled all night and still breathe easy.

"When did I ever bully you, sister?"

Yala shook her head. "You have a poor memory, Brada. When I was small, you used to lift me over your head and threaten to throw me over the small wall to the men. You said they'd cook me up and eat me!"

"What harm was there in that?" Brada asked. "You're so small and stringy, they'd only have thrown you back. Besides, you got too fierce to bully." She paused in her pulling and looked to see that the other women were out of earshot.

"Maybe you're too fierce still, sister. Tral has a wind up her cloak about you. She thinks you challenge her authority among the women. I love our mother, but she acts like her name is Tra instead of Tral. Listen sister, if she can lift herself up by pressing you down, she will. So, don't be fierce, Yala. Be meek and mild . . . like me!"

Yala stared at her sister and, without warning, launched herself on the larger woman, tripping her and wrestling her to the ground. By the time Brada freed herself, both were laughing so hard that they didn't notice a small figure come up behind them.

"It is good to see sisters who love each other with such violence," Ke said. Neither of her granddaughters had noticed her stay behind while they talked and pulled the sled.

The two scrambled up and brushed the sand and red dust off their cloaks.

"Sorry, Grandmother," they said in unison, then giggled again.

Ke smiled. "Joy is the rarest wind," she said, and the smile disappeared. "Brada, take the sled to the wall and set the goods out. Yala, come with me. The women must hear more of these slavers. The one-souled must hate living, since they keep coming into our lands."

Yala took a package from the sled, a cloth-wrapped bundle of silver ingots and looped wire. It was small, but not small enough to escape Ke's notice.

"You have someone in mind for that?" she asked, one white eyebrow raised.

Brada hid a smile behind a broad hand. She winked at Yala and pulled the sled away.

Yala felt her cheeks flush but answered as calmly as she could. "Yes, I do know someone who can use this," she said.

"You are young to show favour," Ke said. She might have been discussing the weather, but Yala felt judgment again come down upon her head.

"Favour for favour," she said to her grandmother. "He gave me much to take to the Mother of Waters, and they valued it, as you saw."

They said no more as they walked the twisting path to the well. Yala did not want that path to end, despite the stretching silence between them, for once in the well she would again be questioned, criticized, and perhaps punished for her actions. She hoped Dorict and his friend would have a better welcome among the men. At least they could look to the small one's leg.

Ke did say one thing before they came out into the pocket of green among the red hills. It was not what Yala was expecting.

"Granddaughter, how has Chit-chit been acting?"

THE HUT WAS small and empty, save for a bed, pads on the floor for sitting, and a low workbench. The tall, broad-shouldered man now talking had to crouch to stand within it.

"The leg must be off," the man said. He held up a snake-toothed length of metal as bright as a sword.

Dorict paled at the sight of the saw. "Can't you drain the wound and bind it up again?" he asked. Marick lay between them, wrapped in a blanket against an onset of chills, his thin face pale and sweaty.

The man, who the others called Before Dawn Field Man, shook his head, his scarred face frowning. "Listen, town-dweller. Wound is bad. Leave the leg, lose the life. Might yet die. Fever has him. If dies, must be outside the well. One-soul become wind, trouble our fields."

"Let me think on this first," Dorict pleaded. He didn't know what to do, but he knew that a Marick who couldn't jump and run might curse him for saving his life.

Before Dawn Field Man drew back in surprise. Some of

the other men crowded outside the low doorway laughed. "Animal, not your choice. Ours only. Bad enough women put you here! Bad thinking," he said, and tapped the side of his head, touching one of the many scars that tracked across his blunt, dark face. He gestured with the saw towards where Marick shivered.

"Still, get use out of him, get use out of you," he said. "Animal good in fields," he added, and laughed.

Dorict snarled at that and lunged towards him, but was knocked back and smothered by others rushing in. He struck out, and was glad to hear grunts of pain, but an arm wrapped around his neck and the hut went black. His last squeezed vision was of Before Dawn Field Man slicing the boot off Marick's leg.

HE WOKE with a fierce headache and reached up to find a wet cloth laid across his forehead. He pulled it off, feeling the coolness of it as he dragged it down to rest on his chest. Opening his eyes was difficult, for they were swollen. His nose felt bigger too, and very sore.

Slowly, his surroundings swam into view. Another hut, smaller, empty except for a single man, who came over and took the cloth from the bane's limp hand. He dipped it in a bowl of water and put it back on Dorict's forehead.

"Simple," the man said. "No . . . easy. I don't speak town words so well as Yala. Here, sit and drink."

He helped Dorict to sit against the mud-brick wall and put a cup of hot liquid in his hand.

"Help head," the man said.

As Dorict drank, he examined his benefactor. Where most of the men he had seen so far were big, broad figures made fiercer by the scars they sported on their faces, this one was slim, with a face marked by only a single old cut running from the corner of his right ear across his cheek.

The drink cleared his head and tamped down the pain in his skull.

"Thank you," he said, then tried to stand up, making it only halfway before the man had to grab him to keep him from falling. The cup clattered on stone flagging, and the greenish liquid within made a small puddle at his feet. While the world spun, a calf's head pushed between them and licked at the floor.

"Eh!" the man said and pushed the animal into a reluctant retreat. "Sorry," he added. "Sandcats hunt when calves come. Keep inside, like you."

"Marick," Dorict said, sliding back down into a sitting position. The hut stopped spinning, and he could focus on the other. "What happened to Marick?" he asked.

The man sat cross-legged across from him. He leaned on a small table covered with polished stone, pieces of glass, and a variety of small tools. "Ah, your friend," he said, frowning. "He lives! Be glad. But his leg is gone. Sorry."

"Heaven shield him! But, at least he's alive," Dorict said. "Would he really have died if they didn't do it?"

The man nodded. "Maybe so," he said. "The cut was bad. Bad smell. You are Dorict, yes? I heard your name."

"Dorict, yes," the bane said. "What is your name?"

"I am," the man said, and stopped. "How do you say this?" he asked, and brought his two hands, palms facing each other, close together.

"Thin?" Dorict said. "Narrow?"

The two hands clapped. "Yes! Narrow. I am Narrow Field Man. People say I am small like my field!"

Dorict nodded, not quite understanding. "Narrow Field

Man, why did the others beat me?" he asked. He touched his nose and felt the sharp pain that meant it was broken.

"Don't touch!" Narrow Field Man said. "I make straight already. They beat you because you fight. Only humans should be allowed to fight other humans. Fight, get big scar to make you look good. Some fight so much, all scars, no face anymore! They say you are animal. They beat you because you fight. I say, 'I take animal and feed' and they say 'good.'"

Dorict remembered Yala's talk about souls and humans.

"Do you think I'm an animal?" he asked. He felt like one, caged and beaten. It made him want to see Marick even more. He wanted to take him away to someplace safe, someplace where they weren't treated as beasts.

Narrow Field Man shrugged. "Don't know. Like animals." A hen wandered into the hut and climbed over his legs before moving on to probe the corners of the hut for insects. "I think animals so easy, people so hard. Maybe two souls too much? Don't know." He helped Dorict lie down again and replaced the wet cloth on his forehead.

The bane closed his eyes and heard Narrow Field Man say, "Animals sleep, like humans, yes? Sleep, Dorict. I go see your friend."

ON THE OTHER side of the wall that separated men from women in Old Carving Well, Yala endured a full day of answering the same questions over and over again until she wanted to scream out her replies.

"Yes! The slavers are coming north again. Yes! I'm sure they met sandwalkers. At least ten, including the one who tried to kill us. Yes! They gave them men from a well and took a chest in payment. No! I don't know where the slavers are going, except it is in the desert and to the north."

Each answer caused a corresponding uproar of accusations and near-panic:

"The northern wells are all thieves. Now they are traitors too!"

"My fear lizard is stirring; is this because of the slavers?"

"We have to rouse all the southern wells and catch those slavers!"

"Quiet!" Ke shouted, and the babble slowed to a muttering, then silence.

"Yes, we must kill the slavers," she said, and many, including Yala, murmured in agreement. Then Ke looked around the circle of red-robed figures and asked, "But can we kill sandwalkers too?"

At that, there had been much shaking of heads. Many seemed shocked by the idea.

Ke struck the ground with her hand. "Sandwalkers have not fought each other for many lifetimes," the old woman said. "For good reason. Can we trade and fight at the same time? Can the men farm and make trade goods under the threat of arrows from the darkness? Those days were bad, full of hunger and death, or so the tales say. We should not fight."

Many women, especially the older ones, had agreed. Brada stood and held up her hand for attention.

"Grandmother, you speak words of wisdom, but where is the wisdom of letting them get away with this? What if the slavers come to this well, guided by those northern sandwalkers? With human aid, the animals will be harder to defeat, and maybe they will kill us. I agree with those who say to kill the slavers. Let the traitors in the north see that they'll get no profit. Call on the nearest wells to help us. We will send a storm of arrows against them!"

Tral smiled at that, and Yala wondered if those were her words coming out of Brada's mouth.

Ke looked at them both, and Tral's smile vanished. There was a rustling, and all those with the shortest names came to stand behind Yala's grandmother.

"There is danger on all sides here, and more than one, as those who carry lizards know," Ke said, and touched her shoulder. "That threat may or may not be, and we will deal with it separately, but about these slavers, we must decide now. Brada is right, though I'm sure that will surprise her! We must kill the slavers, and we need the help of other wells, but not just the southern wells, the northern ones as well. No, hear me! Not all will be traitors. This might be a single well. The others will hate them as much as we do. We must act as one – all sandwalkers against the traitors in our midst."

The other old women nodded. One stepped forward.

"Ke is right," she said, and smiled. "Which will not surprise her. We must be cautious. The slavers first, yes? Let runners go out to the nearest wells. Tell them of this and ask for women to make up a raiding party, small enough to move unnoticed but large enough to kill – how many slavers were there?"

"Two dozen minus one," Yala said. "And maybe minus their sandwalker guide."

"To know their well would have been useful," Tral said. She turned to her daughter. "Didn't you get any of their arrows?"

Yala shrugged. "The one she shot wide was lost. The other I gave back," she said.

"Gave back?"

"In her shoulder," Yala said, and the women in the trade-house slapped their thighs and whistled out praise.

Tral did not. She waited until the noise died down and asked, "You didn't stop to find the other arrow?"

Yala stared back at her mother. "No," she said, "for if we had stopped to do that, I might have had more arrows than I wanted, because she was going back for help."

"Better she should have died," Tral said.

The silence was heavy then, until Ke broke it with a short laugh.

"She will, for Yala marked her and we'll find her so Yala can finish the job to please her mother," Ke said. "Now, all of you with long names go. We have other matters to discuss."

"First time I've been happy to be Brada and not Brad," Yala's sister said as they walked towards the tents of their family. Yala's was the smallest of eight placed in a circle around the cooking fires. When they arrived, she ducked in and out again only to run straight into Brada.

"Hah! I thought you might want to take that package to the wall. Tell me, is it Blue Stone Field Man? Leaning Tree Field Man?" she demanded. "Come on, tell me or I'll burst."

"Burst then," Yala said, and left her sister there, chuckling.

None of her business, not with Brada going to the night huts with Northmost Field Man – and trying to keep it secret!

She did not see the one she was looking for near the wall. She walked its long length, ignoring the men and women sitting or standing close to it. Most were gathered in one spot, for a knife dance was going on. Two men,

Before Dawn Field Man and Plum Soil Field Man, were circling each other, their knives flashing from one hand to the other. The came together, turning, blocking, slashing, and blood flew from Plum Soil Field Man's chin. There was a cheer from both sides of the wall, and the two men clasped hands and began their loud, poetic praise of each other, which the crowd cheered as loudly as they had the victory.

Yala turned back. She saw a lone figure approach the end of the wall where it petered out into the space between the rock and the fields. She walked there, as nonchalantly as possible, holding the package in a sweaty hand.

She stopped near where Narrow Field Man lingered and said, "These silver ingots and wire are probably useless, but maybe a good maker can use them for something."

She did not say it loudly, for the crowd had broken up now and were ranging farther along the waist-high wall. The man standing on the other side, looking with no interest at the green fields of the men, replied, "I'm sure it is good, Yala."

She stumbled a bit at that, caught turning away from what should have been an indirect conversation.

"Thank you," she said, after a moment needed to compose herself. "And thank you for the goods you gave me to take to the Mother of Waters. There was a woman there from the City of Fountains who said to tell you how much they praise your work."

Narrow Field Man smiled. "It is good to hear such words, and to talk to you instead of away from you. Listen, Yala, those two you brought are safe. Dorict is with me, but the other is in Before Dawn Field Man's hut. They took his leg, but he still lives. I looked at him before I came here. He does not speak, but he breathes more easily."

Some were coming closer to where they stood, curious no doubt. Yala put the package of silver on top of the wall. "They are my friends. Please help them if you can."

She walked away and heard him say, loudly, "These things are of poor quality, but I'll take them and . . . try my best."

Yala let out a held breath. That last part was the answer she had hoped for. She touched the hidden tube at her shoulder, wanting nothing more than the reassurance of another life close to her, but Chit-chit did not stir. It had not come out for a full day, and Yala decided to ask Brada if her fear lizard was also acting oddly, but when she came back to the tents, Brada was nowhere to be found, and Yala decided sleep was the best choice left to her.

CHAPTER 27
A CITY OF SAND

"They went in there?" Son-neen asked. "But it's too big. We'll never find them now!"

Vinir wrapped her arms around the girl and looked over her head at the ruins stretching out for leagues before them. Since her horse had died in the desert, Son-neen had lost much of her usual confidence. Now, she was sure they would never recover the bills of lading and promissory notes her tower had entrusted to her care, and without them, she could never make a strong name for herself in the City of Fountains.

Vinir could not find words of comfort for the girl.

If Toosha-lun lied and there's no water here, your papers won't matter much.

They had first seen the ruins from a distance, in the light of the rising moon. Bright against the darker sands, the sight had encouraged them to a last, desperate push that strained them to the utmost. Only the promise of water and an end to their chase kept them going when the dawn threatened.

"By my tower's name, look at all that," Chal-lat said. He held a reed hat between his eyes and the morning sun.

The low light drew stretching shadows from hundreds of half walls and broken buildings. Between those ruins lay desert-choked streets and smothered gardens, canals full of red sand and a few still-standing structures ranging from tiny to tremendous. But for all that, the eye was first drawn to the centre of the city. A hill rose there, one made by human hands. From a broad base it soared, white and curved, into an elongated dome towering over the dead city.

"Chal-lat, Vinir! It's strange, isn't it? A city full of sand!" Son-neen said, looking more closely at the strange vista and awed out of her self-pity. Chal-lat didn't answer. He was busy sketching on the roll of paper he had carried all the way from the City of Fountains. Vinir shaded her eyes from the low sun and scanned the humped and rutted buildings for smoke or other signs of their prey. Her eyes fixed on a point near that huge central dome.

"I don't know what this place is," Mor-ra said. She pointed to where Vinir stared. A thread of smoke rising was rising into the air. "It's only on your map and none of ours, but it seems our friends found it too."

The guard loosened the short sword in her belt and shoved Son-neen forward. "Come on. Let's get off this dune before we're spotted. We'll find a good hidey-hole and see if we can track any water in this sand city."

They brought the surviving horses down the dune face and into the city. Stetta led them down the half-buried streets in a large circle to the west, hoping to slip past anyone the slavers might have left to guard their backs. The ruin of an old barracks, or so it seemed by the faint, soldierly paintings on the walls, gave them the cover they needed, space for their horses, and a well that trickled water when they dug out the sand. They drank as the water bottles filled, taking turns with the horses to wash the desert from their throats.

After a long discussion, it was agreed that they would rest and recover their strength before investigating the smoke. They kept a cold camp again and took watches from the remains of a second floor.

Vinir's turn to replace Mor-ra on watch came as the moon was rising. The silver light softened the lines of broken roofs and empty windows, making the city seem asleep rather than dead and long abandoned.

Mor-ra nodded and slipped down the stairs to the larger rooms below, leaving Vinir crouched beside a shutterless window that looked out into the night. Somewhere out there, she knew the slavers were keeping watch too.

That smoke must be from their fires, and Marick and Dorict must be with them. Heaven shield them both!

Something moved along a sand-choked street, not a man but a four-footed shadow, low-slung and quick. It paused to sniff the air, then vanished into some narrow place where the moon could not follow, leaving Vinir with no company but her own fears.

CHAPTER 28
DEATH AND POTIONS

"The little animal is dead," Before Dawn Field Man said.

He filled the doorway of Narrow Field Man's hut, not bothering to come in. When he turned to go, Dorict called out after him.

"You said he'd live if you took his leg! You lied!"

The bigger man said nothing, but Narrow Field Man did. "Was it fever?" he asked.

The other grunted and walked off, leaving Dorict stunned. The calf nudged his arm, but he ignored it.

"All those adventures," Dorict said. "All his stupid, dangerous risks, and then he goes and dies from a fever?" He shook his head and wondered why he wasn't weeping.

But there were no tears. Instead, there was an emptiness where there should have been anger and grief. Now, he would never get the chance to ask Marick why he had betrayed his fellow banes or how he could have turned his back on their friendship. His friend had taken those answers to the grave.

"A clawed fever," he said, and slumped down.

The calf gave up and wandered over to Narrow Field Man, who stroked it under the chin. "No. Fever broke last night," he said and pushed the calf away to stand. He picked up a hoe from tools stacked beside the door and went outside, pausing only to look back at Dorict.

"Saw the boy. He was better. Eyes open, talking. No fever."

Dorict was up and ran to the door, only to find his host blocking it, the hoe held across his path.

"Let me go see him," the bane said. "I have to know!"

He tried to wrest the hoe from Narrow Field Man but found him stronger than he appeared.

"Go see him, they make him die. Make you die too. Ahh! Town words hard to make. Listen! Later time, we go see Yala. Make way to help. Yes?"

Dorict released the shaft of the tool. He nodded, for there was little else he could do. He might overpower Before Dawn Field Man, but not the rest of those scarred, strong men. He sighed and leaned against the door frame. There might be nothing he could do to help Marick, or himself, but he had no wish to stay in the hut and brood in the company of a lonely calf.

"All right," he said. "All right! Give me that hoe and show me what a weed looks like in this clawed land."

Narrow Field Man raised his eyebrows. He stood aside to let Dorict out into the hot morning.

"No weeds, only good plants," he said, clearly hurt by the accusation. "You help clear water channels."

They worked until the sun rose enough to make Dorict weak. Then they retreated to the slightly cooler shade of the hut, and he watched his host's clever fingers bend silver wire into intricate, beautiful shapes. They spoke now and then, talking about the life of a man of Old Carving Well or the life of a bane of Shirath. The calf slept until it was hungry, then Narrow Field Man took it to its mother to feed and brought it back to sleep again.

~

YALA WAS EATING a simple meal of dried beef and fruit when her mother yanked back the tent flap and stuck her head inside.

"He's dead," Tral said.

She left and Yala followed, going to the second largest of the family tents. The sides were rolled up to catch any breeze, but both entered through the door flap and sat in the appropriate places: Tral facing north-west and Yala facing south-east. After a moment, Yala moved over to take a place on the south-west corner of the woven mat, the direction of loss. She sat down and covered her face.

"You mourn for an animal you barely knew?" Tral asked. She picked at the threads of an old cloak, clipping the stray ones with a pair of shears.

After some time, Yala raised her head. "I mourn for a life, Tral. I also grieve for the sorrow of his friend, who will feel the pain of his loss as much as you or I would."

"Always you have been this way, looking at something and seeing it differently from everyone else," her mother said. She set down the shears and folded the cloak in quick, savage movements.

There was a silence between them while the bar of sunlight admitted through the open tent flap moved across the rugs covering the ground. At last, Yala stood and made the sign of parting.

"I will take the other one back to the Mother of Waters," she said. "When he is rested, and I have more trade to take."

Tral looked up, her eyes narrowed. "There will be no trade, not for Yalasa. And the other animal will stay here. He can be useful. If you could see clearly, you would look to your fear lizard. Something bad is coming – not just the slavers, something we have not suffered since Ke's time. Go now, and help the old women do what is needed."

Yala, for she would not think of herself as Yalasa, left and went to the trade-house, the long wooden building that held cargo, food, and the oldest short-named women of the well.

"It is Yala," she said as she entered.

I must show them that I am who I am.

"Do you think I don't know my own granddaughter?" Ke said, and grabbed her arm. She led her to the north end of the long room. There, a ring of old women sat in a circle. Her grand-aunt, Bo, held a tube much like the one Yala had to house Chit-chit but made of silkstone. There was no stopper, and she could see it held a fear lizard, probably her aunt's. It twitched but made no attempt to escape. Bo rotated the tube slowly, and Yala saw that the other end of the tube was also open, making it a poor container for a sandwalker's companion. After only a few degrees of turning, the small lizard jumped free to run across the circle and hide under the draped cloak of another ancient one. Bo coaxed it out and replaced it in the open tube. She repeated the odd process, and the little creature ran out at the same exact point in the tube's turn. Bo shook out the little creature so it could go back into its leather-tube home. "Three fear lizards tested, and they all agree. Sister, it is like it was when we were children."

Ke nodded. "I'd hoped to die and be with the wind before it happened again, but I wasn't fast enough, it seems. Have the others returned?"

Bo nodded. There was a strong resemblance between the two sisters, made stronger still by their shared, grim expression.

"Tral sent them last night. They've gone and come back again, and with the worst news. The angles of their tubes crossed not far from our well. That poison wind will blow right over us unless . . ."

Ke held up a hand and nodded towards Yala. "Some here are too young to hear that, but not too young to help, I hope. Yala, do as Bo tells you. I must speak to your mother."

Yala nodded and went with her grand-aunt. She spent the morning chopping herbs and crushing bright-coloured rocks with a mortar and pestle. When she was done, Bo brought a wide-mouthed glass bottle, an expensive item, as Yala knew, and then a smaller one filled with a bright blue liquid.

"From the stomach of the blue flier," she said, and Yala stepped back.

Why would we need that? Fliers are beautiful. They glow like blue stars, but they also lay pit-killer eggs and make their nests with that liquid. One drop will eat through a foot of rock!

Bo smiled. "You are wise to be careful, but don't worry, grand-niece. Mixed with these herbs and minerals, it will not burn the skin before it can be washed off, though to drink it is still to die."

"What is it for?" Yala asked.

Bo looked around to make sure they were alone and reached out to clutch Yala's shoulder with a bony hand. "When you are Ya – and you will be – you will know what this is for. I say this much because there is the beginning of strength in you, whatever Tral says, so remember how to make it."

Under her grand-aunt's severe gaze, Yala repeated the

older woman's recitation of the ingredients and steps until it was set in her memory. When she had chanted it back three times without mistake, Bo nodded and released her shoulder.

"Good, now let's do what you just said."

Bo poured some of the deadly blue liquid into the larger glass bottle, then Yala added the other ingredients, one at a time and carefully. The last bit of herb went in, dissolving as soon as it touched the surface of the mixture. A wooden stopper went to seal the bottle, and Bo said, "Keep it upright or it might seep out. Now, there is a question you have been wanting to ask, or so your fidgeting has told me. If you cannot stand still, girl, ask! What is it?"

Yala reddened. Everyone wanted to treat her as a child. She stood straighter. "Bo, when we learn to walk the desert, we get a fear lizard. We're told to watch it and tell our elders if they act oddly or a poison wind will take us. Now they act oddly. So tell me, what is coming with that wind?"

Bo coughed out a laugh. "Hah! Have patience. In thirty years, you'll be wise enough to know such things. Until then, don't ask questions that will lengthen your name. Tral already wants us to call you Yalasa, but Ke says no."

"And you, grand-aunt?" Yala asked. She picked up the bottle and carefully swirled the blue liquid, now darker, less vivid, in the bottle. Bo took it from her and placed it back on the table before answering her.

"I fear you are drifting away from us, Yala, and if it takes a hard hand to pull you back, well, it's better than what waits for you among the animals."

CHAPTER 29
THE SLAVERS FOUND

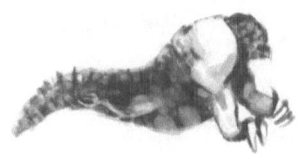

"I tell you, no one that young is with those cursed slavers," Stetta repeated for the third time, but Vinir was just as incredulous as before.

"They have to be!" she said. "There were no bodies, no graves that we found. They must be there."

"They could still be dead," Mor-ra said. She broke a piece of stale bread, the last of their supplies, and handed it to Son-neen. The girl took it silently and watched Vinir's face as the bane frowned at Mor-ra's words.

"How?" she asked. There was a menace in her tone.

Mor-ra held up a hand. "Now don't get angry at me! I just mean that, if they were dead, the bodies could have been left out for the animals to take. There's many out here that could make a body disappear: sandcats, sandsnakes, pit-killers, even the sand itself!"

"Or they could have fed them to the animals they brought along," Stetta added.

Vinir stood up. "No! They aren't dead. You just haven't found them yet. Keep looking!"

She balled her fists and took a step forward.

Stetta stood as well. His voice was mild, but he had one hand on the short sword slung from his belt. "Let's not go falling out over something we can't change, yes? I'll go again when the moon goes down, and Vinir, you come as well. If I've missed something, you'll see it and we'll be sure. Agreed?"

Vinir spun away and half walked, half ran to where Chal-lat kept watch.

"Leave her be," Son-neen said when Mor-ra made to follow. "I know how she feels. She's lost something precious and needs it back."

"You're wise for your years," Stetta said, and tousled her hair.

Mor-ra slapped his hand away from the girl's head. "I wish you were," she said. "Wise, I mean, you big oaf! And she's a child, not a dog."

"I'm not a child!" Son-neen said.

Vinir climbed away from the argument, coming up to where Chal-lat kept his post in a broken upper room. The artist was looking out over the city, one hand holding a piece of charcoal and tracing the half-seen skyline on a broken tile.

"Do you watch or draw?" Vinir demanded, a little more harshly than she had intended.

"Both, since it's the same thing," Chal-lat said. "Don't worry, I must be doing my duty, since I saw you coming, though I heard you stomping first. Did those two get on your nerves?"

"Yes," she said, and picked up another tile, one of many spread out on the floor. She angled it to the moonlight and saw a feline shape reclining on a large stone, its eyes focused directly on the artist.

"This sandcat must have liked you to stop long enough for such a noble portrait," Vinir said. She handed the tile to Chal-lat, who held it up for a more critical examination.

"It likes our horses more, or the smell of them," he said. "Which makes it less noble and more dangerous, I think."

She dropped down beside him and folded her arms across her chest.

"Stetta couldn't see them," she said. She leaned back against the wall and drew up her knees.

"Your friends?" Chal-lat asked. "Well, maybe some slaves are kept out of sight, just like our horses. Don't give up hope, Vinir."

She said nothing, for in her heart she was close to doing just that. She wished she had never come to this sun-blasted land. When Hallmaster Branet made her a master, placing a red sash on her shoulder in front of all Shirath's banes, she had been proud and confident. She had promised herself that she would not disgrace her own masters, Relict and Tarix, or let down her friends.

Now she had. Badly. First, she neglected her duties to pursue a selfish dream of making art. Second, and worse, she had let Marick drift away when she should have pulled him back, counselled him, persuaded him to . . . what, grow up?

"He did this, not you," Chal-lat said. He smiled at her look of shock. "I wasn't reading your thoughts, but they weren't hard to follow from the expressions on your face. That last one was puzzlement, and I guessed you were wondering at Marick's motives. Were you?"

Vinir nodded, keeping her face set. She didn't like being so obvious, though it wouldn't have bothered her before. In Shirath, she had always been open to others, too easy to read. Maybe she had some growing to do too.

Chal-lat scanned the streets again before continuing.

"I know you said you have no time for us, the two of us, I mean, but you can't ignore emotion just to do your duty. You'll become like a mosaic that's technically perfect but lacks all heart. We've both seen works like that. You can find no flaw, but it still leaves you cold. That's why I like your work, Vinir. It's full of emotion. The spirit of it makes up for any flaws—"

"Flaws? What flaws?" Vinir demanded. She let go of her knees and crossed her legs, tailor-fashion.

"Not serious ones!" Chal-lat said. "Or Sarth would never have taken you on. Like that cat I drew. The paws are too big, the tale curved a bit too much, and it didn't really recline like that, but the spirit is there, isn't it?" he asked, suddenly nervous.

"Yes, yes!" Vinir said, leaning forward and grabbing his hand. "The spirit is there, truly, and I feel it in both of us, too, but I don't know if . . . I have to get those two back and go to make my report, though Heaven knows if I'll still be a master after that. Then, maybe, we can see about those other things."

Chal-lat put his other hand on top of hers.

"Then I'll keep quiet about everything else for now and just help you find them, yes?" he said. At her nod, he released her hand and leaned back to look out over the city.

"Aha! That sandcat is back for another portrait. Your turn now. The fresh tiles are over there."

When Stetta came quietly to get her, she waved him away. Chal-lat was asleep, rolled up in his blanket, and Vinir whispered, "Tomorrow, Stetta. We'll try by day to see if they move the slaves around."

She looked over the streets and let her hand move auto-

matically over the slate, memorizing the positions of the
larger buildings and their distance from that central,
brooding dome.

CHAPTER 30
THE POISON WIND

Dorict and Narrow Field Man sat huddled against the wall, far from where most of the people of the well gathered farther to the north.

"Will she come?" Dorict asked. He was frantic with worry over Marick's fate. Was he really still alive? If he was, why would they lie to him about it?

"I'm here," Yala said. She sat down on the wall top, facing the hubbub to the north as if she listened to that instead of the two crouched below her. She spoke again, in a strange language and at some length.

Narrow Field Man answered in the same tongue, with a fluidity and speed that momentarily confused Dorict.

I've only heard him using words that weren't his own, so I thought him simple. It seems I'm the simple one!

Yala spoke to his host once more and then switched to the tongue Dorict understood.

"Marick is alive," she said.

Dorict let out a huge sigh. "Heaven shield us all! Why did they say he was dead?" he asked.

Narrow Field Man put a warning hand on his shoulder as the bane's voice rose beyond caution.

Yala leaned over and lowered her own voice. "Some things the old women have told me, and some things I have heard by listening when they thought I was asleep. There is a poison wind coming, a curse on the wells that falls only once in many years. Ke and Bo will not say what it is or how they will stop it," she whispered. "But Marick is part of their plan. They will take him at dawn in the direction our lizards fear."

"Can we save him?" Dorict asked, then shook his head. "No, I mean, can I save him? You both have helped me so much already, and I don't want you to fall out with your people."

Narrow Field Man smiled, though it was barely visible in the dark.

"You are good guest. You think on your host! But . . ." He turned to Yala and spoke again in his own language. He went on for some time.

Yala nodded and translated. "He says that he has always wondered about the world, but never expected to see it. He has learned much from you, and for that gift, he owes you something. He also knows a way for us to get free after we rescue your friend."

Dorict frowned. "Us? All three of us?" he asked.

As series of shouts came from the crowd and two men began to walk around, yelling at the top of their voices.

Yala shook her head. "No, not him," she said, and pointed at Narrow Field Man. "He will stay behind and say you hit him. He will also tell the others that he woke up much later and you were already gone. I will go with you, for my own reasons."

"Will you be punished?" Dorict asked Narrow Field Man.

The other shook his head. "Others will . . . laugh, but not hit. Maybe I go soon, anyway."

"Where?" Dorict asked. "You can come with us," he added.

Narrow Field Man shook his head. "No. Go south to City of Fountains. One year, two years from here maybe. Make glass, learn their glass, come back."

Yala smiled and spoke to him again. He blushed and handed her a small wrapped package. After a moment's awkward silence, they clasped hands and Yala stood up.

"He will bring you to me at dawn," she said and walked up to the crowd as if she were just another watcher of the knife dance.

Narrow Field Man pulled at Dorict's arm.

"Come," he said. "Sleep, be strong."

DORICT HAD MORE worry than rest. Before the sun rose, and after feeding the calf and tying it so it wouldn't follow, Narrow Field Man took the bane along the edges of the fields. They passed a round stone building, much larger than the men's mud and reed huts.

"The water is there," Dorict's guide said, and made a slow two-handed gesture towards the building. "Soon, many men there too. We must hurry," he added.

Past the building, they stayed close to the sand, a slow flood pushing in where the well's boundaries failed. Few were up this early, and those who were kept at a distance. Dorict wore a borrowed tunic of linen over his dark brown trousers, looking just like the other field men, save for his boots. His yellow hair was hidden under a woven reed hat, and he had a bag slung over his shoulder to look like he had some business wandering about so early in the day. They came to the last field and Narrow Field Man took back the bag and handed Dorict a full waterskin.

"Soon everyone come out, work," he said, taking the bag back. "Go up hill, find Yala. Careful, friend."

Dorict took his hand in his own. "I will be careful, and thank you, friend."

They parted there, and Dorict climbed the terraced hill until he saw Yala standing beside her sled, waiting for him. Her bow was strapped to it along with a full quiver of arrows and a leather bag. Her shovel was hanging at her belt, and a knife was fixed beside it.

"I could not bring another bow or shovel," she said. "I hope we do not need to fight."

They went east, Yala using Chit-chit's anxiety to adjust their path every half league. The sun was two hands-lengths into its rising arc when she crawled back down a dune and gestured for silence.

"I can see the women," she said. "They left earlier than I thought and are sitting by some rocks. I saw the boy on a sled."

"What do we do?" Dorict said. He crouched beside the sled, twisting the harness straps between his fingers.

"Go around," Yala said. "We must trust Chit-chit now. I think they will take the boy to where the poison wind will be, and they won't stay, not for the poison wind. Chit-chit can lead us there, but first we must go in a big circle to the south."

"Are you sure of this?" Dorict asked.

"I *think* more than *know*," Yala replied. She bit her lip before going on. "These are things only those with very short names are supposed to know, but when I was working in the trading hut, I heard more than they thought, and guessed more than that. It is bad, Dorict."

At his look of confusion, she spat out her next words. "Don't you see? He will be bait! Bait to poison a poison wind! And I am part of it, for I made their poison. Death and deep water! We are as bad as that one-eyed man, using your friend to catch a pit-killer. We are . . . animals."

She could not continue. Dorict stepped back, staring at the sandwalker in disbelief. There was no sound save for what might have been the wind, or a young woman's weeping. As what she said took hold, the bane felt anger rising up in him and took a step forward, then stopped. He stood there, fists balled at his side, the hot wind blowing against his skin. He looked at the young woman with whom he had shared so many dangers. This wasn't Yala's fault, no matter what she said. She was right here with him, two fools rushing to rescue another.

Marick would have laughed at us.

"Listen, Yala," he said, stepping close enough to put a careful hand on her shoulder. When it was not shrugged off, he continued. "I'm angry, but not at you, maybe not at anyone. I think your people are afraid of this poison wind, just like my people are afraid of demons. We do some bad things too, taking children from their parents, forcing them to train and fight monsters. Sometimes I think everything bad in this world has a fear behind it! Let's fight that fear and keep going, together. All right?"

Yala wiped her eyes, leaving smudges of sand and grit across her cheeks. She smiled and took up the harness once more. "The wind is in your words," she said. "I should call you 'Dor' for all that wisdom in your head. Yes, we'll go together, against fear. But we still must go around."

Dorict nodded and began pulling. He strained at the ropes, agonizing over the time lost by avoiding the other sandwalkers.

"Easy," Yala said. "Who knows what waits for us? Ease off a bit. We must save some of our strength for the end."

They slowed and followed the lizard's lead until they crested a last dune and found Marick. On an island of hard ground in the middle of the dunes, a trap had been set. The boy was strapped to a light wood frame, three limbs bound fast and the last, ending in a bandage just below the knee, hanging free. Dorict had to swallow hard at that, and the smell, for a fire was set in front of the bound bane, a smouldering pile whose acrid stench rose and then trailed off in the light breeze. The wind shifted, blowing the smoke back towards the prisoner, and he coughed.

"He's still alive!" Dorict cried out, and made to run down the dune face, but Yala held him back. Her face was pale. With shaking hands, she untied a leather bag fixed to the sled. Carefully, she removed a length of thick, doubled linen wrapped around a glass bottle. She left the bottle leaning against the sled and raised the cloth to her face.

"Dorict, I can barely move! Please help me," she gasped, and began to wind the cloth around her head, leaving but a single slit for sight and another for breath. It was no light bandage but a bulky, doubled strip holding many hard and hidden objects.

Dorict stumbled back and looked at Yala, then at Marick. He rushed to tie the ends tight for her, though it took a while to manage a knot. What was wrong with his hands?

"Its heavy," he said. "What's in this?"

"You told Narrow Field Man that silkstone keeps away fear," Yala said. "The poison wind brings much fear. That's why . . . that's why Chit-chit feels it so. Narrow Field Man, he uses silkstone to polish glass, and he put many slices of it inside these wrappings, like the masks you told him of."

He stood still, looking at Yala while she strung her bow, slipping the loop off the tip twice before it set. Why would she want silkstone? He shivered again and then stood stock-still, the truth of it falling on him like a mountain. Something was coming, something too familiar and too terrible for words. The fear he felt hadn't just been for Marick. No, they had been wrong about the Far South, horribly wrong. He turned his head back and forth until his fear fixed on a distant shifting mass, a blur in the heated air, but one that moved with purpose, coming straight at them.

"A demon! Heaven shield us!" he said and ran down towards the sacrificial frame. Marick was unconscious, his clothes and skin covered in a sticky blue liquid. The ropes were thick, and the knots complex. Dorict looked for Yala and her knife, but she was still by the sled, standing still as a stone, looking at that approaching doom.

"Yala!" he shouted, and ran back up to her, sending scuds of sand from his heels as he scaled the dune. He grabbed her arms and yelled at her, "Help me, Yala. It's a demon! A demon from my lands. I need . . ." He stopped talking and pulled at the strap holding the shovel to her belt. Wrenching it free, he paused only to shake her one more time. She turned wide eyes upon him and stared.

He held her shoulders and shouted, trying to force his words past the demon fear. "Yala, the silkstone will help. It will! But it won't keep it all out. Listen, a bane fights her own fears first!" he said, yelling into her ear. "If you can beat them, you can beat a demon's fear too!"

He turned and raced down the slope, just as the demon came over a last mound of sand and into full view.

It was grotesque, stumbling on four unsteady legs, an immense, rattling mass of horns, each one waving in its own tempo as the demon moved towards the smoke and the boy tied behind it.

Yala twisted her head, as if she could shake out Dorict's words, and the fear trembled before steadying. She shook her head again, and the same thing happened.

Perhaps Narrow Field Man's gift works after all.

She tried to calm her breath and found she could slow it from a gulp to a shivering gasp.

Fight my own fears? I've been doing that for years. Every step I've taken these last months has been a battle against fear, and every next step another.

Slowly, trying to keep her head level so that the bindings would not slip, she reached down and picked up her strung bow from the sand. With her other hand, she pried the wooden stopper from the glass bottle. She had made this extra batch last night, taking the ingredients to her tent so the old women would not know. Slowly, so as not to overturn the precious liquid, she thrust a handful of arrows into the bottle, coating the tips in the sticky blue substance. With those loose arrows and her bow held in one hand, she slung her quiver over her shoulder and picked up the bottle.

The first step was the hardest, the second easier only by comparing it to the first. While the monster approached and Dorict hacked at the ropes, Yala stumbled down the slope, her eyes never leaving the demon's quivering bulk.

The creature reared up and sniffed the smoke, taking in the reek of burning meat with great gusts of air. Filled with the scent of its prey, the demon opened its leathery, needle-toothed beak and let out a hooting, echoing call. The very grains of the dune face trembled and slid at the sound, and Yala froze again.

223

That mouth is big enough to swallow me whole! I am dead. We all are. I can't . . . No, I am Yala of Old Carving Well. I am the friend of Narrow Field Man, of Dor of Shirath, and even of the fool who brought us to this horror. I will stay. I will fight. If this is my death, I meet it on my feet, my bow in my hand and defending my friends.

That made the next step easier, and the next, until she was running down the dune. She skidded to a stop beside Dorict and shoved the bottle into the sand. While the bane still hacked at the frame with Yala's shovel, the sandwalker pulled out her quiver's remaining arrows and plunged them into the broad mouth of the bottle to stand upright and ready.

"So," she said through gritted teeth. "This is the last truth of my people."

Dorict parted the last rope and lowered Marick to the ground. The boy opened his eyes and looked wildly about him. "Dorict," he cried out, "I feel it, even over the pain. It's a demon. Where's my shield?"

"Back in Shirath, fool!" Dorict said. "Yala, give him your knife, please!"

She did so, not taking her eyes off the shambling thing. It took another heavy step towards them, its bizarre coat of horns rustling and scraping against each other. It moved like it was in pain, but it didn't stop coming towards the fire and the boy now lying on the ground beside it. Yala laid an arrow on the string and tried to pull it back. Her fingers slipped, and it went only a few feet before hitting the sand. The monster twitched at the twang of her bow and stopped to paw the ground.

"I'll draw it away," Dorict said. "If you can't shoot, save Marick!"

He ran at the beast, swiping at the forest of horns that

sprouted from its beaked face. The sharpened shovel sliced one horn away and drops of blood fell to the sand.

"Its eye, Yala," Dorict shouted. "Shoot its eye!"

Yala shook herself, felt the ripples of fear move across her mind, and tried to focus. She looked hard at the creature and saw what the bane meant; the demon had but one eye. The other was gone, a horn thrusting from the socket at a sharp angle.

Like the slaver, though without the horns. If I could shoot an arrow into that good eye . . .

Breathing out her terror, she set another arrow to the ready. Seeing each movement in her mind before making it, she made it to full draw, then loosed.

A miss. The arrow buried itself in the demon's front leg.

A miss? At this range? I can hit a leaf at sixty yards, and this is half that distance. Sand take it! Even I will call myself Yalasa if I can't do better.

That anger warmed her muscles and steadied her aim. The next shaft cut its brow. The beast raised its head, and Dorict attacked again, trying to slice the remaining eye with the sharp edge of the shovel.

But the demon was too well protected. The blade twisted off a horn and fell from Dorict's hand to land on the hard earth in front of the beast. The massive head twisted, and the bane jumped back, and back again as the demon, torn between hunger and rage like the rest of its kind, began to pursue its tormentor.

Yala ran after it with the three arrows she still held. The first she shot between the horns crowding the demon's rump. It brought the expected reaction. The beast tried to turn and snap at the wound, but the forest of spiked horns only snapped back, cutting its beak and breaking off more of its protective armour.

Frustrated, it raised its head and hooted out its rage. The wave of fear increased, and Yala collapsed onto the hard ground.

In a daring roll under the very teeth of the beast, Dorict recovered the shovel. He jabbed it at the creature's side, in a spot with fewer spikes, but failed to pierce the thick, tumorous skin. That cost him a cut across the cheek as the demon turned again in its pursuit of this irritating, uncooperative meal. Shuffling back, Dorict regarded the beast and set his mouth in a grim line.

"Yala, for Heaven's sake and our lives, hit that eye!" he shouted, and charged the demon.

The sandwalker crouched there, trembling. This close to the demon, the fear battered her like a midday sun. She could not raise the bow. Wave after wave of horror called up terrifying memories: and they all came in her mother's voice. Every past complaint, every criticism played out until one came that she could use.

"Hold that bow steady! By sand and wind, Brada was much better at this! Don't release the arrow until you can breathe out slowly! Not even a child does so badly!"

"You are nothing," the demon fear whispered to her. "Not even a child."

Yala clenched her teeth and stood, daring her mother's voice to continue.

"Even a child can set an arrow on the string."

So, she did.

"Even a child can pull a bowstring back."

So, she did that too. A wind stirred in her chest, a mere breath at first, but it held steady against the rush of terror. She missed, of course, but the arrow flew between Dorict and the demon, and the beast shied away from the movement, giving the bane a chance to attack again.

226

Dorict struck it on the side of its beak once, then again as it dropped back down. There was blood this time, a gout of it dripping down its jaws and running in rivulets along the nearest horns.

A weak spot!

She touched one hand to the silkstone wrapping, moving it slightly and feeling again that strange tremor in her mind.

Dorict is right. The feeling is a thing outside me . . . It uses my own fears against me.

She felt her bow creak under the pressure of her grip. A bow was one of the few things a woman made for herself. She had trimmed and sanded the wood under Ke's direction. The cord had come from her aunt's trading, silk from the South. She had fashioned arrows over and over again until Ke approved them, then she sewed and filled her cloth quiver. She had practised so much that even Tral found other things to criticize. This bow was as much a part of her as her cloak, and it was here, ready to be used.

My bow doesn't care about fear. It only knows my hands and the flight of the shaft! So be like that. Pull yourself like a bowstring, Yala or Yalasana, or whoever I am! The world wants to break me: my mother, my well, now this demon. Everything wants me to crack and splinter. Let them try! Whether I'm Yalasana or Yala or Ya, I am here now. I'll bend, not break, for my friends are in danger, and I have an arrow to add to this fight.

Her muscles loosened at these thoughts, and the next shaft flew true, slipping between the jaws to lodge inside a mottled cheek.

"Chew on that, you un-souled thing!" Yala yelled and saw Dorict grin back from where he still circled the monster. But if it felt good to curse, she might better have waited until the thing was dead, for the demon turned on her words, fixing on the red-robed figure standing twenty yards away. It shook itself, and after another deep hooting challenge, rattled towards her.

For a moment, she was paralyzed, but only for a moment. She let her last arrow fly, and then sped off herself, running away from where Marick lay, out towards the sand.

Let's see how fast you can move when these dunes grab you!

But the creature did not pursue. Instead, it sniffed the air, and turned its back on her. She slid to a stop and Dorict caught up with her as she came back onto the hard ground.

"The meat! It smells the burning meat," Dorict said, gasping for breath. "And Marick's too weak to move. Look, you go help him while I lead it off again. I'll try and get it out into that sand; that was a good idea! You just get Marick out of sight."

"Then what?" Yala asked. They followed the demon as closely as they dared.

Dorict put a hand on her arm and smiled. "Well, since you seem to be a demonbane, why don't you come back after that and help me kill this clawed beast."

Yala smiled back, though it was hidden under the wrappings. "I will," she said and ran in a circle to the left of the slow-moving demon while Dorict went right.

"Hey! Heeey!" he shouted, waving his arms and keeping within sight of the demon's one good eye. "Over here, you piece of filth!"

He darted in and struck but failed to get the beast's attention. The demon seemed transfixed by the smell of burning flesh. It lifted its beak and sniffed the air, sucking in gallons of it and then snorting it out only to take more in.

Yala reached Marick and saw his horrified focus on

something behind her. She turned to see the demon coming towards them again, ignoring Dorict, who danced around its head trying to turn it. She snatched up the last of her arrows from the bottle.

The old women wouldn't say, but this must be poison to the beast. The boy's clothes stink of it! But if it does not soon kill this demon, then we are dead.

For a terrible moment, the fear returned, pushing past the wrappings and freezing her heart, but the wind blowing between her souls stirred again, warm against the night-cold of the fear, and she raised her bow.

Her arrow was already half pulled when Dorict jumped between them and thrust the sharp edge of Yala's shovel into the angle of the demon's jaw. He screamed as he did so, the muscles of his shoulders bulging, and his legs braced hard against the stony ground.

The skin of the mouth split, and still the shovel cut into the beast. The demon tried to wrench its head away from the agony, doing even more damage until the shovel was pulled out of Dorict's hand and the demon's mouth flapped open, useless now, for the bone was broken through on one side.

Dorict had been thrown off his feet by a last convulsion. He sat upon the ground, bleeding, shaking his head and not even trying to rise.

"Get out of there!" Marick said. He might have thought he was shouting, but he only had enough strength to whisper.

Yala, fingers still pinching the nocked arrow, could do no better. Any shot into the beast's vulnerable face would likely hit Dorict, especially with the fear chewing at her aim. The demon stopped its shuffling charge, trembled, then rose up on its hind legs and stiffened, hanging there for an endless moment while Dorict looked up at it, blinking.

No! Please let the poison kill it now before it kills him. Oh, wind's blessing, please . . .

But the wind blew its own way, and the demon fell on Dorict like a mountain of spears.

"No!" Yala screamed. She fired the arrow, stepped and fired again. And again, and again until her hand grasped an empty string. The demon shivered but stayed on the ground. The poison was a torment in it, and it groaned like any dying beast.

Draw and fire, draw and fire, wind scour it! And beat it with the bow if it still dares to live!

As she ran, she picked up her first arrow from where it angled in the sand. It pierced the beast's good eye, fired from two feet away, her bow held just beyond the thicket of horns. The demon whistled out a long last breath, and died when it was done.

Yala dropped her bow and fell to her knees. Behind her, Marick groaned, and she turned to see him crawling towards her, ropes still trailing from his remaining limbs and the knife held in his teeth. He pulled himself across the hard earth, trying to reach his friend.

Yala looked down. She reached out, drew back, and then knelt on the ground. His soul – or souls, she was ready to grant him as many as he wished – had already fled. She stood up. Dorict's body must have been pierced through in many places, and she knew that the blood flowing from under the creature must be his.

The demon shifted, then shifted again, the limp horns rattling like dry bones. Something silver pushed out from beneath it.

The tip of the shovel.

Yala watched, incredulous, as the notched blade, the wooden handle, and then a scratched, pale hand followed. The hand waved the shovel like a flag.

"Mmphhh!" Dorict said and waved the shovel again.

Yala snatched it from his hand and began digging. Sand and clumps of hard dirt flew over her shoulder until the hand became an arm, then a shoulder, then a very dirty face. She dropped the shovel and began pulling, despite Dorict's protests.

"Careful, there're still horns down here," he gasped. "Ouch! Let me twist around. There, pull now!"

He emerged from under the demon, clothes torn, hair missing in clumps, and holding one of the beast's horns in his other hand. He fell into Yala's grip, and she lowered him to the ground.

"I thought you'd be stabbed in a hundred places," she said, but looking, she could only find scratches and cuts, no gaping holes.

"Not many horns on the underside," Dorict managed between panting breaths. "Broken or torn off as it moved, I expect." He looked at the beast's hulking corpse. "I've never seen a demon move so slowly, not even a Tunneller demon, and so many horns! It's . . . not right."

He tried to breathe deeply but grimaced and held his ribs.

"Get Marick," he whispered.

Yala turned but Marick was already there, lying on the other side of the demon's massive head, stabbing at it with Yala's knife.

"Claws take you," he howled, finding his voice in his mistaken grief. "You killed him! You killed him."

Yala grabbed his arms, for his hands were already

slashed by the dead beast's horns and he looked ready to throw himself onto them in his despair.

"Stop!" Yala said and shook him. "Stop! He's not dead. Here, see?"

She pulled him around the maimed beak to show him the other bane lying on his back, his chest heaving up and down and one arm thrown across his eyes.

"Dorict?" Marick said, unbelieving. "Dorict! Claws, you could have died, you fool!"

His smile turned into a grimace as he clutched his knee just above the bandage.

Dorict glared at the bane. "Me a fool? It'll take me a year to list all your idiotic actions! Wait till Tarix gets a hold of you. She'll tear the skin off you with a look!"

Tears rolled down Marick's face. "I know. I'm sorry, all right? I'm sorry! I didn't think . . ."

"You never do," Dorict said, and crawled over to where Yala held the boy's head in her lap.

"No," Marick said. "I did think, but the wrong way. I didn't know if I could go on being a bane, and now I know I can't."

Dorict carefully shifted his friend to his own arms. "Why, because you've lost a leg? Don't think Tarix will let you get away with that excuse," he said, and coughed. "Once a bane, always a bane, right?"

Marick wiped his face into a striped pattern of dirt and blood. "You're wrong, as usual. Garet stopped being a bane. He's a king's agent now."

"And acts more a bane than he ever did before, and you know it," Dorict said. "Look, no matter what you do, even if you have to hop, you'll still be a bane. I know that and Vinir knows that too."

Yala stood up and approached the demon. Something

was different. After a moment, she began to unwind the silkstone-laden wrappings from around her head.

"Vinir will forgive you," Dorict said. "If you apologize and moan enough. Even I'll admit you've suffered for your sins, though don't think I'll ever let you forget how foolish . . . Yala! What are you doing? That beast is still able to freeze you with its jewel, even when it's dead."

"No," Yala said, "it isn't. I don't know what this jewel is, but there is very little of what I felt before, and it's fading."

Dorict and Marick looked as she removed the last of her protective covering. She carefully reached between the spikes on the demon's head and touched the rough skin.

"Nothing," she said. "Save for a smell that would kill a sandcat."

"Dorict," Marick said. "Those women covered me with this foul stuff before they tied me up. I think they meant me to poison the beast, but the demon never touched me."

"The points of my arrows were covered with it," Yala said. "Maybe that's why it died."

"It must be a powerful poison then," Dorict said. "Yala, will it hurt Marick?"

The sandwalker shook her head. "No, not unless he drank it, or so my grand-aunt said, though we should wash it off – with sand if we don't have enough water. I helped her make it. Some of it comes from blue fliers, the ones that lay pit-killer eggs and can eat stone."

"Eat stone!" Marick said. "Dorict, maybe it ate away the jewel and that's why we can't feel it anymore."

"I think it is eating the bones too," Yala said, and pointed to where the legs bent and sagged against the ground.

"Eating a demon's jewel?" Dorict asked. "That poison would be very useful to the banehall! And what about the fire? The demon breathed in a lot of the smoke. Maybe it was poison too. What were they burning there?"

Yala, who had seen what was burning, did not answer. She went over to the smouldering fire and kicked dirt over it, burying the long bones and the small ones from sight.

"It did not hurt the beast," was all she said. "I think it died because I used that blue poison on my arrows, of which the beast ate many."

Dorict looked to the frame and the mound of sand and ashes in front of it.

"Yala, what was being burned?" he asked. His face, which had recovered some of its colour, paled again.

"No!" Marick said. He looked down at the bandage on his leg. "They wouldn't. How could . . ."

He pointed the knife at Yala, and though his hand shook, he kept it raised between them.

"Monsters! Your people are all monsters, claw you! You took my leg!"

Dorict reached around and plucked the knife from his hand. He said nothing, but his eyes were fixed on Marick's wound.

Yala came and knelt down by the boy. She grabbed both his hands in hers and said, "Yes, monsters. Our well is full of them. So is the Mother of Waters, and maybe the City of Fountains. Even your city, Shirath, has many, from your friend's stories."

She took the knife from Dorict and handed it back to Marick.

"Now it's your choice, to be a monster or not. I have not harmed you. I have saved you three times, by my count. If you kill me now, Marick of Shirath, what are you?"

Marick looked at her, at her unflinching gaze that ignored the knife and waited for his decision. After a moment, he dropped the knife between them and lay back against Dorict.

"This doesn't mean I like you," Marick said, and his eyes abruptly closed.

She brought down the sled and they tied the boy to it, cushioned by both their cloaks. She tore down the rest of the scaffold and scuffed the land around it until it looked like the beast had ravaged all over the place. Before she left, she recovered all her arrows and stuck a piece of rope in the dead demon's jaws. With Dorict's help, she wiped their tracks clean. From the dune above, Yala and Dorict looked down on the scene.

"You want them to think it worked, don't you?" Dorict asked. "That the Horned demon ate Marick and was poisoned."

Yala shrugged. "Horned demon? A good name for it! Yes, it might fool them until they come near enough to see its wounds, then they'll guess we were here, but that might buy us some leagues before we are followed."

She looked up at the sky, shading her goggles with one hand.

"We cannot go south. I doubt we'd make the Mother of Waters before the women of my well catch up with us."

"What would they do?" Dorict asked. He bent over and brushed a lock of dirty hair away from Marick's face. "Kill us?"

Yala shook her head. "No. You two would be kept prisoner until the next poison wind – demon – came near, though they might trade you to another well for that purpose."

The sun was still high, and the heat rose from the sand, engulfing them.

"As for me, I'd be named a child for the rest of my life,"

she said, "bound to do the duties of a child and never walking the open desert again. We must go now. And in a direction they will not easily guess, one that Narrow Field Man told me about when we met at the wall."

They raised the harness and began pulling towards the south, retracing the detour they had taken before. The wind cut across them, from north-west to south-east.

From change to wisdom. The wind always knows.

"That was dangerous, giving that knife back to Marick," Dorict said. "He wasn't in his right mind, if he ever is, and he might have harmed you. Why take such a risk?"

"For a greater reward," Yala said. She kicked a runner to free it from a soft patch of sand, and the boy they spoke of murmured but did not wake.

Dorict tugged the sled a few feet further on, then paused as they reached harder ground and Yala switched to the wheels. By his reckoning, they had come far enough south to avoid meeting the sandwalkers who would still be watching their little lizards and waiting for the demon to die. Now they could turn west, return to the well, and discover Narrow Field Man's promised escape route.

He turned to Yala. "Well, what did you get?" he asked.

Yala looked to where the young man stood panting, holding his sore ribs. She smiled.

"The last part of an answer," she said. One side done, she circled around and placed the third wheel on its axle, fixing it with a bronze pin. After setting the last wheel, she took pity on Dorict's obvious confusion and continued.

"We'll pull and talk, yes? First, you have to know why I needed this answer. You need to know the question in my souls. Long ago, there was a woman in our well named Seena. She was older than me and went off with the men before the old women thought she should. She gave birth the year I was nine years old. It was a boy, but it did not live."

"That's a sad story," Dorict said, grunting as he pulled the sled at Yala's quick pace.

"But not all the story," she said. "In the wells, babies who are born sick are left for the wind on the tall rocks near our well. 'The wind decides,' the old women say, and if the baby lives a night and a day up there, it is given back to its mother to keep fighting for its life. Seena's baby was left for the wind, but not given back to her."

"Because it was too sick and died out there?" Dorict spat.

He hates the thought of this. Did he lose someone so young, a brother or sister?

Yala shook her head. "No," she said. "I held him the day they took him away. He was healthy and hungry. In my arms, he cried and waved his arms and legs like any other child."

Dorict paused for a moment to readjust the strap or perhaps calm his temper. Yala waited for him to start pulling again before she continued.

"Quickly now! We must pull faster if we are to escape the others. Where was I in my tale? Yes, in the year before Seena's baby was born, the sand came over the hills and we lost three fields and parts of many others for that growing season and the next two. Also, there had been many boys born already that year, and there were no fields for them when they grew big enough to apprentice to an older man."

Dorict turned his head to look at her. "You think they killed a baby just because there'd be no field for him when he grew up?" he asked, frowning.

Yala nodded. "Yes," she answered. "Though I didn't know this until later."

They continued to pull to the west, waiting until they were nearer the well to turn north again. It was a long way off a more direct route, but he hoped this detour would save them from an awkward meeting. He put these thoughts aside as Yala continued her story.

"Three years ago, long after the child's death, I was in the tent of my mother. Ke was there, and Bo, and some others. They were talking about the births that year. Few boys had been born, and the last of the sand had finally been shovelled from the fields. Tral said something that made me think, too much, perhaps. She was complaining about a different woman named Calla who, like Seena, had a baby when she was too young. My mother said, 'Calla was a fool to go with Third Terrace Field Man and have a child, but at least there are enough fields now, so she won't have to suffer like Seena did.'"

Yala stopped pulling and tried to slow her breath. Speed was good, but for her plan to work they must have some strength left when they reached the well. When she could speak easily again, she said, "The others told her to be quiet and sent me out of the tent, but I saw the guilt in the old women's eyes."

Dorict bent over, hands on knees, and coughed. He waved away her arm and said, "Claw that demon. It had a whole desert to fall on. Why pick me? So, how did this make you . . . doubt your whole life?" he asked.

Yala took sip from her waterskin and handed it to Dorict.

"Because," she said, "I saw it wasn't the wind that decided, it was Tral and Ke, and the other short-named women of the well." She took back the waterskin. "This is not our way, or it shouldn't be. A child is told, 'You must listen to the winds. Only animals make decisions without their guidance!' That's why we have two souls, a small one for the earth and a greater one to listen to the wind."

"And animals like me have no such wisdom," Dorict said. He did not say it with malice but with his usual thoughtfulness.

"So I thought," Yala said. "Before Seena and her baby." She scanned the sky. They had travelled far to avoid the others. Red showed in a horizon-touching glow, tinging the wispy clouds in the west. Soon, the sun would fall into the sea, where it would fight all night only to emerge again in the morning, triumphant over its vast watery foe.

They pulled for another league before Yala spoke again. "I could not shake that death from my thoughts," she said. "How could real people, my people, act like animals and kill a child, then go and talk about how the wind willed it? I was angry! So, even when I stopped being Yalasa and went out into the world as Yala, I pulled a question behind me like a stone sled: What makes a person and what makes an animal?"

She paused for a moment to let the battered bane catch his breath again.

"The answer came in parts. Inla-phor was the first part I found. He was a wounded slave, but I watched him die like a person, not an animal. An old woman trader in the Mother of Waters was the next. She was honest, fair to me in trade. I also saw the one-eyed man and some guards, even other sandwalkers. Everyone answered a part of the question. Then there was you and this one," she said, pointing back to Marick.

"You said you had the final part of your answer when Marick dropped the knife," Dorict said. He wrapped an arm tightly around his aching ribs and waited for her response.

"Yes," Yala said. "This was his part. He had a chance to

be a monster – a demon, you would say – but he did not take it. He chose to be a person. With Seena's baby, we chose to be monsters. We were monsters with Marick, too. It wasn't his place to save my well from the poison wind. Why do we not use a cow? Are your demons so fancy about their food? Or is it because it has never been done before that it can never be thought of?" She kicked up a gout of sand, then did it again. "Listen, even if it must be a person, one of us could go, not a stranger."

She picked up the harness again, and Dorict did the same.

"So," he said, "if your question was 'Who is an animal and who is a human?' what's the whole answer? You've only told me bits and pieces."

"Ah," Yala said. "You, me, everyone are people and animals – and monsters. It is all mixed together like sand dancing in a spirit wind. Saying I am only one and you are only the other is a lie to make us feel . . . strong, stronger than our fear. Like you say, fear is behind all the bad in the world. Now I know Yala is only Yala, and she will have to decide what she will be."

She stopped and spread her arms out to the dying light.

"It is her choice, and it is her answer."

CHAPTER 31
A SMALL VICTORY

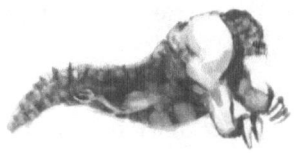

"Twenty-two," Vinir said, and Stetta nodded.

"That's my count," he said. "And forty-nine slaves, plus a bunch of animals we don't have to care about, as long as they stay in those cages."

They were watching from a half-buried cellar near the dome at the city's centre. Their shelter was close enough to see the slavers' base, a low building, better preserved than most, built of well-cut white stone and boasting an entire roof. They seemed ready to camp there for some time, with many lounging in the shade of a stone porch, drinking and snarling at each other. To Vinir's eye, there was no watchfulness in their actions. They wolfed down a morning meal sitting on the steps, in plain sight, with no guards set to keep watch. After gorging themselves, they fed the slaves, giving Stetta a chance to make his count and curse the brutes when they threw the food on the ground at their captives' feet before driving them back inside with whips and curses.

Vinir and Stetta checked each other's calculations and then watched the majority of the brutes return to the shade of their camp. One of the slavers stayed to keep watch from the shade of a broken statue, its stone legs ending abruptly at the thighs. The statue's base, a block of stone the size of a small hut, was covered with symbols that seemed half familiar to Vinir. This block was one of many facing the avenue surrounding the dome, but Vinir ignored them all to concentrate on the slavers.

This is the first sign of wisdom, claws take them! A guard here and maybe one on the other side of their camp, I'd guess. Everyone else is inside, save for one other.

That one was an old man, one of the slaves, Vinir guessed, chained to a pillar facing the slavers camp. That stone might have once helped to hold up a roof, but if so, the building would have been immense, for there were hundreds of columns, in various broken lengths, running around the sand-filled square that fronted Vinir and Stetta's hiding place.

"That old man must have angered them," Stetta said, and spat. "Or maybe they figured he wouldn't last to this Dry Hills place anyway, so they left him to die in the sun to frighten the others. They do that in the Far South, and worse things, storm take them."

Using her fingertips, Vinir brushed a little more sand out of the cellar window and scanned the plaza for any other movement. "The guard's keeping in the shade, so he'll be on the other side of that big stone now," she said. "Let's go."

"Where?" Stetta frowned at her. "You don't mean? No, Vinir. If we help him, they'll know we're here and scour the ruins for us! We'd never take on that many in a stand-up fight," he said. "I'm sorry for the old fellow, but we'd only kill ourselves, and he'd still burn."

"They won't know it's us," the bane said. "We'll make it

look like he slipped the ropes himself and ran off. Come on, Stetta. We can't leave him like this, and he'll know what happened to Dorict and Marick."

She waited, hands on hips, until the guard nodded. He slipped his short sword from its scabbard and weighed it in his hand, doubtfully.

Vinir hefted her axe with more confidence. Despite Stetta's protests, they had left their bows with Mor-ra. The round-faced guard had clipped Stetta's ear and told him it was better to be badly armed and afraid then bristling with weapons and stupidly heroic – especially if you were supposed to be sneaking around.

Vinir smiled at the thought. Mor-ra reminded her of many banehall masters, women and men of long experience and little patience for misplaced bravery.

They skirted the plaza's edge, keeping one eye on the statue hiding the guard. They came to the point where they must break cover. Vinir ducked and ran to the first pillar, then the second, and Stetta followed. In this way they moved, one then the other, until the very next column held the punished man. Vinir slipped over to stand at the back of the pillar

"Say nothing," she said, putting a hand on the man's thin shoulder, but she could have saved her breath, for the old man was too ravaged by thirst to speak. His eyes, however, were eloquent, pleading for rescue, which Vinir was happy to provide. Before leaving their hiding place, the bane had found a shard of stone sharp enough to suit her purpose, and now she used it to saw at the thick ropes binding the prisoner.

"Must you take all day?" Stetta whispered from behind his own pillar. He switched his gaze back and forth between her slow cutting and the still invisible guard.

"Wait!" he hissed and pulled his head back.

Vinir did the same. A rock flew past her ear, missing the intended target. The second one didn't, and the bound man groaned, a dry rasping sound that made the stone-thrower laugh.

"Hah! Still alive, grey-beard?" the slaver called out. "Won't be long before the sun takes you, gut-ripped fool! Weren't for you, I'd be inside where its cooler. Gods take you, I'll go get some water, or something stronger if they haven't guzzled it all. Sorry, old man, none for you!"

A last rock flipped past the pillars. Vinir and Stetta held their breaths.

"Wait," Stetta whispered and slowly moved his head until he could peer around the curve of his hiding place. "He's gone, but not for long, I'd wager, unless there is some wine left for him, which I doubt with this drunken lot, and why in the name of the Mother's Mouth are you cutting rope with a stone?" The usually calm man's voice was rising into a panic, but Vinir kept cutting.

"A clean slice would give us away!" she said. "This has to look like he did it. Almost done . . . There. Put him on your back and let's go."

She dropped the flake of rock on top of the cut rope and followed Stetta, using the broad blade of her axe to smooth over their footprints. Once back in the ruined palace, they joined arms, slung the old man between them, and fled as quietly as possible.

There must have been wine left, or something that kept the slaver distracted, for they never heard a hue and cry from the slavers, and none came searching the outskirts of the city where they hid.

"He'll PROBABLY DIE on us now," Stetta said, looking down at the rescued man.

"Was it worth saving him and maybe losing your lives?" Mor-ra demanded. She glared at Vinir. The bane sat cross-legged beside the freed slave, staring at the sleeping old man, willing him to wake up and speak.

The guards looked at each other and left to climb up to the second floor and relieve Chal-lat and Son-neen. When they were alone, Stetta said, "Pray to the Mother that the old codger wakes before he dies. If he can tell us about those two boys, at least we'll know what to do next."

Mor-ra looked out into the sand-choked streets. "You should pray very hard," she said, "because if he dies without talking, sure as sand and storm she'll send you back to fetch another!"

CHAPTER 32
ESCAPE

"Do they know I'm gone?" Marick asked, rubbing his eyes. "Have they found the demon?"

The wounded bane raised himself from the sled, balancing on one arm as all three looked over the green fields of the well. There were lights by the low wall and near the tents beyond it, but all the closest huts were dark.

"I don't think so. Look," Yala said, pointing to the brightest patch at the wall. Figures danced there and a howling of voices rose into the night.

"Knife dancing," she said. "They wouldn't do that without the women watching."

"And if they're watching," Marick said, his voice still thick with sleep, "they aren't chasing us."

"You are clever when you are not dying," Yala said. "They will wait until morning, I think, then use their fear lizards to make sure the poison has dissolved that 'jewel' you told me of, the one that spits out fear. Now, let us go. Narrow Field Man said he'd leave us supplies near the well-house."

They slipped down the dune to the first field and Yala motioned Dorict to pick up the back of the sled. They bore it like a stretcher, carrying Marick over the narrow paths between the fields where they had to go single file. When the path broadened, Yala told Dorict to lower the sled again. They stood with green fields on one side and grazing grass on the other.

"The way is wider," Yala said. "We can pull from here."

It was half a league still to their destination, the round stone building Dorict had seen earlier.

"Our well-house," Yala said when they reached the stone building. "See, this is where our rock walls end and the sand needs constant shovelling. In the day, there are many working here, but not now." She dropped the sled harness and peered into the darkness. "Narrow Field Man told me a secret of the men that lies beneath it, though I think Ke and some others know about it too. Look, there's the food. Help me secure it on the sled beside Marick."

She worked quickly, looking up now and then to see the distant fires and the shadows dancing before them.

Stay there and let us leave in peace, let us be free.

Tral, her red cloak covered with streaks of sand and sweat, stepped from the shadows of the well-house door, blocking their way.

"You followed us," Yala said. "How did you know?" She went to stand between Tral and the others.

The sandwalker glared at her daughter. "How did I know that you wouldn't obey? How did I know that you would think yourself wiser than those with shorter names? Hah! This was not hard, Yalasa. I came back early and kept watch, only to find you again with these animals!"

Marick raised himself on one arm and pointed shakily

with the other. "Claws take you! You tied me up to die out there," he said, rasping out the words. "I'll cut your throat."

He grabbed one of the demon horns Dorict had brought to show to the banehall masters and tried to crawl towards the sandwalker, forgetting that he was still tied to the sled. After a moment's exertion, he fell back, and the horn fell to the ground.

Dorict picked it up. He stepped forward to stand beside Yala.

"For Yala's sake, I'll forget that you captured us and tried to kill my friend," the bane said. He held the horn point down, like one would a dagger. "But if you try to stop us now, I'll fight you," he said. There was a calmness in his tone, but his body had a tension to it, a readiness to commit violence.

Yala said nothing, but her hand slipped beneath her cloak to free her shovel.

"Come. Be truly wise and leave them," Tral said to her daughter, ignoring Dorict's threat. "He is one-souled, an animal. Animals are given to us by the wind for our use, and you know the small one's use was to be put out in the sand to protect true people."

Yala flicked her robe aside to show Tral the shovel in her hand. Its edge was not as shiny as before, for the demon's teeth had been tough enough to notch it, but it was still a weapon.

Tral's eyes narrowed. "Are you an animal too, to threaten your mother?" she said, and held her cloak open to show that she too was armed.

"Yes," Yala said, slipping to the right to force the other away from the door. Dorict stayed between Tral and the sled. "I am. You say they are animals and we are true people, but what does that mean, Tral?"

I will not call you "Mother."

Tral hesitated, then stepped to her right, perhaps confident that even if Yala slipped past her, the sled and its "useful" animal would remain.

Yala took another step. "What do 'true people' do to their own kind, Tral? What do they do to their own children? Do you remember Seena's child? I do."

Tral frowned. "Still you speak of this? We did what was needed with Seena. That's a woman's duty. When a woman's name is short, she protects the well, even if it means—"

"Murder?" Yala said. "Killing the weak, the ones who don't fit your needs?"

Tral brandished her own shovel, a longer, sharper version of the one Yala held.

"The well's needs, not mine," the older woman said, and feinted with her weapon.

Yala did not flinch. "I have seen how your needs and the needs of the well's fit so closely together, Tral, but this is your will, not the wind's!" She raised her shovel so that it pointed straight up into the dark sky. A sudden gust blew sheets of sand between them. "Move aside. I'm taking the dark road with this one. The poison wind is dead, by my arrows. Let that be enough."

She slid her front foot forward one inch.

Let her see the strong wind in my souls and go.

Tral took a tentative step forward and then jumped back to avoid a downward slash to her arm. Her eyes widened, and she looked at Yala as if seeing her for the first time. "You would do this? You would kill you own kind?" she asked. "You truly are an animal!"

Yala did not move from her position between Tral and the door. The shovel was now held horizontally across her body, ready for another attack. She would not willingly kill, but neither would she run.

Tral stepped back, then again. A shadow passed over her face, and she dropped her shovel onto the flagstones. It rang like an alarm, but the sound quickly faded into silence. The sun was far below the horizon. The dimmest stars were now visible, and from far away came the sound of the men and women cheering on a new pair of knife dancers.

Unarmed, she crossed her hands at her chest, palms out, and spat between them onto the ground. "You are not Yala. You are not even Yalasa or Yalasana. You are nothing. Leave here and never return, or we will know how to use you."

"Yes, Tral, I am leaving," said Yala, who knew who she was even if Tral denied it. "But I'm taking them with me," she added.

Tral turned away and ran, her cloak flapping behind her as she went back to the noise and light of her people. Yala snatched up the harness and yanked the sled to the entrance and through into the true darkness within.

Dorict followed quickly, Tral's shovel in his hand. When Yala lit a lamp hanging from the wall, she saw this and frowned.

Dorict tied it to his belt. "She owes us for what she did," he told her. "This is just a part of the payment."

"Here, then," Yala said, pointing at bundles left beside the mouth of the well. "Narrow Field Man has left us food and blankets . . . and look, your pack! That is more payment, and our freedom is the final coin. Help me move aside this well-cap."

Dorict and Yala had to use all their strength to do so, for it was made of hammered bronze, a great shield covering a hole in the stone floor. There was barely room to move it aside, for the inside of the well-house was crowded with waist-high jars, many full of water, giving the air a wonderful freshness compared to the smell of sand and dust outside.

Yala pulled a hook down from a nest of pulleys hanging above the well-hole. She yanked it up and down until she found the loose end of its line and threaded that through an iron ring set in the floor.

"I'll go down first and then you let down the sled with him on it," she said. "And bar that door, for Tral will have them all after us in a moment's time!"

While Dorict manhandled heavy jars in front of the door, Yala took the lantern from the wall and hung it on the hook. She lowered the light into the hole. The room darkened until the only light shone upwards from the opening. Looking down, she could see a rock floor thirty feet below. She felt a draft plunging into the hole, trying to draw her in, and she heard a dull roaring, deeper than any wind she had ever known. Dorict came to hold the other end of the rope tight and she began to climb down.

"Yala," the bane called out. "I'll lower Marick and the sled now. What's that noise down there?"

There was no answer, so he pulled the rope back up and set the hook in the frame of the sled. He tipped it into the hole and used the pulley to lower it. Marick made no sound, but his eyes were opened wide. When the rope went slack, Dorict tied it off, put on his pack, and swung out over the empty space. His ribs hurt as he climbed down, but, from much experience with injuries, he guessed they were just bruised and not broken.

At the bottom, he found Yala with the sled set on its wheels and the harness already around her shoulders. The space here was a match for that above, though instead of a door, a hole in the rock led away from the lantern's light.

"Where are we?" a small voice said, barely heard over the rushing noise that surrounded them.

"Underneath Old Carving Well," Dorict answered, bending over to make sure Marick's bandages hadn't come loose while he dangled.

"Come," Yala said. "Narrow Field Man says we go down that tunnel to find the dark road."

"Sounds lovely," Marick said, yawning at the end of that pronouncement and closing his eyes again.

Dorict stood up. The bandage around the stump showed flecks of blood but no great bleeding. He used his cloak to cushion it and followed Yala down the tunnel, walking backwards with Tral's shovel ready in his hand.

Light showed from above, and a torch dropped down to sputter out on the stone floor. An arrow followed, skipping across to blunt itself on a curved wall. More danced down, then another torch, this one flaring into a real blaze.

"They've dropped down oil and set it alight," Dorict shouted, coughing at the smoke that followed them rather than rising back up through the well-hole. Something was drawing it past them. Now he felt the wind he had heard, a great rushing of air that dragged him down the tunnel until Yala caught his arm.

"Careful," she said, her voice strained. "We must stay to the side."

She held the light above her head, and Dorict saw why. This was the source of the water, the reason the well had green fields and not dead, dry dirt. A torrent flowed under Old Carving Well, a roaring current that rushed through a channel of cut stone, polishing the sides and spraying the paths that ran along each artificial bank.

"A river!" Dorict said. "And not natural. This tunnel is of cut stone. It must be forty, no, fifty paces across. How deep is the water?"

Yala pulled him away from the tunnel entrance. The smoke went past them and was carried off to the right, following the direction of the current.

"Narrow Field Man said nobody knows how deep the Dying River is. The men only dare to come this far to get water in jars and barrels, enough to irrigate the fields and provide for the people," she said. "Now come, to the left, for he said that is north on the dark road."

"Will they follow us?" Dorict asked. He had to shout to be heard over the sound of the water.

Yala did not answer. Despite the light, she ran her hand along the arching wall, making the sled bump and scrape against the rock.

Dorict caught up with her and shook her shoulder. Her face was pale, and there was a wildness in her eyes.

"I remember now!" he shouted. "You fear the water, don't you?"

She nodded. "A little is life, but this much is death," she said, then shouted it when she saw he couldn't hear her mumbling voice.

"Only if we fall in," Dorict said and smiled, but Yala shook her head.

"Your people don't know! The sun fights the sea every night. One day, the sea will win, and there will be darkness. Darkness and water, like here. Oh! Dorict, I can't."

It shocked him to see the sandwalker, who had been so calm in their travels and so brave against the Horned demon, fall apart like this.

"Listen," he shouted. "Use those wrappings your friend

gave you to cover your eyes for now. Keep near the wall and put a hand on my shoulder. I'll pull!"

She fixed the silkstone-laden cloth over her eyes and stretched out both hands, one resting on Dorict's shoulder and the other brushing the spray-washed wall. Dorict pulled as fast as his ribs would allow and they made good speed, for the road beside the river was broad enough to take three sleds side-by-side and was as smooth as polished glass.

After a third stop to rest, Yala uncovered one eye.

It is only water. I drink it, I wash with it, I capture it in jars and waterskins! It has no hold over me unless I allow it.

This was a feeling like the fear the demon cast. She fought it the same way, taking one step after the other. The sound and the darkness never relented, but the sandwalker kept moving.

I wish my people had a poison to kill this darkness or this noise – or both!

"There's a side tunnel ahead," Dorict shouted, and held the lantern up to examine the void.

"It only goes back a few yards before it's blocked," he said, and pulled the sled inside. There was a comfort in stepping even a few feet away from the underground river, and Yala felt her muscles uncramp as she leaned back against the sled. Dorict stripped Marick of his blue-stained clothes and used water from the river to rinse the last of the poison from his skin.

"At least we'll be clean," he shouted to Yala, but the sandwalker shook her head and gave him a severe look.

Dorict grinned. The dark and noise were oppressive, but they were free again and travelling towards home. He dressed the wounded bane in a clean shirt from his pack, glad he'd had the foresight to take it with him when he'd woken up all those mornings ago to see their tent cut open, their coin gone, and shadowy figures fleeing up the road.

The small bane looked like a child in the oversized shirt, and Dorict wrapped a blanket around him before going out to the edge of the path to rinse Marick's tunic and pants in the river. Given what they had gone through, the clothes were little better than rags, but he washed them all the same. The water was cool on his hands, and he left them submerged for a while, thinking of snow and ice and anything except sand. He returned to an anxious Yala and set the wet clothes in a sheltered corner of the blocked passageway to dry as best they could.

While they rested, Yala and Dorict conversed in raised voices.

"Are you sure they won't follow us?" the bane yelled.

"Follow us?" Yala shouted back. "No, for they fear the water as much as I do, I think! They will not go too far past the entrance, but they will send fast runners to the next wells along the Dying River to guard against us. We will not be able to leave by those wells."

Dorict poked through the food Narrow Field Man had left them and pulled out a flat loaf of bread. He broke it in three pieces and tried to rouse Marick to eat. He had no luck and finally stuffed it into the clean shirt to keep it dry.

Dorict chewed both the bread and Yala's words for a while before speaking again. "That's a problem! Are there any other ways out of this tunnel?"

Yala thought back to what Narrow Field Man had told her of the dark road.

"Perhaps," she said. "Though we must go far to find it. There are ruins, some of them very big, that lie under the sand. Sometimes the wind clears away enough to see them for a season or two. We might find wells leading up to such places. If not, we must go to where the Dying River starts, and even Narrow Field Man does not know where that is."

She sipped from the waterskin and handed it to Dorict. It felt sinful to drink with no thought of saving enough for later, but there was no need for that while they travelled along the Dying River. Beside them, Marick slept on. Yala tapped the boulders blocking the passageway.

"This tunnel must have led to one such place," she said, "but it fell in long ago. We'll have to look into each side tunnel and hope that there is one that lets us out on this side of the river."

Dorict nodded. "I hope we find it soon. The oil in this lamp won't last forever."

Yala pointed to the basket tied by Marick's feet. "There's more oil there, and a smaller lamp," she shouted. "But put out that one now. We'll rest here, if we can bear the darkness and noise."

Dorict laughed. "He can," he said, nodding to where Marick slept, one hand thrown over his face. The smile faded from the bigger bane's face. "It's a healing sleep, I hope. The wound was well cared for, I'll give the men of your well that, but he needs rest, not hard travel." He blew out the lantern's flame, and darkness fell on them faster than a thought.

Between that and the buffeting noise, both felt alone in the world, unable to even hear a comforting word as they lay there. Unconsciously, they each edged towards the other until their stretched legs touched, and so comforted they could at last sleep.

And dream. Yala floated above the desert she knew so well, seeing day and night flash below her in rapid drumbeats of time. She hovered there, bodiless, it seemed, until she quickened on a chasing wind, raising little clouds of sand when she dropped low over the red dunes, illuminating them.

What am I? I am light. I'm glowing green, but if I were a blue flier I'd be blue, wouldn't I? And I wouldn't be Yala, would I?

Her thoughts fluttered like her wings, and she saw that she now flew above a dune littered with corpses: slavers and sandwalkers lying side-by-side while sandcats moved among them, licking blood from their faces.

She tried to fly higher, to escape this vision, but the smell of death pulled her down. Her wings stopped beating and she fell, leaf thin and tumbling, until she touched the red ground.

Yala sat up, crowding back until the sled stopped her panicked retreat. She felt Marick's shoulder against her spine and let out a breath.

A dream. I was a night flier. I flew over a battlefield. I was glowing . . . I am glowing!

The light was still there, a green luminescence that gave some sight to what had been a formless, eternal night. Squinting, she could make out Dorict's huddled form nearby, could see the waterskin by her hand and the runners of the sled. Slowly she crawled, hand over hand, towards the source of that light. It came from the water. Her stomach churning, she reached the lip of the riverbank and stuck her head out just far enough to look over the edge.

Things moved there, sleek, swift, and bearing their own lights. Some were brighter, some dimmer, some were as small as her finger, others as long as her arm, but all were lit with that green glow. These weren't the only things in the water. Strange jointed creatures crawled along the stone below the waterline, picking at the rock with nimble claws and pushing unseen food into their busy mouths. There was a flash of movement as a glowing swimmer as long as her sled broke the water and disappeared again. The tiny ones dived deep, and the light faded a bit.

They glow like blue fliers but in the water, not the sky. Even Narrow Field Man did not speak of this.

Slowly, very slowly, she raised herself to a kneeling position and stayed there until Dorict woke and joined her. She tried but could not explain the absolute wonder of it to him, that the sun's enemy could have such a gentle light of its own.

CHAPTER 33
SMALL HOPES

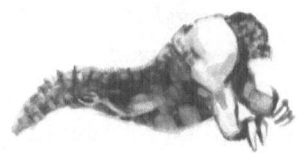

"He escaped?" Vinir asked. "Marick is free?"

The horse nickered and nudged her to continue brushing.

Mor-ra sat down on a weathered well curb and nodded. "So the old man just told me. According to him, your friend escaped some days ago," the guard replied. "He said the boy was badly wounded in the leg because he tried to help him, and that one-eyed thief we should have locked up in the town did it, sand take him! He said Marick never came back after One-Eye took him off into the desert one night. The other slavers searched but found no trace of the boy or their chief."

Vinir ran the brush down the horse's mane. "Claws! What did the slavers think happened, or doesn't the old man know?"

Mor-ra shrugged. "Goz, the one left in charge, swore the boy ran off and was chased by their chief. The sandwalker that came with them, storm curse her for all the trouble that bit of news brings, went after them and disappeared as well." She offered Vinir a piece of dried meat, but the bane, who had liked the horse it came from, shook her head.

Wounded and vanished into the desert with a slaver on his trail! Why couldn't he have stayed put and waited for me, for us, to rescue him? And where is Dorict? Claws! Two days until the old man stays awake long enough to talk, and this is all he says!

"Nothing of Dorict?" she asked.

Mor-ra finished chewing, which required both time and effort, before answering. "Never saw him. Seems the old man and the rest were kept a day's travel north of the town until One-Eye showed up with more of his bully boys and your friend in a collar. Just the one, though."

"So, where is he then?" the bane demanded, but Mor-ra was chewing again, and the horse beside her had no answer except for a more urgent nudge. Vinir resumed brushing the sweaty hide of the animal while it leaned into her efforts and sighed out a bushel of air.

"He's smart, that Dorict," a voice said behind them, and the two women turned to see Son-neen standing there, holding a bow and two blunt practice arrows.

"It's time for practice, Mor-ra," she said. "And if I were Dorict, I would have followed those slavers and found out where they were going."

"Would he be so foolhardy?" Vinir asked, to herself rather than the others, though the horse responded with a stomping hoof.

Maybe, if he thought he could catch Marick and talk sense into him before it was too late.

Mor-ra stood and scratched her head. "To save his friend, maybe he would," she said.

Son-neen stamped her own foot. "Not for that, Mor-ra! To get back my papers."

The guard grinned and slapped the girl on the shoulder.

"Maybe he wanted to do both, see? Well, let's find a target and move you back a few more feet this time."

Vinir watched them walk away before leaving the horse and going back to where Stetta tended the old man. Challat was on watch, or maybe drawing again, and Vinir looked up to his tower post. She wanted to go to him so she could hear his calm, reasoning voice, maybe so they could just sit together while she decided what to do next.

Before she could make up her mind, Stetta waved her over. The guard had a pot in his hand and held it over the small fire they had managed out of the very old wooden beams they had found among the stones. There was a large pile of it ready, for it crumbled more than burned. The only thing to be said for it was it gave off very little smoke compared to the oily bushes of the desert.

When Vinir stood beside him, she wrinkled her nose at the smell.

"Here now!" Stetta said. "No criticism, please. You should be thankful that horse gave his life. Now we can eat a fine stew."

"Many thanks," Vinir said. "To the horse, which died of thirst, not generosity."

Stetta smiled and pointed a thumb at the old man, who watched them with hopeful, if frightened, eyes.

"He says your Marick was the bravest boy he ever saw, taunting the slavers with a rude song just so they'd stop whipping him. He thinks Marick killed One-Eye and got away. Says maybe other sandwalkers saved him. Seems they do that sometimes."

"Only sometimes?" Vinir asked, alarmed.

"They're a changeable folk," Stetta said. "As you can see by some of them helping slavers. Never thought that would happen! My grandmother would have spat blood to hear that. She was one, a sandwalker. Came to the City of Fountains when she was kicked out of her well. Nice and nasty in the same breath, she was."

Vinir left him there, still holding the pot. She started to climb the tower stairs, then stopped. There were shards of stone on each step, and she moved one about with the toe of her boot while she thought.

Maybe, maybe one saved the other, and the sandwalkers saved them both.

Maybe.

CHAPTER 34
BURIED IN STONE

Marick woke for breakfast, such as it was, for when he demanded it, Dorict shouted that he should reach into his shirt and get it himself.

"Well, at least it's dry," he shouted, then coughed, a racking sound heard even over the roar of the river. Dorict fetched him water and he choked it down.

"Don't talk," Dorict said. "Just nod or shake your head. Does your leg hurt?"

A grim nod.

"Can you eat?"

A pause, then a tentative nod. Marick pointed to where a light bobbed ahead of them.

"Yala," Dorict shouted. "She's a friend. I don't know if you remember much of the last few days . . ."

A shrug.

"But she killed that slaver, the one-eyed brute, with an arrow and kept you alive until you got to the well. After that . . ."

Marick held up a hand and grimaced before falling back on the folded cloaks.

"We have to keep going," Dorict told him. "Yala says there are ruins that we have to find to get out of this tunnel. That's why she's scouting ahead."

Dorict helped the smaller bane to sit up again and held him while he chewed the round of bread. When he was done, Dorict gave him more water and laid him back down. He stood to see Yala coming back from her scouting.

She shook her head and picked up the harness. When Dorict went to take the position nearest the water, she pushed him to the other side, by the wall.

"Are you all right?" he yelled.

She glared at him and shouted back, "No! I am not. We are in the middle of death and darkness with only a lantern and a bit of green light to show us the way. So why don't you pull and help us get back to the wind!"

Pull they did. There was wind enough in the tunnel, dragged by the current and always in their faces, but Dorict did not point this out to the sandwalker. They fought that wind, and the dark when they extinguished their lantern and waited for their eyes to adjust enough to see glow, and now they fought the path itself, for long stretches of it had cracks and ridges that caught at the wheels of the sled, stopping them again and again.

"Careful," Yala said, and pulled Dorict back from a hole that would have swallowed his leg.

They eased the sled over it and rested for a while, but the urge to escape soon put them in the harness again, and they pulled until they could barely stand.

"We must rest here," Dorict shouted, but Yala shook her head.

"Farther," she yelled back. "Find a side tunnel to get out of the spray."

"What about that one back there?" Dorict asked, for they had passed such a refuge not too long ago.

"No," Yala said, and pointed the way they travelled.

Dorict shrugged and took the pause as an excuse to catch his breath. He knelt beside the sled and gave Marick water. The wounded bane looked better, more alert than before. He motioned Dorict nearer.

"I don't need to drink," Marick said in Dorict's ear, for he couldn't yet shout over the sound of the river. "All this spray will just sink in sooner or later anyway."

Dorict snorted. A bad joke was a good sign of Marick's recovery. He held out the waterskin, and Marick took it. He signalled Dorict to lean back down again and said, "What's the matter with you two? Lover's quarrel? And what about that girl back in the City of Fountains? Do you think you can handle two girlfriends at once?"

Dorict growled loud enough to be heard over the roar of the river. "Fool! Do you think you can swim with only three limbs?"

Marick smiled and lay back down.

"What did he say?" Yala asked, seeing the look on Dorict's face when he picked up the harness straps.

"He's almost back to normal," Dorict said. "Which is a great shame." He put his irritation into his pulling, and Yala tried to keep up. She looked at the boy from the corners of her eyes.

Maybe it's something about men. Ke always said they were moody.

Since day and night were only memories in this glowing, eternal twilight, they slept when they were exhausted and pulled while they had strength. This tedium was broken by eating and passing the occasional side tunnel, most of these completely filled with rubble and some going off only a few yards before yielding disappointment.

The open passageways they had found so far led to other wells, and they knew that those exits would be guarded night and day. For several, they had to wait at a great distance until lines of men filling water jars left, taking their lamps with them. When the green glow returned, they would pass with great care, carrying the sled so the wheels made no sound on the stone.

They kept going until day and night were only matters of opinion, and time was measured by aching muscles and empty stomachs. At last, they came to an opening that was different from the others.

"Light the lamp," Yala shouted. "This one goes back farther than most."

"Careful," Dorict said. He pulled the lantern from the sled and hurriedly lit it with tinder fired by flint and steel.

The tunnel did indeed go back beyond sight and was free of any fallen rocks. They pulled the sled up a gentle slope for many, many, many yards before coming out into a round chamber much bigger than the one under Old Carving Well. The walls were also more ornate, being carved and bearing traces of paint.

"Look," Dorict said, surprised by the sound of his own voice, for they were now far from the river and the current's noise was not so overwhelming.

"Writing," Dorict added, and pointed at half-seen symbols.

Yala shrugged. "Not from sandwalkers," she said. "And this is no well of my people. Look up."

The banes did, and saw a darkness stretching above them. Yala picked up a chip of stone from the floor and threw it upwards at an angle. It passed out of sight and did not return.

"It didn't hit a well-cap!" Marick said. "Can we get up there?"

"How?" Yala asked. "By throwing you up too?"

Marick scowled at her. "Why not? Your friends did their best to make me lighter."

Dorict held up a hand to forestall Yala's angry response.

"Enough! Yala is our friend, Marick. It's harder on her down here than it is on you and me. Besides, your crimes should have taught you some humility by now."

He lifted the lantern as high as he could.

"Yala, could you take this and stand on my shoulders. Maybe you can see some way we can get out of here."

The sandwalker folded her cloak and laid it on the harness. She clambered up to sit on Dorict's shoulders and took the lantern from him.

"Hold still," she said, and pushed up higher to stand on his broad shoulders, holding up the light to examine the void above.

"Let me down," she said, and slithered down the bane's frame into a brief and awkward embrace.

"He's got a girlfriend," Marick called out. "So don't think he's free."

"What I think," Yala said through clenched teeth, "is that I liked you better when you were asleep."

"I almost died," Marick said, looking aggrieved.

"Almost doesn't help," Dorict said, "as I've told you before. Many times, in fact."

"Yes," said Yala, picking up her robe and throwing it over the boy's head. "Next time do better."

And at last free of that all-consuming noise and darkness, they laughed, an echoing sound in that round room. It lasted a long time, for even looking at each other brought another bout of stomach-shaking mirth, and some of the anger and grief they bore eased from their souls.

"There is an opening, but there are no hand-holds I could reach," Yala said, when she could speak again.

"Well, what about a rope?" Marick asked, wiping his eyes. "Could you shoot it up on one of your arrows?"

Yala shook her head. "The rope is too heavy, and a shaft, even if it caught, would break under our weight."

Dorict was examining the sled and its contents.

"I have an idea," he said, "but you won't like it, Yala."

It took them a long time to disassemble the sled, for it was well pegged and glued together, with some joints strengthened by a braiding of lacquered twine. They set Marick the job of prying off the silkstone bottoms of the runners. After chipping the knife, he asked for Dorict's shovel – Tral's actually, as Yala reminded him.

"A woman's weapon," she said. "It is strange to see you use it."

"Men use shovels," Dorict said. "Narrow Field Man had one in his hut."

Yala shrugged. "Men's shovels are not women's shovels" she said.

She looked to where Marick worked, expecting some comment, but the boy had fallen back on the floor of the room, the knife still held loosely in one hand. She went over to him and took the blade away, then felt his forehead with the back of her hand.

"He's asleep, but the fever has not returned," she told Dorict, and handed him the unfinished piece.

"That he can wake at all is a marvel," Dorict said, running the shovel blade between stone slices and the wood of the runner. "He lost his leg . . . wait, how many days has it been?"

Yala shook her head and hammered loose a peg using the haft-end of her knife.

"Five days? Six?" she finally said. The piece came loose, and she stacked it with the other slats. "Does it matter?"

Dorict paused in his work. "Yes, I want to keep track of the days. I can't think down here, in this darkness and noise! Claws! I thought that if I didn't go deaf, I'd go mad, which is why we are going to use these runners to shoot a hook of some kind up into that opening."

"Like a bow?" Yala asked. When he had suggested taking the sled apart, she thought he meant to tie the pieces together into a long pole and lift up a loop of rope, but this was more ambitious, or foolish.

"This is not bow wood," she warned, holding up a board that once made part of the sled's cargo bed. "It will break if pulled too much."

Dorict had already tied the runners together and made a makeshift bowstring out of blanket strips rather than Yala's rope, which he was saving for the arrow. The arrow was to be a railing pole, with a line tied to the middle of the shaft so it would twist and catch on any convenient edge. The bane notched its centre for the line to bite but did not bother to sharpen the end.

"Even if it stuck in something," he explained, "it would just pull out again."

It took some time to figure out how to draw it, for the draw length was as long as Dorict's body. They finally managed a strange configuration with Dorict standing and holding the bow in hands wrapped against the string's bite and Yala lying on the ground, her boots planted firmly on the bane's buttocks as she held the end of the arrow with aching fingers.

"Lower your head, or the string will take off your hair!" she said, and when he had done so, she let the arrow go. There was a deep twang, and the pole flew up – and crashed into a hidden wall, falling to the ground at Dorict's feet.

"Again," he said, and they tried, over and over, until Yala was sure the sled runners would crack at each attempt. Dorict aimed at different points in the darkness each time, but with no success, until the arrow did not fall back down to the stone floor, but vanished, leaving nothing but the taut rope, its lower end tied around his waist.

Yala pulled the line back, fearing each tug would send the arrow tumbling down again. Dorict smiled when the rope went taught and held.

He stopped smiling when Yala tied the small lantern to her belt by a length of cord and made ready to climb. Dorict stopped her.

"I'll go up first," he said. "I'm used to difficult things like this, and you might break your neck if you fall."

Yala looked at him. "It was my sled that made the bow," she said. "It is my rope that is tied to the arrow. And it is my neck! Storm and sand! I don't know why you are so . . . irritating, you town-dwellers. Is it sandwalkers you look down on, or only those who are not banes?"

Since Dorict had no answer for that, he held the bottom of the rope while Yala shinnied up into the darkness. Peering up after her, he saw those shadows dispelled by the lamp swinging below her. There was indeed an exit, a hole in the side of that chimney-like structure, and he watched her climb through it and pull the lantern after her.

It was some minutes before she looked out again and called down.

"The rope is better tied now. I'm coming down."

They repeated their descent into the river tunnel in reverse: Dorict ascending and Yala tying the rope around load after load of food, sled parts, and a still-sleeping Marick. She was the last to rise, but it was easier this time, for she put her foot in a loop of the rope and Dorict brought her up like any other cargo.

"This is just another room," Dorict said, rubbing his sore arms. "Round like the one down there. Is there a door?"

"I saw three," Yala said. She held up the lamp and walked towards the curved wall. "Metal doors in the stone. And colours on the walls, pictures, I think."

The walls bore designs of red, yellow, and black. Some were intricate geometrical patterns of angles and lines. Others were people.

"Why are some so small?" Yala asked, peering at the image. "Are they children?"

"Holding swords and spears?" Dorict said. "Very bad parenting." He traced a finger over the larger figure, a man holding up a whip and a type of axe, both in the same hand.

"A fight maybe," he said. "Maybe a war, and the small ones are the enemy."

Yala laughed. "Not much of a battle then, but I've never heard of a people so small, unless that big one is a giant. Some say they live in the far east, among the big stone hills."

"Mountains?" Dorict asked. "There are many mountains in the east, past the Midlands, or so Garet told me. No, I think this picture is fashioned to make the big man seem more important, a conqueror."

"And the little ones?"

Dorict frowned. "Easy to crush, I suppose."

"I do not like this big man," Yala said, "and I see the small ones have dark skin and black hair like me. The big one has hair the same colour as the sand."

The sandwalker turned from the paintings and tried to open the nearest door. Despite her best efforts, the wide panel of bronze would not move. She looked at the seam but was reluctant to mar her shovel's edge against the metal.

Dorict had no better luck. He looked to the centre of the room, where a small figure lay sleeping in a pile of robes and blankets. "Well," he said, "if you want to open a locked door, talk to a thief."

He walked over to the sleeping bane and gently shook his shoulder. It took a while, but Marick opened his eyes and yawned.

"Go away," he said. "I was asleep."

"Now you're not," Dorict said. "Come, we need your skills." He gathered Marick up in his arms and carried him to the door. Yala stepped aside to give them room.

"It's a door," Marick said, still yawning. He closed his eyes and rested his head against Dorict's shoulder but was shaken awake once more.

"Thank you for that, wise one," Dorict said. "Open it!"

He moved close so Marick could examine the barrier.

"All right! All right," the small bane said. "No keyhole, which is just as well, for those clawed tower people took my lockpicks. It must have a catch or something like that."

He ran his fingers over all the ornamental projections, ordering Dorict to lower or raise him many times.

"Are you done?" Dorict asked, his voice somewhat strained. He was on one knee now, letting his friend feel under the door frame.

"Almost," Marick replied. There was a satisfying click, and the metal door swung out a half inch.

"There," he said. "Aren't you glad I'm here?"

Dorict set him down against the wall. "Hah! If you think this redeems you, think again. That would take a thousand doors at least."

"Let us hope there aren't so many between us and the air," Yala said.

Dorict pulled the door wider and wedged it with a slat from the sled. That done, he used the rope and a blanket to make a sling that could hold Marick on his back. The boy twisted until he found a position where his stump did not rub and closed his eyes again. The other bane hefted his shovel and nodded at Yala, who carried the small lamp and her strung bow. They stepped through a yard-deep stone frame and held up the lamp.

"Heaven's shield," Dorict murmured, and Marick opened his eyes and whistled over his friend's shoulder.

"Claws and teeth and screams in the night! Is that what I think it is?"

Yala looked at them, then at the walls, floor, and ceiling of the spacious, empty chamber.

"Your silkstone," she said, and raised her bow hand to touch the protective wrapping she kept loosely curled around her neck. She calculated the amount and shook her head in wonder. Every sandwalker of every well could have protection from the poison winds, and all that could come from a single wall of this room.

"Thousands of masks," Dorict said. "And armour too. A real army. An army to help us defeat the demons."

"We'll have to get it back to Shirath first," Marick reminded him, but his eyes shone as he took in the possibility of that green-veined stone.

Yala wished to move on, but Dorict first chipped a small sample from one of the pillars that held up the low roof.

"Hallmaster Branet and King Trax will both faint when they hear of this," he said, and handed it back over his shoulder. "Keep this safe."

Marick nodded. "Don't worry, I've got a few hiding places left," he said, and the stone disappeared.

Yala led them to the left, for the light glinted off another bronze door. The small bane opened this one as well, and quicker, having the hang of it now. The next room was like the first in size and height but was fashioned of regular stone – much to the banes' disappointment. It was crowded compared to the silkstone chamber. Stone shelves lined every wall and held the ancient remains of wooden crates, and piles of dust that might have been anything, once. The floor had even more of this, most of it crumbled into waist-high mounds of rubbish.

"Food, maybe," Yala said, stirring one such pile with a toe. "There are animal bones in here, and bits of clay pots."

She edged between these remains and began to examine the shelves. Dorict did the same on the other side of the room. He found rolled carpets that had survived almost intact and boxes that time had reduced to hinges and intricate locks. Something shiny caught his eye, and he fished out a small, bright stone. It was a jewel, something a lord or king would wear. He shrugged and pushed it back into the dust. He was a bane, not a lord. There being nothing else of interest, he went back and waited for the sandwalker.

Yala soon returned with a piece of brocade made into a bag.

"Did you find food?" Dorict asked and stiffened when Marick laughed at his eagerness.

"At least that hasn't changed," the boy said, grinning over Dorict's shoulder.

"No food," Yala said, holding back a smile of her own. "That is all dust and bones, but I found a few useful things."

She put the makeshift bag on a shelf and opened it. Arrowheads spilled out, as well as two larger spearheads and a double-edged knife, its haft rotted away, but with the tang and pommel still intact.

"There are many of these over there," she said, nodding towards the back of the room, "but no door, and most of the weapons are useless now, for their shafts and handles are gone."

"Then why did you take these?" Dorict asked. He poked among the bronze points.

Yala picked up the knife. It was a broad-bladed, deadly looking thing.

"I gave my knife to Marick," she said. "I need a new one, and these arrow points will be useful if I break my own points, and the spears . . ."

"If we ever find a tree to make shafts," Marick said. "All right, and I suppose I did forget to thank you for the knife."

Yala shrugged. "You did not kill me with it. That is like thanking." She looked to the darkness on the other side of the room.

"I will search for more doors," she said, and went off, the lamp bobbing as she held it higher and lower to examine her surroundings.

It did not take long, and she brought no new treasures back with her.

"Some gold and jewels, but nothing of use," she said. "Though Narrow Field Man would like them for his making. I found only two doors, one back to the round room we started in and the other to the silkstone room. No outside doors, sand take this place!"

They returned to the round room through the doors the sandwalker had discovered. There, Dorict crouched down by the last unopened door, and Marick found the catch.

"So, what's in those?" the small bane asked, looking to where Yala's lamp illuminated rows of long stone boxes and metal stands that might once have been lamps.

The sandwalker looked into the basin of a smaller brass bowl. "The oil in these lamps is thick now, like tar," Yala said. "But it still may burn." She lit the nearest one from her own lamp and a smoky light sprang up. The smoke travelled upwards, into a dark corner of the ceiling. She lit more of the brass lamps until her own light was unnecessary.

Dorict tapped the stone lid of one of the boxes. "More weapons, you think, or a treasure of some kind?"

Yala shrugged. She stood beside him and they both pushed at the heavy slab. It groaned, stuck, groaned again and moved. The two set themselves and pushed harder, using all their strength to move it clear of the rim.

Yala peered inside and then jumped back, one hand over her mouth.

"Sand and storm! There's a man in there!"

Dorict looked at her, then at the stone box. He took a deep breath and looked within. There was a man there, long dead with shrunken features and skin like pooled wax. Covered in plates of silkstone, the corpse bore a crown on its head and one withered hand loosely clasped both a curved axe and a small whip.

Steeling himself, Dorict pulled the crown free, and unfortunately the head as well, which went rolling across the floor.

"Aii!" Yala screamed and glared at the bane. "What

are you doing? It is a one-souled ghost, trapped in stone for some great crime. Would you make it wake and curse us?"

"Not trapped," Marick said, reaching out a hand to grab her shoulder. "Buried! Listen, the people of the City of Fountains bury their dead too, in big stone caves they call tombs. I thought it was strange, just like you. How would Heaven take you if you weren't made into smoke? But they say it keeps the spirits of their people in their city, so they can stay part of it forever."

"This is wrong," Yala said, standing by the door, hands crossed at her chest and palms facing out towards that box.

Dorict ignored the two and held the crown near the lamp. "I thought so," he said. "Silkstone and jewels! Look, he's dressed in it too. This crown goes with us. It will get King Trax's attention and buy us some good will with the palace."

Yala snatched the lamp away and made a fist-down gesture several times.

"This is one-souled magic," she said. "Leave it with the dead."

"It isn't magic, Yala, just another way of . . . being dead," Marick said. "I guess you don't bury your dead, do you? I mean, when you're not feeding them to demons."

Yala shrugged off Marick's hand and backed away from the stone graves. "No, but you know that. Dorict, you freed that woman, the sandwalker the slavers killed."

"I did that so her people could find her body and know what happened," Dorict said. Despite the burden on his back, he caught up to her and took her by the shoulders. The crown rested around his forearm, the jewels twinkling in the unsteady light.

"Easy, easy, Yala. This is just like the demon fear. It's on the outside, their business," he said, looking back towards the tombs, "not ours."

She was shaking, and he held her closer until she calmed.

"Two girlfriends, Dorict," Marick said from his position of forced observation. "Who would have thought?"

Irritation interrupted the moment but also broke Yala's panic. She reached over and slapped the little bane's head lightly.

"I am well, Dorict," she said. "Release me, please."

When he had done so, and given the crown to Marick's care, they returned to the round room.

"We have to go back to the river," Yala said, with little enthusiasm.

"Maybe," Dorict said. He untied Marick and, after setting him back upon the blankets, took to pacing back and forth in the limited space.

"Why silkstone, and why was it all over the room, even on the ceiling and floor?" he asked, perhaps to himself, for he did not wait for an answer. "It was even on the inside of the door," he said.

Marick and Yala looked at each other.

"They were afraid of the poison winds," she said.

Marick nodded. "Was it a refuge from demons?"

Dorict stopped. "Look, this place is ancient, so that means demons must have been coming here for a long time," he said. "Long before they ever attacked Shirath, but how can that be? And another thing bothers me: what good is a refuge if you can't escape from it, or get into it from the outside?"

"They could use the Dying River," Yala said, and shuddered.

"The river tunnel is deep enough that they wouldn't

need the room," Dorict said. "That much rock between you and a demon would blunt most of the fear anyway. No, that refuge is meant to be filled up fast. That's why it's so empty, no benches, no beds, just room for people to crowd in. So, why are there no doors to the outside?"

"Maybe we just didn't find the door," Marick said. "It's hidden in one of those rooms."

Dorict kept pacing, muttering to himself. Marick slapped his own head and said, "Think, fool!"

Yala looked at the lamp, remembering something about a room she would rather forget.

"The room of dead boxes," she said. "The smoke from those old lamps went up and out somewhere."

Dorict smiled. "So it did! Brilliant, Yala." His smile faded when he saw her expression.

"Sorry, but you can wait here, if you wish."

She shook her head and picked up the lamp. She would not let her friend go into that cursed room alone. She shouldered her bow, for ghosts did not fear arrows, only being trapped in a turning, twisting spirit wind.

When Marick opened the door, the light from the lamps still flickered, burning the last of their ancient fuel. Knowing what waited there made braving the door worse this time. Yala concentrated on those smoky lamps, watching the fumes rise to a corner of the room, thankfully past the last of the tombs.

"Here," she said and pointed to the notches cut into the stone. Fragments of wood stuck out of some of them, hinting at a ladder or stairs that had once aided those fleeing the poison winds. The holes led up to a stone sill, and Yala climbed while Dorict and Marick watched.

"There's a tunnel here," she called down. "Send up our gear and the child."

"Hey!" Marick said, but had to complain on the move, for Dorict turned to make his way back to the round room. It was a heavy load, but he stuffed their diminished supplies into his pack and tied the sled parts into an awkward bundle. Holding all of it in his arms, he stumbled back, much to Marick's dismay.

"Hey! Slow down. If you fall on me with all that, I'll be dead for sure!"

When Dorict dropped his load at the foot of the wall, the bundle of sled parts fell to the stone with an astonishing clatter in that enclosed space.

Yala frowned down at them. "Would you wake the dead?" she hissed and caught the coil of rope he tossed upwards.

Marick went up first, worrying that Yala might drop him, or at least want to. Despite his misgivings, he soon found himself in a square tunnel. Yala hauled up their belongings, and Marick, tired of being carried, pushed the pack and sled parts down the shaft as far as he could, despite the pain that jolted through him every time his stump touched the stone.

Dorict joined them and found he couldn't stand up straight in the stone corridor. "Hah!" he said, head bent to one side. "It seems those builders weren't as tall as their paintings made them out to be!" He crouched and joined the other two at the far end.

That was blocked by another metal door, this one smaller, and Yala, with the dead behind her and the free air somewhere ahead, rang blow upon blow on it with her boot heels.

Dorict gritted his teeth and looked to where Marick grinned in the lamp light.

"Good idea, Yala," the little bane shouted. "If you do

wake those corpses, they'll probably run away from all the noise you're making!"

She did not answer, at least not in words. The drum of boots on bronze increased in speed and ferocity, and then the door gave way, falling with a metallic clang of defeat beyond the exit. Yala reached back for the lantern and stepped through. The banes saw the light bobble and swing as she scanned her surroundings. Dorict, mindful of how little oil they had left, extinguished the larger lamp he carried.

Marick went next, finding that he could keep crawling if he kept the stump of his right leg off the floor. The corridor came out level with a new floor. He moved over so that Dorict could come next, dragging the roped bundle of their gear and the parts of Yala's sled.

She pointed to the lamp in Dorict's hand. "Light it again," she said.

Dorict frowned. "We don't have much oil left. Why use both?" he asked, then looked up as the sandwalker pointed to where a ceiling would be in any sane room. His voice echoed strangely.

"Because I think we will need much light," Yala said. She gave Marick her shoulder so that he could lean against her and see.

With both lamps lit, the mad dimensions of the space they inhabited became clear.

From where they stood and stared, stone tiers rose in retreating levels, seven of them in all, and each one at least eight feet high. The white walls of the gigantic chamber curved upwards and inwards, narrowing until the shadows became too deep to be lit by their little flames.

"It's like being inside a hollow hill," Yala said.

This tremendous space was too much after days travelling the cramped confines of the river tunnel and passing through the rooms below. The stone steps swung before her eyes. She crouched, pulling Marick down beside her, the lantern clanging to the floor.

How can it be so big and still be inside? Oh wind, I need the sky on my face or I will die!

Dorict sat down beside her, just as awed. He righted the guttering lamp, and Yala, who could only look at the floor, was glad to see his hands were also shaking. By degrees, she raised her head, counting the tiers to slow her panic.

"Three, four, five, six, and seven," she said. "And all to hold up that empty hill, I think."

"A dome, not a hill," Dorict said. "We have domes in Shirath over our temples, but this! What a task it must have been to build! You remember all the things I told you of? The temple, the banehall, and the palace? They're small compared to this. Only our city walls could match it for height. Oh, I wish Dasanat and Mandarack were here. The mechanicals would go mad over this! I suppose I should sketch it out, though if Vinir was here she would do a better job."

"I wish she was here too," Marick said.

Dorict turned to see his friend looking out into the great space that opened above them, tears running down his cheeks. He shifted about to face Marick.

"Don't worry too much about what she'll do. There'll be harsh words at first," he said, and put one arm around his friend's shaking shoulders, "but you know Vinir is too soft-hearted to stay mad forever."

Marick did not reply.

Dorict went over to the nearest rising stones and ran his fingers over the surface.

"There's writing here, carved into the stone," he said

and came back to find his pack and take out a scrap of paper and a well-wrapped bottle of ink. With a glass-tipped pen, a parting present from a young woman in the City of Fountains, he began copying what was written on the nearest block, stopping now and then to peer upwards.

"Look! There are images too, and not just on the tiers," he said. "I think I see traces of big paintings up in that dome. Claws, I'll have to use every piece of paper I have just to get a hundredth of this." He began writing faster.

Yala glanced at Marick and saw his eyes open, but with little focus. Pain was deep in them, and his mouth was twisted into a grimace that would have scared off a sandcat.

"You are wounded, and all this moving around must pain you," she said.

"I guess," Marick finally said. "I can still feel it. The rest of leg, I mean. And it hurts, which makes no sense since its all ashes now." He took the waterskin she offered and poured a stream of liquid down his throat. "Claws! I wish this were wine. I've never liked it, but I'm beginning to see the point of drinking yourself into a stupor."

Yala looked to where Dorict moved along the bottom tier. She watched him scramble up to the next one, a difficult task since each level was taller than him. Watching him climb, she realized that she and Marick might speak privately for the first time since the desert.

"Marick of Shirath," she said, and put a hand over her heart, fist clenched. "I am sorry for the actions of my people, even if they aren't my people anymore. I brought you to them, but I did not know their plan. I wish they had treated you better."

Marick frowned. Sweat beaded his forehead and he clutched at his thigh.

"Ahh, claws that hurts!" he said, and lay back on the blankets, his head turned towards the sandwalker. "I've no love of your people, Yala, but I don't blame you, I guess, since you worked so hard to keep me alive, even if you do hate me."

Yala raised her eyebrows. "I do not hate you," she said, then added, "but I do not like you much either. You are very, what is the word? Troubling."

She took back the waterskin and shook it. It had been filled before they had climbed up here, and she guessed she would have to climb back down to fill it again unless they found their way to daylight and a new source of water. She looked to the boy's bandage but could do little but wash the wrappings and put them back on again. The men of the well had sewn the skin together quite neatly and done something to reduce the boy's bleeding to a mere seep. Marick bore her attention with his usual complaints and insults but stopped when she had finished.

"Look, just why are you helping us?" he asked, twisting his head back and forth to concentrate against the pain. "You're not a bane." His voice was drifting again, falling from wakefulness to a troubled sleep. "And I told you, he's got a girlfriend," he said, a last slurred thought before the darkness took him. "So don't think . . ."

She pulled the blanket over him and looked to where the other bane walked along the third tier now.

You are wrong, troubling boy. If I would think of anyone, it would be Narrow Field Man, but there is no use doing that. Not now, maybe not for years. I hope he goes to the City of Fountains. I want him to know what it is to be free.

She blew out the lamp, for there was no eerie water glow here to take its place and they were low on oil. The blackness rushed in, broken only by the distant bobbing of

Dorict's lamp. She clenched her fists and pounded them on the floor, gently though, so as not to wake the boy. *What next? Another room, only bigger?* They needed to find a way to freedom, to the outside, but how? If only there were some way to track the sun, even if it came in the dark like . . .

"The light in the river!" Yala said aloud and called Dorict to come back.

The bane returned reluctantly. He juggled lamp, pen, paper, and ink bottle awkwardly, and Yala took the last from him as it slipped from of his fingers.

"Put out the lamp," she said. "If there is a crack in these walls, we must wait for our eyes to see it."

He looked at her, then looked up. A slow smile spread across his face. He blew out the flame and vanished from her sight as the darkness rushed in.

It took a long time, longer than with the river, but she had been right.

"There," Dorict said, and took Yala's hand to point it towards the direction he could not otherwise show.

Yala looked, waiting, trusting, and saw it, a yellow-red patch of light, fainter than a dying candle, but still standing out in this artificial night. They took one lamp and left Marick sleeping. Climbing the tall stones was easier with both of them helping each other, and they soon reached the top tier and the approximate location of that hopeful light.

By touch, they found a thin line between two blocks and snuffed out the lamp flames to see if this was where they had spotted it. After many anxious moments, the dim glow reappeared. Dorict traced the gap with a finger until he found a bronze door set hidden behind a facing of cracked stone. He struck a flint to the iron rim of his tinderbox and used a piece of reed to transfer the flame to the lamp.

"We can get out now!" Yala said. "We can escape this stone-cursed place."

Dorict laid a hand on her shoulder. "We can go out, yes," Dorict said. "But we, or at least I, have to come back." At her uncomprehending look, he said, "I need time here, Yala. I found something here. Something more precious to my people than that crown."

Yala rested her hand on the door. Her heart beat wildly, and she had to clench her fingers into a fist to keep from clawing at the door.

It will still be here ten breaths from now, a day from now. I can wait. I am Yala.

"What have you found?" she asked, when she could breathe easily.

"The same thing you wanted," Dorict said. "Answers!"

In the flickering light, there was a look of excitement on his face that made Yala turn from the promise of freedom and follow him back down into the stone prison.

CHAPTER 35
SHADOWS AND DEATH

Vinir found Chal-lat at his usual post in the half-roofed upper room, looking out through a window made bigger by time. He pulled her over to sit beside him and pointed out into the darkness. Vinir could barely see his finger.

"Is something out there moving?" she asked.

Chal-lat shook his head. "No."

"What is it, then?" Vinir demanded. "The moon's only a thin crescent, I can't see anything but shadows."

"That's what I see," Chal-lat said. "But it's the shadows that worry me."

Vinir nudged him to explain while she scanned the heavy darkness in the street below.

"See that corner by the fallen blocks, the one to the right?"

"Hmm," Vinir said. "So what?"

"It's rounded where it should be square. There are two more places where the shadows are a different shape."

Vinir looked at him, seeing little but a blur of dark hair against the white of the walls.

"You're imagining this!" she hissed. "Or maybe your sandcat has come back. There's no chance those slavers snuck up on us without showing more than a bent shadow."

"I've watched for six nights," Chal-lat said. "I know every shadow like my own. Go get Stetta and Mor-ra."

Vinir went back down the stairs and found the two guards on the floor, unable to help, for each had a drawn arrow pointed at the backs of their necks. Son-neen was held by a tall figure in a red cloak, her mouth muffled by a fold of cloth and her kicking legs held well off the floor.

The old man was still asleep.

One of the intruders stepped behind Vinir, and the bane felt an iron point between her shoulders. There was pressure. The meaning was clear: move.

Vinir folded her arms and said, "You're not slavers. Did they pay you to attack us?"

A trickle that might have been blood ran down the skin below her tunic, but she held her ground.

"Answer me!" she said. "Are you with the slavers?"

A small figure made its way through the mass of red cloaks. She stopped in front of the bane and pulled back her hood, showing grey hair and a wrinkled face under glass and leather goggles. She poked Vinir in the arm and shook her head.

"You're big for a town-dweller. You'd make a match for Brada, no doubt," she said and hooked a thumb at the one who held Son-neen. "But no, girl, we are not with the slavers."

A short-handled shovel appeared in the old woman's hand, the shaft dark with age but the steel edge shiny with a recent sharpening. The old woman held it between them, letting the light of the oil lamp glint off the tip.

"But now you should convince us that *you* are not with the slavers," she said.

Vinir laughed, a long laugh, gut-deep and shaking, a laugh that let out all the tension, all the guilt she had carried on this pursuit. When she stopped, still with an arrow at her back and a blade at her front, she was herself again.

"With the slavers?" she asked, still chuckling. "With respect, elder, you are wrong. We have chased those scum for days, losing horses to the desert and nearly dying ourselves until we came to these ruins and found water."

She wiped at her eyes and turned to see the woman behind her, younger than the ancient in front but older than Vinir.

"If you wouldn't mind taking that arrow out of my back, I'll tell you all about it."

The old woman made a motion, and the other lowered her bow and let the tension off the string, but she didn't put the arrow back in her quiver. Another motion and the two guards were allowed to rise and Son-neen was lowered back to earth. The first thing the latter did was kick her captor's shin. That one, Brada, yelped and hopped away from further attacks.

Son-neen came over to stand with Vinir and the others. Chal-lat soon joined them, brought down by more of the "shadows" he had seen from his post. Everyone ignored the old man who still snored.

"Sit," the old woman said. "I am Ke. Tell me why we should not kill you for being in our lands."

Vinir sat down and offered Ke a skin of water. The old woman shook her head.

"I will not drink with you, not yet," she said.

"I am Vinir," the bane said, "from the city of Shirath in

the North, one of Five Cities on the River Ar. Have you heard of that place?"

Ke nodded, but said nothing. Four equally ancient women came to sit beside her, leaving Vinir feeling rather outnumbered until Chal-lat moved up on one side and Son-neen crouched on the other. The guards filled out the edges, Mor-ra sitting beside the angry girl and giving her a warning look.

"Well," Vinir continued, "we came to the City of Fountains, and then the Mother of Waters to seek out a type of creature, a monster that has attacked our cities for six hundred years. We hope to find where they come from so we can destroy them once and for all."

The woman who had held Vinir at arrowpoint frowned. "Now you have found us. Are we your monsters?" she asked.

Ke waved the words away. "Tral, sit down and listen. Vinir of . . . Shirath? What do these creatures look like?"

Vinir whispered to Chal-lat, and he stood up – very carefully – and got Vinir's flat drawing case from the pile of gear next to the most intact wall of the stables.

The bane laid out several drawings before the sand-walkers, and Tral held a lamp low over the pages.

Ke looked up sharply at Vinir. "It might be that we will speak of this later, or not," she said, and pushed the papers back towards her captives. "But for now, tell us why you hunt slavers, not monsters."

Vinir told the whole story of Marick's crimes and Dorict's disappearance. She described their chase and what they had seen of the slavers' camp near the pyramid.

"He was a slave," she said, pointing at the blissfully snoring grey-bearded man in the corner. "He said that Marick and Dorict escaped. Have you any word of them?"

At this, Ke rocked back and forth a bit, before looking at her fellow ancients. They hemmed and hawed in their own tongue, and at last reached some kind of agreement, for Ke spoke.

"We have seen them, but they escaped us also, helped by my granddaughter and Tral's daughter, Yala. She told us of these slavers and that they have allies, so we have brought many wells to fight them."

"We aren't their allies!" Chal-lat said. "The City of Fountains has fought slavers since before I was born."

Ke snorted and stood up, a fluid movement for one so old, and the shovel disappeared within the robe.

"That is true, and it seems you are their enemies. We will not harm you. Stay here. At dawn, we will kill the slavers. You can take the slaves that live back to the Mother of Waters."

She turned to go, but Vinir stood up too. Tral stepped between them, but something in the bane's eyes made the sandwalker drop her restraining hand.

"I will come with you, and these guards as well," Vinir said. "I have suffered through the fire of this land to find my friends, and nothing will stop me."

"An arrow might," Tral said, and many bows were raised but halted in their movement when Stetta started shouting.

"This man is not very good at things, but he might be useful in fighting slavers, because he has done it before and still lives. This woman is better at it, even though she is hard to get along with!" His eyes were fixed on the roof, the only place in the room that avoided the encircling eyes of the sandwalkers.

Mor-ra pinched him. "Who are you talking to? And what are you doing?"

Ke laughed. "He's being polite, for a man. Some sand-walker blood, I think! Very well. That man is probably too weak to help, but we will bring him along. . . and the difficult woman too!"

There was much laughter at this, and the sandwalkers took up spots along the wall, wrapping their cloaks around themselves. Some closed their eyes, but a few went out to guard their shelter with more shadows. Others looked to their bows and arrows in preparation for the dawn.

Vinir sat down next to the old man, who opened his eyes, looked around the room, and then back at the bane.

"Go back to sleep," she said. "These are friends, of a sort."

He closed his eyes again, but Vinir's stayed open and watchful until the sun tinged the east with streaks of red. At some point in that anxious waiting, Ke came over to sit beside her, and the two talked for a very long time.

CHAPTER 36

BLOOD IN THE CITY OF SAND

"I'll need more paper," Dorict said, when they had returned to where Marick slept on the bottom of that vast, pillared space. He fished out his other shirt and used Yala's knife to cut it into strips. "I'm glad Narrow Field Man lent me the one I'm wearing. It lets me cut this one up! This will have to do for the writing. I had only a bit of paper in my pack, since Vinir and Chal-lat both carried more for their drawing."

"What do they draw?" Yala asked. Her own people made some designs on common things like pots and goggles, but she knew the town-dwellers covered everything, even the walls of their towering huts, with pictures.

Dorict sat back. "Anything! Everything! People, animals, buildings, even the desert with that aqueduct running across it. I thought it too desolate for a good picture, but Vinir said it helped her develop perspective, which has something to do with making a drawing seem more real."

He drank from the last waterskin and passed it over. "She really is an artist," he said, "as much as she is a bane. I can see now that this bothered Marick. He's loved her like a moon-struck calf ever since he came to Shirath, and it must have pained him to see her change."

He rolled the strips up into balls and stuffed them in his belt pouch. "Not that she saw him as anything other than, say, a younger brother. Now, where is that ink? It's funny about her, I knew Vinir liked to make drawings, but in Shirath she was always a bane first and foremost. Now she seems different, since coming south."

Yala drank. "How so?" She had heard much of this Vinir and wondered if they would meet before this journey was over.

"She's so . . . intense," Dorict said. "Like she'd be willing to leave the banehall and live a new life." He shrugged and added, "Well, I suppose I thought about it too. Not with art, but with books! There were so many of them, and they tell you such interesting things. I could see myself staying there forever, reading books and being happy. That was hard on Marick. It was like we had both turned away from him."

Yala nodded. "It is bad when everyone else is going a different way. I know this!"

Dorict nodded. "So do I. Back in Shirath, there was a time when a few of us stood against the banehall and the whole city. But there's another reason, I think, that pushed Marick into doing what he did."

Yala tilted her head and looked her question.

The bane blushed. "Well, it's not my business, but Vinir's very close with Chal-lat, another art student. She's in love with him, I think."

"And this bothers him but not you?" Yala asked. She heard Marick's change of breath.

He's awake, sly as a sandcat!

Dorict laughed a bit. "Vinir is my friend, and a fellow

bane. Both of those things mean a lot to me, but I have no fantasy about her looking at me that way," he said and shrugged. "I've always been an ugly lump."

Yala looked at him in the lamp light. "You are not ugly, Dorict of Shirath, though your face is pale and your hair is very yellow. Besides, you are strong. Even Narrow Field Man said that," she said and nodded towards Marick. "This one said you had a friend in the City of Fountains."

It was difficult to tell in the low light, but she thought he blushed.

"Yes," he said. "I do, or at least I did. I think seeing Vinir changing into a new person gave me the courage to be one too. The bookseller had a niece, Vella, and we got along! Laughing and talking with her was like a dream, though I knew I'd have to wake up sooner or later." He waved his arms at their surroundings. "And I suppose I did!"

Yala nodded, thinking of Narrow Field Man sitting by the wall, talking to her in his quiet voice.

What is sadder, a dream that ended or one that may never begin?

"You might see her again," she said. "The right wind can change a dream into a future, my people say."

"Or you can have no future," a small voice said from the blankets.

Marick sat up, carefully, and looked at them both. "What about me? My dream was to be a bane, for the world to keep on going like it always had," he said. "With Vinir and this lump here. Now I can't even walk, so how can I still be a bane? How can I be anything when I'm so useless?"

Dorict frowned. "You've made mistakes," he said, "bad ones, but you can still make amends if you want to! It should say something about your 'use' that we risked our lives to save you. If your life has worth to us, it should have worth to you, shouldn't it? As for your leg, well, there're still plenty of jobs in the banehall you could do."

Marick spat out a laugh. "What, like Senerix in the Old Torrick banehall? Handing out sashes and boots and snarling at everyone?"

"You snarl enough already," Yala said. "Listen, you are still alive and have more years ahead of you, and a choice."

She held up two hands, one palm up, the other down. "Give up. Don't give up. I will help you to return home, and that will end any debts between us. It is up to you what you do then."

She picked up the waterskins and slung them over her shoulder. Taking the small lantern in hand, she stood up. "Give me the rope. We need more water."

Dorict coiled the line and gave it to her. When she was gone, he looked over at Marick. The bane lay back on his blankets, frowning.

"She's right, you know," Dorict said. "It really is your choice. I hope you make a good one, this time. As for the banehall, it could still use you, and you know it! But Shirath is a big city, and you're smart enough to find a place in it."

Marick stared down at the absence that was once a leg, a strong, nimble limb that had carried him over Shirath's rooftops, down its alleys, and into so much wonderful trouble.

The silence grew, became part of the emptiness around them.

He shifted on his blankets and rubbed his nose. "Is there enough wood left in that clawed sled to make me a crutch?" he demanded.

Dorict smiled and picked up the two cargo rails.

"I doubt we'll need any more giant arrows," he said,

and began to poke through the remaining bits for a cross-piece to sit under the bane's arm.

When Yala climbed back up, laden with sloshing water-skins, she found Marick using her old knife to cut notches in the poles so that they could tie snugly to the crosspiece.

After a long time looking at the remains of her first sled, she took out the blade she had found among all that treasure. She wrapped a cloth around the bare tang and tied it tight.

"You will need two of these to walk," she said, and began working on the second rail.

"Thanks," Marick said. He was tearing strips off a blanket and using them to pad the pieces that would fit under his arms. His hands moved with some confidence. This was not the first time he had needed crutches.

They worked quietly for some time. Yala fed the last of the oil into the small lamp. "We have to open that door, Dorict," she said. "Now, while we have light."

"You could always burn my other leg," Marick said. He was standing now, crutches under both arms and leaning against Dorict.

"I'd burn your tongue first," Yala said, "and that other business is finished between us. Save your breath, for we have to climb to that top level."

It was more difficult than before, for they had to haul up both Marick and their supplies as they went, all wrapped into one complaining bundle.

"Careful, you're scraping half my skin off."

Yala and Dorict looked at each other, then up to the last tier and perhaps their way out. The lamp was set as low as possible, but Dorict kept his tinderbox handy in case the flame went out before they found the sun.

On the seventh tier, they leaned against the blocks and

sat there until they caught their breath. Yala found the bronze door behind the stone façade and ran her hands under it, looking for a catch.

"I can't open it," she said, and Dorict took over, pushing hard against it, but to no avail. The door stayed stubbornly shut.

"My turn," Marick said. The others moved aside. Yala picked pieces of a reed basket out of their supplies to make a small fire if needed.

As the lamp guttered and died, Yala lit the reeds, one at a time. The light was less than a candle, but she pushed a few into the lantern's housing and held it up to illuminate the little bane's work. Marick leaned against the door, pressing it here and there, bringing small, clicking sounds out of the metal.

"Clever," he said. "Whoever built this place was clever in big ways like this dome and clever in small ways like this door. Maybe this entrance is more important, like an escape route, because its mechanism is more complex than the others. Dorict, hold down this stud. Yala, push up here."

They did as they were told. A clank sounded from the other side, and Marick wedged a crutch in the seam between the door and the wall. The square of stone and bronze shuddered and edged a fraction of an inch away from them.

"Just about," he murmured, and used his crutch to push it back again.

Dust exploded from around the frame. The metal moved, a shrieking, grinding motion that drew the door away from them, down a rectangular tunnel cut into the stone walls. Yala added more reeds to the lamp and held it out in front of her.

"Grooves," Marick said, panting and pointing to the

walls and floor, "to guide the door, and gears to move it. Dasanat would swoon over this."

The door continued its retreat until it stopped ten yards away from the watchers and descended into a slit cut into the floor.

Or almost descended, for it stopped halfway, and no gear or kick could force it further. It did not matter though, at least to Yala. There was a bright gap in the stone beyond.

A red sky! A sun rising or setting, I don't care which as long as I'm under it.

She slipped over the frozen door, Dorict and Marick following with crutches and supplies more slowly.

"Somebody tried to force the door from the other side," Marick said. "They bent it, with hammers maybe. That's why it's stuck."

Yala did not turn to see what he meant. They were free. She stepped out into the open air and looked out onto a vast sand-choked plaza. The lower, tiered-part of the great space they had just escaped must have been buried, for they came out no more than ten feet above the level of the ground. Twilight showed a vast, ruined city stretching before them. Lights glittered below, campfires and torches, and rough voices rose to greet them.

"Goz! I heard more noise up above, on that first level," said one, and the other answered with a curse.

Yala frowned. *What freedom is this? From darkness into the hands of slavers!*

"Waterskins, blankets, and food," she told the others. "Put them in Dorict's pack and give it to me." She strung her bow and put an arrow on the string. There was more movement below, feet shuffling upwards, grunts as tired men climbed over tumbled stones, but she knew those men were armed, and it would be slavery or worse if they were caught.

"Dorict, can you carry him?" she asked. The dome's base was terraced, as it was inside the massive structure, but broken into smaller steps. They could easily carry Marick and climb down. Then it would be a desperate dash across that plaza, hoping low light would hide them from pursuit. Rows of pillars and cracked walls would give them even more cover – if they could make it there under the slavers' noses.

With no time to fashion another rope sling, Dorict threw Marick over his shoulder, holding his hands at his chest and letting his one leg dangle. He kept the sand-walker shovel in his other hand, ready to fight or flee.

"Claws!" Marick said, looking a little green at the rough treatment, but he held his crutches tight, so that the other wouldn't trip.

"Go for that big broken pillar to the right," Yala said. "I'll follow and slow them down."

Dorict looked at her for a moment and nodded.

"Now!"

The bane thundered down the steps, managing to keep on his feet all the way down before setting off at a laboured run towards the pillar. A yelping chorus of voices rose behind him, and he moved his legs as fast as he could through the thick layer of sand. Marick bounced up and down, but he didn't drop the crutches or complain.

Yala ran a dozen yards behind them, then slid to a stop. She turned and fired at the nearest slaver. That one went down with a shaft in his chest, but many more followed. A thrown spear fell short, but an arrow barely missed her head, cutting a lock from her black hair that fell to the sand. By the time it touched the ground, she had spun and followed the banes, angling back and forth but always keeping between them and the slavers.

A fallen block gave her cover for more shots, and she took down two, wounding a big axe-wielder in the thigh and sticking a smaller bowman in the throat.

Time to run again, to hope each dodge took her out of an arrow's path and not into it. She was almost to the pillar when her legs flew out from under her, tied in mid-stride by a whip swung from behind. Her bow fell out of her hands, and the arrows scattered from her quiver. She pulled her shovel free to cut the leather braid, but a booted foot kicked that away as well. Yala looked up at the one she had seen carrying Marick at the Mother of Waters, the one called Goz. The slaver grinned and raised a huge fist. She lashed out at his leg with her bound feet, but it was like kicking a tree trunk. The slaver's smile widened, showing brown and broken teeth, and then a sand spirit came whirling across the open space between the building and the broken pillars to engulf him, blinding the brute and filling his mouth with red grit.

Yala closed her eyes against the flying grains and untied her legs by touch. She scooped up her shovel and raised it to strike, then held back the blow. Goz was half buried, and the spirit still twisted around him, locked in place. It spun faster, and the slaver cried out as his skin was scoured raw. At last he stumbled from the pile of sand and collapsed at her feet, his clothes torn and blood seeping through the rents. Yala looked up at the sand spirit and saw a face form for an instant, lean and bearded, etched with pain, but its eyes looking at her with compassion. The whirling stopped, and the captured sand fell to the ground. Yala stood there, open-mouthed.

I know that face. Inla-phor! You said you would help me, if you could.

Goz tried to rise, but Dorict flashed past Yala and kicked him hard enough to send the big man rolling. Not stopping, he charged the knot of thugs who followed. They were armed with swords, clubs, and knives, but they might have been holding feathers for all the good it did them. Yala watched as the shovel flashed back and forth, and the bane's free hand punched men with such force that they left their feet to fall onto the sand-choked plaza. In a few breaths, it was done, and the nearest slavers were down.

But there were many more coming, and at least three with bows. Dorict backed up and stood between them and Yala. The sandwalker snatched up her scattered arrows. Her bow appeared at her elbow, and she turned to see Marick holding it up, having crawled from his hiding place to help as much he could. He had the long, rough length of the demon's horn in his other hand and a fire in his eyes that matched his friend's.

"Heaven's shield, start shooting!" he said, and a slaver fell from an arrow, not Yala's but one shot into his back. Then another fell, screaming and clutching at the point protruding from his stomach.

Marick and Yala both looked at her bow, then each other.

"Good trick," the boy said, and grinned.

"Not a trick of mine," Yala replied and pointed to where sandwalkers boiled out from the last shadows of the night, firing deadly shafts and moving to encircle the slavers.

A group of the men broke away, but before they could return to the building they had taken for their own, a tall woman, blond braids flying and bearing a fierce double-bladed axe, charged them. The fleeing slavers raised their weapons, but to little use, for she knocked down the first, then a second, taking both their heads in whistling arcs of steel. She was joined by four others, two with slashing swords and two more with bows, one of them quite small, who danced around, firing arrows in odd directions.

The noose of red cloaks tightened, and the slavers fell one after the other until none were left standing, though some still lived, begging for mercy on their knees.

"It's over," Yala said. She retrieved Marick's crutches and helped him to stand again. While he swayed, she went to Dorict. He was standing over the slavers he had fought.

"Are you all right?" she asked. "Did they wound you?"

Dorict shook his head. "For all their bluster, they weren't good fighters, not for somebody who trains as much as we do. Heaven shield me! Garet was right. Killing a demon is one thing. Killing people is another."

He turned and stumbled behind the pillars. Yala heard him retching, and her own stomach churned.

I have killed too. One-Eye, these slavers – shouldn't I feel it as he does?

She decided to think on this later and felt a tugging at her sleeve.

"I don't know why he's upset," Marick said. He'd retrieved his crutches and stood beside the sandwalker. "If I could have, I'd have killed them all myself."

Yala shrugged. "Be quiet," she said.

"Why?" he demanded.

"Because I don't like agreeing with you," she said and straightened the young bane's shirt, brushing off the sand.

"Don't fuss over me!" he said but smiled.

Dorict came back, pale but moving with purpose. He knelt and examined the slavers.

Three of them were dead, or soon would be. Two others

might live, if the sandwalkers let them. Two of those who had fought against the brutes, but were not red-cloaked, were arguing about that now.

"Look, let us take them back to the Mother of Waters," one said, a short round-faced woman whose sword was red to the hilt. The tall man beside her nodded and shouted strangely into the air.

"Yes, they are useless, but they might have some information that maybe could help us all in the future, but probably not!"

"Such scum are better off dead," a sandwalker woman shouted back, again up to the heavens.

Marick shook his head and looked at Yala, who shrugged. Dorict smiled.

"Like at that wall in your well, Yala," Dorict said. "Heaven's shield! I think the whole world is mad some days."

While the odd argument went on, the woman who had fought so savagely near the palace door dropped her axe and came walking, then running over to them. She grabbed Dorict and lifted him into a bear hug, his feet leaving the ground.

"Dorict!" she said and dropped him to grab Marick. "Oh, Marick! Oh, your leg. I'm so sorry . . ."

"No," Marick said. "Listen, I'm sorry! I'm an idiot, Vinir. I didn't think . . ."

Vinir reached out again for the stumbling Dorict and hugged them both, at least until Marick yelped in pain.

"Sorry," she said, wiping away tears. They were all crying, and Yala was surprised to feel some wetness on her own cheeks.

Vinir transferred Marick to Dorict's support and wrapped her arms around Yala.

"Last night, your grandmother told me how you helped them, Yala," she said. "I'm so glad to meet you."

This woman, who was as tall as Brada and seemed even stronger, held her for some moments before letting her go. She looked down at the dead and wounded slavers and then at Dorict, who looked away.

"It was necessary," Vinir told him. "Don't forget that, Dorict. You were fighting for your own life and the lives you care about."

"Like me," Marick said. He was leaning against Dorict, tucked under his arm like a little bird under a branch, and he still wept, for it was a sanctuary, and, after all his sins, he had been allowed to return.

"Oh, claws," he said, trying to twist around to hide behind his larger friend. "Here come's Son-neen!"

CHAPTER 37
FRIENDS REUNITED

Under the portico of the slaver's camp, Vinir, Dorict, and Yala watched Son-neen harangue Marick. Her initial attack had only been stopped by Vinir's long arms and Marick's revelation that the girl's precious papers were still hidden in the secret pocket inside his remaining pants' leg. The washing they had gotten had not destroyed the writing, much to Son-neen's relief, but instead of thanks, she rolled them up and swatted Marick on his head.

"You're just lucky you hid them in the right leg," she said.

"But it was the left leg," Yala said, before understanding Son-neen's meaning. While the girl went into some detail on Marick's character, the sandwalker joined the others in the shade. Vinir produced a waterskin, and they all shared.

"Drink," she said. "There are wells all over these ruins."

"There's one in that dome," Dorict said, "A whole river of water, though it's not easy to get to."

"Hmm, Ke thought the Dying River might flow under here, but no one knew for sure," Vinir said. She looked down to a half-irritated, half-abashed Marick apologizing to Son-neen over and over again.

"Poor Marick! I feel so guilty. I was supposed to keep you both safe!"

Yala shook her head. Son-neen was now counting out loud. Marick's sins, perhaps. It looked like she would soon run out of fingers.

"That boy is a wild wind," Yala said. "You cannot keep him from harm."

Dorict nodded. "It's true, Vinir," he said. "Marick will always be his own master, for all the trouble it gets him into."

Vinir shook her head then stood and stretched. She leaned down and grabbed a handful of sand to rub at a bloodstain on her boots.

"I know that, or at least I should by now," she said. "But I hate to think what Tarix will say, or Salick! Months down here and nothing to show for it but pain and failure. If only we had found something in this wretched land – sorry, Yala. But it would take some of the sting out of my mistakes."

Dorict smiled. "Well, we can help you there! Inside that dome are things we can show you, at least if we can find some lamp oil," he said, pointing to the mammoth rounded building towering across from where they rested. "It's worth taking back to Shirath."

Vinir raised her eyebrows. "Is that so? It seems over-large to pack, but Mor-ra has some oil, I think. She's with Stetta helping the slaves," she said. "I'll go find her."

When the bane had left, Yala stood as well. "I too will go. Your friend says Ke and Tral are here, and I must talk to them, if either one will talk to me."

Dorict handed her the shovel he had wielded, and Yala took it, smiling. When she left, the bane looked down to where Son-neen was jumping up and down in her anger. Marick looked up at him, pleading with his eyes and mouthing words, but Dorict only shook his head. Some things must be endured, especially if they had been rightly earned.

THE SHADOW of a wall made the morning heat bearable. One person sat there, leaning against an ever-present drift of sand. Veined hands sharpened an arrowhead in precise strokes against a whetstone.

"Ke," Yala said. "I am here."

"So you are," the old woman said. She put her work away and pointed to where her granddaughter should sit.

"I'd chasten you for ruining our ambush, but you drew them all out into the open, didn't you?"

Yala nodded.

"And," Ke continued, "you managed to hit some of them, which makes up for letting that Red Rock woman get the better of you."

"Red Rock Well?" Yala asked. "Are those the ones the slavers met?"

"Yes," Ke said. "Thieves and traitors, as everyone knows! We met some coming into this sand city, bearing food for the slavers and forage for their animals. They died badly, running away. Now we must decide what to do next. Will you join us, Yala?"

The young woman looked at the old one, head tilted to one side.

"I am still Yala then, and a sandwalker of Old Carving Well?"

Her grandmother leaned back into the cushion of sand,

winced a bit, and rubbed her knees. "Ahh, I am too old to travel so far just to shoot arrows at fools! Yes, yes, you are, Yala, until you are wise enough to be Yal. Are you a sand-walker of our well? You tell me. Will you come back with us or go farther on with them?"

Yala smiled. "I will go farther, grandmother, but I think one day I will come back."

"Hah!" Ke said, and slapped her thigh. "Brada said you had a field man in mind."

She waved away Yala's angry protests, and they talked for a long time, about what had happened and what might yet occur.

～

THAT EVENING, Ke, Bo and Tral sat outside the arched building's entrance, shaded by a canvas taken from one of the cages. The occupant of that cage, a wild boar from the hills above the City of Fountains, roasted over a fire set at some distance from the three and under Brada's careful eye.

"Our world has changed, hasn't it, sister?" Bo said, and Ke nodded.

"So my granddaughter tells me," she said and looked at her daughter. "Stop sulking, Tral! No one will lengthen your name just because you were wrong about Yala."

Other women joined them, some from Long Valley Well and Three Hill Well, and more from Old Carving Well. Brada brought slices of pork on gold plates and handed them out before sitting down to eat with them.

"What?" she said, seeing several of the older women staring at her. "Do you deny the cook a meal?"

Ke laughed. "No, nor the wisdom you'll learn from listening – not talking," she said.

A Long Valley woman nodded. "Wisdom is needed, Ke. Red Rock has shamed us all. They must be punished."

Bo set down her plate, making a musical note on the cleared paving. "No," she said. "You mean punished more, for they've lost seven women from their well, and that is a hard thing already."

"What of our wounded?" a Three Hill ancient demanded. "Shall we not have blood for that?"

Ke shook her head. "My sister is rarely right, but this time . . . Listen, compensation will be taken from them, enough to beggar them for years! Every well will know the cost of such a betrayal, so let that wind blow itself out. We have more to decide here."

Brada opened her mouth then snapped it shut again.

Ke sighed and shook her head. "Speak, granddaughter."

"Since my mother is so silent, I will speak," Brada said, giving Tral a sidelong glance. The other woman sat, head bowed.

"Before this, we hunted slavers and traded with the town-dwellers on our own terms," Brada said, and many sitting in that circle nodded while they ate.

"Well," she continued, "I may have a longer name than any here, but even I can see that this is a mighty change wind. Slavers going north, poison winds killed by strangers, town people from the Mother of Waters fighting by our side, all these things are new."

"You say what we already know," Long Valley grumbled. "How is that wisdom?"

Brada quailed a bit but didn't retreat. "We need allies, friends to help us survive new dangers!"

"You call animals allies?" a Three Hill woman shouted. "You call the one-souled friends?"

At such heresy, many dropped their plates, sanding their pork and ringing purer tones over the discord.

"Don't waste food!" Ke said, as if scolding children, and they picked up their meat red-faced, brushing the sand and dust off and putting it back on the golden platters.

"Listen," Ke said, smiling a bit at the foolishness of the old and dignified, herself included. "If I had to fight a pit-killer and a sandcat walked up to me and said, 'Hey, woman, why don't we help each other, for I hate pit-killers too,' should I say, 'No, for you are an animal'?"

There was laughter around the circle, and even Tral smiled. Long Valley pointed at her and said, "You, Tral. I have met you three times and always you have talked and talked. What do you say now?"

The Old Carving woman looked down at the sand shovel lying across her legs. She ran a finger along the edge, feeling where it had been notched this day by slaver knives. She frowned and stuck the point in the sand beside her.

"I say my daughter Brada is right," she said. "We must find allies, and these ones have acted well, for animals," she added.

They spoke together after that, many times disagreeing and shouting before they came to an agreement. Their words and meal finished, some made to leave but were stopped when a slight figure came running up and pushed between Ke and Bo to sit down.

"Good," Son-neen said. "You're all here. We can get started!"

She waved those standing to sit back down and unrolled a piece of Chal-lat's paper, now covered with the charcoal strokes of a map.

"We do not speak with animals!" Long Valley said, even though they had spent much time deciding to do just that.

"And I don't talk to idiots!" Son-neen said, and Long Valley sat down abruptly.

Ke laughed, a great giggling sound that shook her thin body. "Talk then, town-dweller! We'll see which is which," she said. "What is it you want of us, brave one – bow lessons?"

Son-neen reddened. "I didn't mean to hit Chal-lat, and it didn't even go through his boot. Forget that, though. I'm better at trade than shooting arrows, and I have the grandest, most name-building plan in the history of my city, one that will make your names bigger as well."

Bo looked around the circle but found only confusion.

"We'd rather shorten our own names, and we trade already, girl," Tral said. "Why do we need your plan?"

Son-neen placed the map on the ground in the centre of the group. They all leaned in to watch her finger trace a line from the Mother of Waters to a spot in the hills near the River Ar.

"Look, five big cities to trade with, not just for you, but for us too! We trade a bit with them already, of course, but ocean travel means waiting months for the right wind, and some ships still sink and everyone drowns. What? What's wrong? Never mind. Forget the sea. You have a road that goes from the Mother of Waters almost to the River Ar and that's close to Shirath, Old Torrick, and all those other markets. Think of it! Silkstone from here, which they really need, and food, cloth, worked metal, salt, minerals, oil, everything going back and forth in weeks rather than months and years."

Tral held up a hand. "Stop this foolishness! Go how? Do you mean to go from well to well? We have water but taking so much freight over the sand is impossible!" she said. "You are the idiot, not us!"

Son-neen stood up and thrust out her chin. "If I am, I'm an idiot who knows about barges and bills of lading, and capital, even if I can't shoot a bow! The answer lies under your feet," she said, and stamped one of hers. "That Dying River took those three all the way from Old Carving Well to this sand city. For every ten leagues it goes, it takes a day or more off travelling through the desert, even with horses, which would just go and die anyway!"

The girl paused to wipe her eyes and nose. "First, let's see how far north the river goes from here, and how far south it goes from your Old Carving Well. Even if the walking paths along the side are blocked, they could still be repaired," she said. "And we could use boats anyway. Now what?"

Several of the women had blanched at her suggestion, and Three Hills had fainted dead away. Tral swayed a bit but kept herself upright.

"We do not travel by water," she said, grinding it out between clenched teeth.

"I do," Son-neen said. Give me a lamp and lots of oil and food, and I'll go look for you."

Faced with such impolite generosity and idiotic bravery, the old women of the wells could do nothing but agree, if only to stop Son-neen from talking.

Vɪɴɪʀ ᴛᴜʀɴᴇᴅ the twisted horn over and over in her hands. After a long examination, she handed it back to Marick. Dorict drew a rough image of the Horned demon in the sand on top of a stone table. Vinir raised her eyebrows at its bizarre armament.

"By shape and size, it's a Horned demon, but those have

only two horns, not a hundred or more as you describe it. And if they broke off so easily, what use would that be to the demon? It sounds like the beast was . . . damaged in some way, sick, maybe."

Dorict nodded. "It did seem diseased," he said. "Besides being slower than any Horned demon I've ever seen, its colour had faded to a patchy grey, and one of these horns was growing from its eye socket! It would have been a very easy kill for a team of banes in Shirath, but why was it so . . . ruined?"

"And why was it here?" Marick said. The other two looked at him and he continued, "I mean, what good does it do to send a demon down here to die by poison? It doesn't hurt Shirath or any of the other cities. If it's a weapon, why shoot it so far off target?"

"Maybe it missed," Dorict said. He looked off into a distant mix of memory and possibility. "Like you say, an arrow shot but missing the target. It wanders south until it dies by poison or too much sun."

Vinir tugged at one of her braids. "Then was it the sun that made it so ill?" she asked.

"I doubt it helped," Marick said. "Since it didn't help us! But weapons break. I mean, you don't really need an arrow after it's hit your enemy, so maybe demons aren't made to last."

"If they are made," Vinir said, "and not a natural terror. That is something we still don't know. Well, however they came to be, they truly are weapons of war."

Dorict nodded. "Yes, and ours isn't the first war that saw them used."

CHAPTER 38
THE ROAD HOME

Vinir and Dorict could not explore the central building until the next day, for many of the slaves were wounded and banes knew something of treating injuries, if only by having watched it done to them. Mor-ra and Stetta worked beside them, along with some of the sandwalkers. Chal-lat had gone back to the stables to pack their gear and bring their remaining horses to the ruined palace. Son-neen was nowhere in sight.

"Probably still chasing your one-legged friend," Mor-ra said. "He's spry on those crutches, but that one, she's determined." The guard held a man's arm steady while Vinir wrapped a cut. She then bound the limb across the man's chest to keep it still.

Stetta came up with a jar of fresh water. The slavers had chosen this building for its deep well, a hole Dorict guessed was fed by an underground pipe from the Dying River. He wondered if the water glowed green at night but doubted he would be able to stay awake long enough to check.

The tall man set the jar on the ground next to Vinir and said, "No, the boy's escaped for now. I saw Son-neen talking to those old women again, Mother protect her. Or maybe them."

Vinir filled a bowl and handed both it and a cloth to the wounded man so he could clean himself. It was a small thing, but washing after weeks of dirty, degrading captivity was a great relief to all the former slaves. They had begun to talk, whispering at first, but when they found comfort instead of whips, they spoke louder, crying, calling out for those left behind, and pleading for help, which the guards and sandwalkers promised to give. Now many of them rested, sleeping away both the day and night to recover their strength.

The surviving slavers, now wearing the iron collars that had so recently graced their captives' necks, were chained together and guarded by red-cloaked women. The brutes showed no willingness to give trouble, for the corpses of their fellows lay within sight through the open door.

"Here is the oil you wanted," Mor-ra said, handing over a sealed jar. "It came from the slavers, but I don't suppose they'll complain." She tapped the sword at her side and grinned.

Dorict filled the large lamp and took Vinir down the passageway leading into the interior of the dome. They found Marick waiting for them, hiding behind the half-closed door.

"Is Son-neen with you?" he whispered, and relaxed when they shook their heads.

"I'd give my other leg if she'd only stop talking," he said, and Vinir smacked the back of his head. "Don't say such a thing!" she said. "I'll rue your wound for the rest of my life. Heaven shield you! Now, Dorict is going to show me what he found. You stay here and pray that your luck outlasts that girl's rage."

Chastened, Marick sat back down and grumbled. Dorict lit the lamp and took her into the vast open space. He held the lamp high, and Vinir whistled.

"Claws!" she said. "I've never seen anything like it, not in all our travels. Even the aqueduct is not so impressive! Was this place known to the sandwalkers?"

"Well, it was a surprise to Yala," Dorict said. "A secret smothered by sand, maybe for a thousand years. We have to climb down now, so take care."

"Have you forgotten I'm a master of the banehall?" Vinir said and ruffled his hair. "I'm supposed to be telling you that."

"Then, after you, Master," Dorict said, and smiled. With Vinir and Marick both here and safe, a weight had fallen from him, and his spirit felt as big as this hollowed-out hill of a building.

He showed her the pictures he had found, images of war and slavery, and drawings of demons obeying the small invaders. Together, they puzzled over the writing, which shared some strokes with Shirath's script but was strangely twisted out of meaning. Dorict unrolled the strips of his sacrificed shirt and copied them down diligently.

"I'll work on this with Barick, if we make it back," he said.

Vinir looked up from where she was sketching a rough copy of a tremendous battle that covered half a tier. She smiled. "Not if, Dorict," she said. "When! Ke says we can have an escort to the River Ar and help from every sand-walker well along the way. They're angry about some of their own that betrayed them, the well of that woman who tried to put an arrow in you and Yala. That shook them up, and now they're ready to accept our help both in trade and against the slavers!"

Dorict nodded. "That might be a good way to go back, despite the sand and sun! The Dying River is hard on the spirit, though easier on the body than climbing over those dunes all night."

He dipped his pen in his diminishing supply of ink and continued his work. Vinir smiled and did the same. It was good to be together again, even if it came after so much hardship and blood.

They returned when the lamp burned low and found Marick had been joined by Yala and Son-neen on the outside steps. Strangely, the girl was ignoring the bane and instead pestering Yala with her questions.

"So how far did you come along the river, and how far would you say it goes? Was that green light bright enough to let people pull a barge and not fall in?"

Yala looked pleadingly at Dorict, and the bane came over and clapped a hand on Son-neen's shoulder. "We'll tell you all we know, but after dinner, for it's hungry work getting up and down those stones."

"I brought food," Son-neen said. Opening a lidded basket, she took out a silver-chased platter loaded with bread and sliced pork. "Even some for him," she added, hooking a thumb at Marick.

"You are very forgiving," Vinir said, and sat beside her on the stone. She took a piece of bread and chewed on it thoughtfully.

"Not forgiving," Son-neen said, holding out the platter for the others to reach. "Practical. He owes me so much it might take years to pay it off, so he has to stay healthy."

"But I'm not healthy," Marick said. He waved a crutch at her. "See? So, you can't squeeze me like you think you can."

Son-neen set the plate down and picked out a piece of

pork with her belt knife. She used it to wave away his protests.

"You might be short one leg, but you still have the other, and your arms. You have a brain too, though it's addled. Don't try and squirm out of your debt. Just because Mor-ra is taking my papers back to the Mother of Waters and delivering them, it doesn't let you off the hook."

"Hooked hard," Dorict said. "Like a fish, or maybe a worm." He grinned around a mouthful of food.

"All right, all right," Marick said. "I'll help you with this crazy plan of yours. Barges along that sunken river. I saw it and I still can't believe it! Who ever heard of a river under the sand! How did it get that way? Does anyone know?"

Yala frowned. "There are tales that the water once tried to drown the world but had to hide from the anger of the sun. Narrow Field Man said it's been down there, dying, ever since. No one really knows."

"We do," Vinir said. "Or at least we think we do." She looked to Dorict, who swallowed a mouthful of pork and spoke to the rest.

"The pictures in that big room," he said, "they tell a story about the Dying River and many other things," he said.

The rest looked at him.

"Tell it then," Son-neen said. She turned towards him and sat cross-legged, elbows on her thighs and her chin cupped in her hands. The others listened in less intense positions.

"Well," Dorict said, "I – I mean we – think that this city was once the centre of a great empire. That crown we found shows it was once a very wealthy land, and there are maps down there that show it stretched from the Far, Far South up to the River Ar and even the Midlands. It seems the empire kept growing until it came up against some people living beyond the Ar. Where that was in the North, the pictures don't show, just very far north of the river. The paintings show them as dark-skinned and with black hair, like your people, Yala."

"And Garet's," Vinir added. "A friend of ours from the Midlands, though his family came from the North." The three banes looked at each other while Son-neen turned to examine Yala.

"But," Vinir said, "the drawings are not very accurate. There's no perspective, and some things are shown cut open, like pots, so you can see what's inside. And if they were your people, Yala, I doubt they were so small!"

Yala nodded in a somewhat confused appreciation of the compliment. A memory came to her of great stone statues and rushing water.

"Maybe it is like the Mouth at the Mother of Waters!" she said. "The big statue stands over the smaller ones who carry burdens."

"Just so," Dorict said, nodding, "That's the story they wanted to tell, a story about who was important and who wasn't. I think they wanted the black-haired people as slaves. Anyway, these two peoples fought, the ones from this city of sand and warriors from the North. If I'm right, that fight went on a long time, though I don't really know because they counted the years differently from us. The Northerners came raiding south along the Dying River, which wasn't buried then. I think these sand city people buried it in a stone tunnel to keep the Northerners from using it. And I think after that the Southerners moved their own troops along it, hiding them from their enemies."

Vinir looked up from where she angled a piece of paper towards the light coming in from the entrance. "I think I'll have to see it to really believe it. Burying a whole river? Claws! And I thought the aqueduct was impressive!"

Son-neen snorted. "They must have been fools!" she said. "If they could build something so big, why is this city in ruins? How could those little people win, if they did win?"

"They did," Vinir said. "By using demons."

Son-neen's mouth dropped open, and even Yala was dumbstruck.

"You mean those baby-eating-monster-things you told me about?" Son-neen asked. "The ones you were looking for? I don't even think they're real!"

"They are!" the others said in a chorus, and Son-neen sat back, surprised at the intensity of the answer.

"Believe us," Dorict said. "We've fought them all our lives, and our people have for six hundred years before that, but it seems like we weren't the first to do so. There's a silk-stone room below us, and maybe others in this city. Silk-stone blocks the demon's fear, a feeling so strong that it freezes you and you can't escape – unless you're protected. We've seen paintings of soldiers in silkstone armour fighting different types of demons. It's all over those walls, and the armour itself is in that tomb."

He wiped the knife against his boot leather and shrugged.

"But even with the silkstone, they couldn't win. The last paintings seem to be all about losing battles. There's much writing on the walls too, but it's different from both ours and the script your people use, Son-neen. We'll copy it down, thanks to Vinir's supply of paper and my poor shirt, and see if we can puzzle it out back in Shirath."

"And Chal-lat and I will copy the maps and drawings," Vinir said to Son-neen, "so we will be here some days. I'll tell Ke and the other sandwalkers about this. I'm sure they will stay to guard us and share their supplies."

Son-neen shrugged. "Well, I can use the time to teach this fool how to think and maybe read better," she said. "How could you grow up so uneducated?"

"Heaven's shield," Marick muttered and collapsed theatrically against the stone wall.

"It will give you time to regain your strength!" Yala said. "Which you will need to pay off your debts to Son-neen and your own people."

She stood and looked north to the red-tinged sky while the others talked and argued.

If these ones speak the truth, there is a new, green land out there, like a field growing that goes on forever.

Dorict came to stand beside the sandwalker. "Son-neen has half convinced us to try the Dying River again, to see how far it goes. Do you still want to come with us?"

"You would be very welcome," Vinir said, joining them on the terrace. "Shirath needs new people and ideas if we are to survive, and Dorict told me of the poison you used to save both him and Marick. Such venom could be Heaven's blessing in our own fight. Come with us, my friend. Bring new knowledge and luck to our city!"

Yala smiled at the bane's enthusiasm. She looked to the west and remembered it was just a day, a night, and another day since they had emerged from the darkness. Would she dare go back into it, travel to an uncertain future in the North, the very home of the death wind?

No matter. All winds bring wisdom in their own time. Let me be wise enough to know this forever.

"Since your people helped me find my answers," she said, and put a hand on her chest, over her heart, "I will go with you and help you find yours."

She left them and walked down to where the sand-walkers gathered by the palace wall putting ancient bits of wood into the makeshift firepits. She had much to say to them, especially to Tral. She didn't know if her mother would listen, but she would say it anyway. A wind blew around her, and Yala felt it fill her souls, storing wisdom and strength for the long journey ahead.

LIST OF NAMES

PEOPLE OF SHIRATH

Andarack: A mechanical, lord of the Eighth Ward, and Master Mandarack's brother.

Banerict: A skilled physician who serves in the banehall infirmary.

Barick: Once the king's butler and now the historian.

Branet: Hallmaster of Shirath Banehall.

Corix: Hallmaster of Old Torrick Banehall.

Dasanat: The master of all the mechanicals in Shirath. She works with Lord Andarack and helped develop the silkstone suit of armour.

Dorict: A Green Sash of Shirath Banehall. He is friend to Garet, Salick, and Marick.

Forlinect: The training master of Shirath Banehall.

Garet: A young man born in the Midlands and taken to Shirath Banehall by Master Mandarack to be a bane. He was a Green Sash who looked to Master Tarix but now is a king's agent.

He died killing the Caller demon, a fearsome beast who

could control others of its kind. Lord Andarack is his brother.

Mandarack: A master of Shirath Banehall who trained Salick, Marick, Dorict, and Garet.

Marick: A Green Sash of Shirath Banehall. Known for his tricks, he is friend to Garet, Salick, Dorict, and Vinir.

Relict: A master of Shirath Banehall and husband to Tarix. Vinir looked to him before becoming a master.

Sacourat: Lord of the Fifth Ward.

Salick: A Red Sash of Shirath Banehall. She looks to Bandat, though she once looked to Mandarack. Friend to Marick, Dorict, and Vinir. She and Garet are very close.

Tarix: A master in Shirath Banehall and wife to Relict. Garet looks to her. She was once restricted to a wheeled chair or crutches by a demon-caused injury but has lately returned to regular patrols.

Trax: The king of Shirath.

Vinir: A Red Sash of Shirath Banehall. She is a friend to Salick, Garet, Marick, and Dorict.

PEOPLE OF THE CITY OF FOUNTAINS AND THE MOTHER OF WATERS

Bortor: A bookshop owner in the City of Fountains.

Chal-lat: A student of art in the City of Fountains.

Fan-col: A guard at the Mother of Waters.

Goz: Second-in-command of the slavers.

Inla-phor: A trader from the Far, Far South who was captured by slavers.

Mor-ra: A guard at the Mother of Waters. Her husband, Stetta, is also a guard.

Norn-i: Commander of the Watch at the Mother of Waters.

One-Eye: Chief of the slavers from the Far, Far South.

Sarth: Old and opinionated art master in the City of Fountains.

Son-neen: An employee of Chal-lat in the City of Fountains.

Stetta: A guard at the Mother of Waters. His wife, Mor-ra, is also a guard.

Toosha-lun: A disreputable trader from the land of the Exalted Nobles in the Far, Far South.

Vella: A book-binder in the City of Fountains, friend to Dorict.

SANDWALKERS AND FIELD MEN

Before Dawn Field Man: A man of Old Carving Well. Perhaps Yala's father.

Bo: A sandwalker of Old Carving Well. Yala's great-aunt and Ke's sister.

Brada: A sandwalker of Old Carving Well, sister to Yala, daughter to Tral, and granddaughter to Ke.

Cheppo: A sandwalker of Old Carving Well.

Chit-chit: The name given to Yala's fear lizard.

Ke: A sandwalker of Old Carving Well. Yala and Brada's grandmother, Tral's mother, and sister to Bo.

Narrow Field Man: A man of Old Carving Well. Skilled in glasswork, he wants to learn more of the outside world.

Shen: A sandwalker of Red Rock Well.

Sota: A sandwalker of Old Carving Well. Yala's cousin.

Tral: A sandwalker of Old Carving Well and Yala's mother.

Yala: A sandwalker of Old Carving Well who is just beginning to travel and trade.

About the Author

Kevin Harkness is a Canadian author who, at a late age, began writing the books he wanted to read. He lives in Vancouver, walks a lot, and occasionally mutters.

https://kevinharkness.ca